THE LAST HERO

THE LAST HERO

Book Two of The Last War

Peter Bostrom

www.authorpeterbostrom.com

Summary: Earth is reeling. American alliances are shaking. And humanity's enemies rally. For six months after the failed alien attack American Admiral Jack Mattis has been ordered to patrol the periphery to stop more alien incursions. Even though he knows the attackers weren't alien, but grotesque mutated super-humans from the future. A truth world governments publicly deny. And now an American scientist witnesses an experimental super-weapon gone awry at a top-secret genetic lab in deep space, while a rebel veterans group storms a Chinese embassy on an American world. Tensions flare, and the American-Chinese peace begins to fray. Admiral Mattis races to put out the fires, while trying to piece together the mystery of the future human invasion, knowing that failure means not only certain death for him, but for the entire human race. The clock is ticking.

Text set in Garamond

Cover art by Tom Edwards

http://tomedwardsdesign.com

ISBN-10: 1548258717
ISBN-13: 978-1548258719

Printed in the United States of America

For my three favorite admirals: Kirk, Adama, and Ackbar

Prologue

MaxGainz Medical Steroid Plant
Planet Zenith
Tonatiuh Sector

Six months after the events of The Last War

Steve Bratta fumbled for his security card, keenly aware of the long line growing behind him. "Sorry, sorry. It's here *somewhere* … hah, I always lose these things…."

The guard, his expression distinctly bored, waited. The people behind him waited. Everyone waited as Bratta's fingers patted over his chest pockets.

His briefcase? No. It wouldn't be there. Left pants pocket. Right pants pocket. Back pocket—back pocket! Back pocket. His fingers closed around the thin plastic card and he withdrew it triumphantly. "Here. My ID card. Doctor Steve Bratta."

"I don't need your name," said the guard, swiping the card. "The computer will tell me." The screen beside him lit up.

DOCTOR STEVE X. BRATTA, PhD, MD

MEDICAL TECHNICIAN GRADE I
ID: XP-379-9951-532
SPECIALISATION: GENETICS
ENTRY: APPROVED

"Doctor Bratta?" said the guard, checking the image of Bratta on the monitor to his face.

Bratta tried his best to squint just like he was in the photo. Why did he always squint during photographs?

The guard looked to him. Then to the screen. Then back to him. "This doesn't look like you."

"It's, uh, definitely me. I just got some new glasses. That might be it."

Nothing.

Time for a joke. Bratta smiled as wide as he could. "Also," he said, "I have a doctorate in applied genetics *and* I'm a medical doctor, so I'm more like, you know, a *doctor doctor*." A pause. "Like, you know, *doctor doctor, give me the news....*"

Silence.

"It's my first day," said Bratta, instantly cringing on the inside. Why. Why did he always mess up the simplest social things? "I, uh, only transferred to Zenith yesterday."

The guard blinked slowly. "Well, good for you, doctor. Next."

Bratta clutched his briefcase close to his chest, keeping his eyes down as he walked past the series of scanners that were probably bombarding his body with radiation—non-ionizing, he hoped—in the search for weapons. No weapons, of course. Just his phone. He preferred to call it a phone, rather than a communicator. Old school.

He walked until he was far enough away from his embarrassment, and then Bratta looked up.

The grounds of the MaxGainz complex were square and fenced in with razor wire, each corner a tall fortified tower topped with a twin-barreled gun that glinted ominously in the moonlight. Squat, prefab buildings lined the central thoroughfare, crammed in next to each other, with modest crowds moving from building to building, the whole area lit up with floodlights. It looked more like a military complex than anything else, but Bratta assumed there was a good reason for the security. Some of these border worlds could be pretty rough.

They'd told him that days and nights lasted nine Earth days on this world, but the fact hadn't really sunk in yet. He'd been here thirty-six hours and it was, technically, the same night. A faint throbbing in his head signaled something else he'd forgotten. Morning coffee. A caffeine-withdrawal headache made his temples throb—part psychosomatic, part chemical dependency. Black coffee had carried him through medical school, but the enduring addiction was a permanent reminder of all the sleep he'd missed.

Fortunately, one of the prefabs was topped with a giant boiling coffee mug sign lit up in neon, and beside it, some Chinese characters he couldn't read. But more than the monolingual signage and the steaming mug of joe, the smell—rich and creamy and bitter—tingled his nose with the promise of relief.

Oh sweet Java, oh merciful Gold Coast blend, deliver me from my lethargy.

He drifted toward the coffee shop in a haze, eagerly

anticipating that first sip. No doubt the prices would be criminal—it was a privately run enterprise with a wholly captive client base on a distant, remote world, hundreds of lightyears from Earth—but it didn't matter. Anything for that sweet, delicious cup of life-giving caffeine. Any price for—

A body landed on the roof of the coffee house, bones breaking with a sickening crunch. It rolled off the roof, crashing down beside him.

Bratta stared in bewilderment. It looked like a Chinese marine. Poor guy had his whole lower torso crushed. Doctor mode kicked in: the patient wasn't moving and the blood was fresh, body absent rigor, with lacerations of the face and scalp and an obvious fracture of the clavarium and skull bones. No obvious breathing. Gaping lacerations of the lower left abdomen and thigh with partial evisceration of sigmoid colon and small intestine—

A shadow fell over the body. Above him, silhouetted by a floodlight, a warped, twisted creature stood on two legs, its back hunched and jagged, gnarled fingers clutching the roof's edge like it was about to leap off.

Bratta slowly reached into his pocket and withdrew his phone, still connected to his combination external hard drive and battery. His own invention. With shaking hands, he held it up and flicked it to record. The act seemed to disturb the creature; it glared down at the crowd.

What the hell was that thing? Bratta kept his phone's camera pointed at it, every frame stored on his external hard drive.

And then the screaming started. All around him. The crowd, seemingly as one, began to run toward the gate. A distant burst of automatic weapons fire broke his trance; Bratta stumbled backward, turning and running, joining the crowd, his briefcase falling from his hands.

Another burst of gunfire, this one much closer, targeting the creature on the roof. Bratta risked a glance over his shoulder—the twin-barreled guns on top of the watchtowers had fired, blasting chunks out of the top of the coffee shop. The creature was nowhere to be found.

Which meant it could be anywhere. In amongst them. Picking them off.

Do not die, he thought to himself. *Do not die! You've got so much left unaccomplished!*

Bratta stumbled and nearly fell, but miraculously kept his footing. His glasses went flying, vanishing into the stampede of people. He kept running, past the gate—now unmanned—and into the car park.

Everyone was looking for their cars. Bratta looked for his. It had been shipped in from Earth and everything. Model IX ESL, with the leather interior and auto-drive features. White. So many cars were white! It didn't help that he'd lost his glasses.

There. There it was, nestled under the scraggly tree, some kind of indigenous flora, crooked and gnarled. Bratta, wheezing, staggered over to it and jammed the key in the car door.

So he didn't see the creature in the tree until it leapt down on top of his car, crushing the roof.

Bratta emitted a startled shout and fell onto his back. In the bright, fluorescent light of the car park he saw the creature fully for the first time. Its skin was black and blue, bruised with mossy green; it was falling off in places, peeling back like the skin of a rotting fruit. Its face was human, almost. It had blue eyes, unnaturally blue and almost glowing, and its face asymmetrical, with a mouth full of rust-colored teeth that were brown and misshapen. It was a woman—or it had been, at some point in the dim past—but it was bulkier than most men. Its fists, huge and gnarled like the tree it had leapt from, were stronger than any man's should be. The monster reeked, almost like old cheese.

It made eye contact with him, looking at him with those blue eyes that betrayed a cunning malevolence to them, an intelligence beyond the animal. Equal to a human.

More than human.

And it was angry.

The car alarm went off, a wailing klaxon. The creature emitted a piercing scream, almost matching it, almost human in its tone and composition, and it coiled like a curled spring. Bratta froze completely; he mentally cried for his muscles to move, to take him away from this *thing*, this horrible monster about to kill him, but all he could do was keep his camera phone pointed at it. Filming his own bludgeoning death and storing it on the combination battery and external drive.

Before it could pounce, another horrible creature identical to the first leapt out of the darkness, crash-tackling the first one. The two fell with combined roars onto the top of his car, their fists flailing, slamming at each other, howling like people play-acting at being monkeys. His windscreen shattered, the bonnet crumpled, and the alarm went ominously silent.

The two monsters fell off, flailing and pummeling each other furiously.

A spray of gunfire caught both of them, blasting chunks of green-blue flesh and blood all over the hood of his car.

Five or six marines, a mixture of Chinese and American, had appeared from *somewhere* and stood behind the bodies of cars, their weapons trained on the monster. Their leader put another burst into both of the monsters, splattering their blood over the pavement.

Bratta mutely kept filming.

"Tangos eliminated." The marine reloaded and, possibly for the first time, saw Bratta. And saw his camera. "Sir, give me that."

Strangely, the idea of having his custom-made phone taken away frightened him more than the monsters. "No."

That, apparently, was not the correct answer. Now the marine's rifle was pointed at him. "Sir, your device. Give it to me. Now."

Slowly, Bratta removed the plug from his phone.

"Slide it to me."

He stared. "That will scratch the surface."

"Do it!"

Without much alternative, Bratta slid the device across the ground. Sparks flew up from the metal, making a horrible screech as it came to rest by the marine.

That would be expensive to fix. It would need a new case, which would be fine, he could fabricate it with a—

The marine bought his boot down on the phone, smashing it into a million pieces. He ground his heel into it to make sure.

"Hey!" said Bratta.

"No pictures," said the marine.

Bratta's eyes drifted back to the pair of dead creatures, still bleeding and riddled with holes, their green vital fluids dripping onto the asphalt. They looked almost human, vaguely, and the more he looked the more truly human they did appear in bone structure, in the way their joints were arranged. But their behavior....

Had he been hired to fix these creatures?

Or create them?

"This," he said, staring at the bloody corpses, "was not what I signed up for."

"No pictures," said the marine, again. Then he and the rest of them walked off.

Bratta shifted into a sitting position, the combination battery and external drive digging into his hip.

At least he still had the pictures.

Now what he needed, were answers.

Chapter One

USS Midway
Shuazzen System

Four weeks later

Six months. For six months the *Midway* had been executing Z-space translation after Z-space translation, jumping to distant border worlds, serving as the first line of defense against further attacks by the aliens.

Aliens.

Admiral Jack Mattis knew they were not aliens. Knowledge he was forced to keep to himself. In truth, not even *he* was sure the explanation made sense.

Time-traveling mutant humans from the future. Even just thinking it made him feel like an idiot. Like he'd been had.

But their effectiveness was undeniable; whatever *they* were, the invaders had thrust into human space, smashed Friendship

Station, wrecked the Chinese ship *Fuqing*, sailed on to Ganymede and bombed it, then made their way to Earth.

The butcher's bill for that battle was enormous. They—the combined American-Chinese force—had barely made it.

And some didn't. His thoughts strayed, just for a moment, to Commander Pitt. He'd been a good man and had died a noble, heroic death. For a brief moment Commander Pitt was the CO of his own ship, until fate had conspired to take it away. Now all that was left was the memory. …

And the distractions. Mattis snapped back to the present, maddening situation.

Why was he here? Out on the edge of nowhere, on the other side of the sector?

Why was he being kept away from the action?

"I'm just saying," his XO, Lieutenant Commander Stewart Lynch, was arguing with Commander Oliver Modi, a conversation that Mattis was only dimly aware of at the edge of his hearing, "it's more complicated than that."

"The position of the Confederacy seemed clear," said Modi, his slight Indian-British accent pleasant to listen to. "The southern states wanted to secede. They were opposed to abolition. The economies of the Union states relied upon slavery. It was a simple war of economics."

A flash of frustration crossed Lynch's face. Even hundreds and hundreds of years later, the American Civil War was a contentious issue. "Listen, you living dictionary, I'm from Texas and I'm telling you—you've been reading too many Northern history books. The War of Northern Aggression wasn't just about slavery." He leaned forward in his seat. "Look. Take the tariffs issue. The North imposed trade taxes to pay for so-called *internal improvements.* But hey, shock-horror, those *internal improvement*s only benefited northern shipping interests and not southern ones. Take, for example, the lighthouse network. The Northern shipping companies demanded more lighthouses in the South. When state governments said no, the North nationalized existing lighthouses and started building new ones with the tariff income."

Modi squinted. "Are you telling me that the American Civil War was fought over lighthouses?"

"No, you damn fool! I told you, it's more complicated than one simple issue. But that lighthouse thing is directly out of the Georgia Causes of Secession document. You can take that to the bank. And another thing—"

They went back to nattering on about a war fought hundreds of years ago that Mattis honestly had minimal feelings about. He was too busy thinking about their *current* problem. And where the next attack was coming from.

Fight the current war. Not the last war.

He sighed. Six months out here, listening to Lynch defend the confederacy and Modi drone on about technological matters that didn't concern him.

So when the long-range communications system flashed on his command console, Mattis mostly felt a profound sense of relief.

"Report," he said to Lynch, pointedly interrupting his conversation.

Lynch swiveled on his chair, palpably reluctant to abandon his current line of discussion, but as his eyes scrolled over his console his obvious reticence evaporated. "It's a distress signal," he said. "Coming in on Z-space, from a nearby Chinese embassy on the planet Sanctuary, in the Omid Sector. It's being transmitted on an open frequency."

Normally the Chinese relied on their own. They must really be desperate. "What's the nature of their distress?"

Lynch read for a moment before continuing. "They're reporting that the building is being overrun by the local inhabitants. They say there's gunfire, and two of the Chinese marines have been wounded."

"Gunfire?" asked Mattis, scowling. "Who the hell shoots up a Chinese embassy? Especially *now*?"

"According to the report," said Lynch, a slight twinge of hesitation in his voice, "the primary bulk of the rioters are US veterans of the Sino-American War. Sanctuary has a disproportionate number of them living there, or so I hear. They call themselves the Forgotten. How dramatic."

Mattis knew why. He'd fought in that war himself. "Sanctuary was the site of one of the first open conflicts between the PRC and the US. The Chinese embassy was the site of some of the first bloodshed."

"This isn't really our jurisdiction," said Lynch, his tone sympathetic. "We're a warship. We have a job to do. This is a matter for local law enforcement."

And yet, whatever served as a police force on that world didn't seem like it was capable of maintaining order. Incapable, or perhaps unwilling. At this point the difference was vanishingly small.

Still, Lynch was right.

"Stay on course and relay the message for anyone else to respond," said Mattis. "We can't intervene."

It sucked, but it was the right call. Right calls were often like that.

The long-range communications array flashed again. Another signal. "Sir," said Lynch, "Fleet Command is responding to the relay. They're ordering us to intervene."

That was *fast*. Suspiciously so. "Lets roll," said Mattis. "Commander Modi, begin Z-space translation. Let's get to Omid and find out what the hell's going on over there."

Lynch relayed some commands, then glanced up to catch Mattis' eye. "That was fast," he said, echoing Mattis's own thoughts. "You think there's something bigger going on here?"

Mattis set his jaw, but shrugged. "Let's hope not."

Lynch mirrored the shrug. "Obviously. But … what do you think's going on, Jack?"

He considered. "After the things we've seen?" He turned back to the command console. "Who knows. Let's just hope it's a disgruntled veteran, deal with him, then get back to guarding civilization."

Chapter Two

Parkland
Georgetown, Maryland
United States
Earth

Chuck Mattis fiddled with the lint in his pocket with one hand, his other hand pressing his communicator up to his ear so he could hear his husband better. "Can you say that again? The reception here is awful."

"Of course it is," said Elroy Lowery-Mattis. "You're out in the wilderness."

Wilderness. Chuck smiled faintly. "You know Georgetown is just across the river from Baltimore. I'm a strong swimmer. I could dive right in, hike to Baltimore, then catch a bus to Washington. I could be at Capitol Hill in, like, two hours."

"Are you sure? I hear banjos in the background. Best make a shelter quick, before you're eaten by wolves."

Chuck laughed. "Okay, okay. I will." He forced his tone to become serious. Elroy always had a way of making him laugh even when it wasn't appropriate. "But seriously—what's this about Jack?"

Jack, formerly Javier. Six-month-old Jack Javier Mattis.

"Oh, nothing. They're just moving him to—" the connection dropped out for a second, then it returned. "For some kind of test, I don't know."

"You … don't know?" A spike of worry shot through him. "Do they think it's serious?"

"What?"

Damn the lack of stable communications connection. His tiny device could send a signal via Z-space relays to distant star systems light years away, but it couldn't get a good signal 30 kilometers from Baltimore. "I asked, is it serious? The problem with Javier."

"Nah," said Elroy. "Honestly, it's totally fine. It's just a heart problem, something they think—"

"His *heart*?" Chuck practically crushed his communicator. "Okay, I'm going to fly out there. He's still an infant, if his heart gives out there might not be anything they can do. Where did you say he was being moved to?"

"He's fine," said Elroy.

"He's not fine! You said his heart had some kind of problem."

"Hang on, lemme read." Faint shuffling in the background. Or perhaps more static. Chuck couldn't be sure. "Okay, here's what it says. It says there's a slight murmur in his heart. It's not serious, but they want to move him to a specialist for evaluation. Worst case scenario—Chuck, it says here, worst case—is that he might need some *minor* surgery."

Minor … no surgery was minor on an infant. "Okay," said Chuck, taking a deep breath.

Elroy was quiet for a bit. "You aren't freaking out about this because of your new job, are you?"

Maybe. Chuck pulled his hand out of his pocket and ran it through his hair. Being a legislative aide was something he had little experience with—how exactly he'd gotten hired was a bit of a miracle—but the work so far was agreeable and his new boss seemed to like him. "I dunno," he confessed. "Maybe. It's certainly different than working as a policy analyst for Senator Pitt, but … the pay is better. I like it."

"Sounds like you're trying to convince me," said Elroy. "That's going to be difficult when you don't know yourself."

Yeah. That was … fair. "It's not exactly where I'd envisioned myself at this age, married with a family," he confessed. "But, you know, it's … genuinely nice. And in regard to Senator Pitt, well—" Chuck grit his teeth so hard they hurt. "I think he did what he felt he needed to do given the circumstances."

"Mmm." Elroy's voice was tinged with humor. "Politics is a *great* field for you, Chuck. If you can lie about that, you can lie about anything."

Yeah, yeah, yeah. Chuck wasn't mad—he was *furious*. But being furious at someone who was politically untouchable was useless. It was a waste of emotion and if he allowed his thoughts to progress unchecked, they would eventually consume him. So he put the anger, the bitterness, the sense of betrayal behind him and focused on the present. On his relaxing walk through the woods. On his new job. On his son.

Or so he told himself.

His communicator vibrated. Annoyed, Chuck glanced at it.

PRIORITY ALERT: HOSTAGE SITUATION IN THE SHUAZZEN SYSTEM

Shuazzen system … the *Midway* was stationed there. Chuck frowned to himself. "Hey, El? There's a situation. I gotta go."

"Okay," said Elroy. He was always so understanding. "Should I send someone to pick you up?"

"Yeah. There's some kind of problem in my Dad's location … and knowing him, he just can't stop himself getting involved."

Chapter Three

Chinese Embassy
Planet Sanctuary
Omid Sector

Marine Captain Mitch Ryan hadn't seen cowering Chinese soldiers in a long, long time. Six soldiers in binders, four men, two women. He still had teeth marks on his hands where one of them had bitten the crap out of him.

"Yeah, that's right," he said, pacing in front of them, his assault rifle slung casually over his chest. "You bastards know why you're here."

"Go to hell," spat one of the embassy guards. She was the one who bit him. The *biter*. "The war's over."

"The hot war's over," clarified Ryan, trying to keep his thick Louisianan accent understandable. "But it didn't end. Not then. Not now. It's still going."

"You're insane."

Ryan had heard too many people say that today. "It's still going, and we're going to prove it."

"But—"

"No. No more talking." Ryan pointedly rested his hand on the grip of his rifle. "You get me?"

She nodded mutely.

One of his men, a fellow veteran, spoke up. "We're ready to stream," he said. "We'll be live once we flick the switch. The video will go to GBC news, to hundreds of local news stations on settled worlds, and as far into space as our Z-space transmitter can get us." He smiled. "We're going to deep six the lies, sir."

Good.

"Is the SAM ready?" asked Ryan. A surface-to-air missile would guarantee their safety from air strikes. "I don't want any … *surprises* when we're filming."

"Yup," said his cameraman. "Any aircraft or spacecraft entering the atmosphere anywhere over this whole city is going to get splatted."

Then it was time for business. Ryan hadn't been on TV for a while. Between that and seeing the Chinese prisoners on their knees, this day had been worth all of the waiting. He moved in front of the camera and took a breath, glancing over his shoulder at the huge American flag flying above him, and the kneeling prisoners below it. They looked suitably scared. Even the biter.

"Ready?" said his cameraman. "Five, four, three, two…" He pointed.

"My fellow Americans," said Ryan, the words feeling good as they rolled off his tongue. "My name is Marine Captain

Mitch Ryan. I'm here to address you all on a matter of great urgency. That topic is … the government. More specifically *your* government, dear Americans. The Office of the President of the United States is a sacred position to all of us. A beacon of freedom for all of humanity." Ryan once again rested his hand on the grip of his rifle. "But that position has been disrespected by the so-called President Edita Schuyler; disrespected in a way you and I can no longer tolerate."

"Go to hell!" The biter shouted, disrupting his thoughts. One of his fellow veterans thumped her in the back with the butt of a rifle.

Slowly, Ryan returned his attention back toward the camera. "Friendship Station," he said. "Most of you know this place. Saw its construction, beam by beam, bulkhead by bulkhead, on the news. Two years of work. Tens of thousands of tons of steel. The blood and sweat of Americans put into creating this … thing. An ideological bridge between us and our enemies. We tried to make peace with our enemies. Because that is the American way. And what did our enemies do? They burned that bridge from under our feet."

He reached down and grabbed the biter by her hair, yanking her face up into the camera. "These Chinese, they aren't like us. They don't think like us. Don't want the same things we do. They don't *want* to live freely. They choose to exist under the iron boot of tyranny and oppression, and extend that oppression to others. That is why they attacked Friendship Station. That is why they murdered our fellow Americans in cold blood."

Ryan released the biter's hair and let her fall face down on the ground. "There's a narrative at work here. A narrative being written by those in power, working for their own interests and against those of the people they swore an oath to serve. Instead, they turn their efforts towards destroying that which generations of Americans have worked, fought, and died to create." He pulled back the charging handle and chambered a round in his rifle. "We believe that which can be destroyed by the truth should be. And we plan on doing plenty of destroying."

The veterans raised their rifles, but right as they were about to fire, the cameraman waved his hand. "Sir, we're off the air."

"What?" Ryan scowled over his shoulder. "Stand down, men. We want them to see this." Then he turned to the cameraman. "What's the problem, marine?"

"Something's blocking the signal. A jammer—a big one, too. Not a local source. Something in orbit."

A shout came from the other room. "Captain, a ship has pulled into orbit! It's the *Midway*, sir!"

The *Midway*. His old float, with the old man himself, Admiral Jack Mattis. They couldn't possibly have asked for better luck.

"Oorah." Ryan's smile became a mile wide. "Power down the SAM and let them land. Ladies and gentlemen, reinforcements have arrived."

Chapter Four

Apartment 13B7, Whitley Building
Planet Zenith
Tonatiuh Sector

Steve Bratta looked between the calendar and his new phone, and grimaced.

The phone might have been an inferior model—although its incompatibility with his multifunction headphone jack and secondary battery port was a serious concern—but it still worked and, thanks to the backups on his external hard drive, he still had all his contacts. A lesser man may have found his efforts to contact anyone stymied by the loss of his phone, but Bratta was better prepared than that. It had been four weeks since the incident and he really needed someone to talk to, but *she* was the only person he could think of to call.

With a significantly diminished sense of anticipation than usual, he connected the new phone to his external hard drive, and dialed.

The voice that came through was thick, familiar, and defiantly Scottish. "Jean Tafola, speaking. Who is this?"

She'd gone back to her old surname? Rude. "Steve. Steve Bratta. Your husba—ah, ex-husband."

There was a long pause. "Alright, Steve. To what, may I ask, do I owe the pleasure?"

"Pleasure? I thought you didn't want to talk to me, after the yelling, and the swearing, and the—"

"I don't."

"Oh. Right." But Jeannie was his only—well, *hope of surviving* was a probably little melodramatic. Probably. Bratta's hand started shaking. "Uh, I do need to talk to someone right now, and I don't have anyone else really so I don't suppose you'll let me talk to you anyway?"

"You … don't have anyone else? Really, Steve?" There was either confusion or pity in her voice. It was hard to tell over the distortion, but it wasn't his fault the signal optimization program he was running was still in beta. It had worked just fine on his other phone.

"Well, I am seeing someone, but I can't talk to her."

"*You?* Seeing someone?" Jeannie asked.

"I'm sorry, how are you both surprised that I have no one else to talk to, and that I am seeing someone? These seem to be mutually exclusive views, Jeannie."

"It's Jean."

"Really? Come on, you've always been Jeannie to me—"

"You have five seconds."

Bratta blinked.

"Four." Jeannie's voice was as cold as the soup he'd

forgotten about fretting over this call.

"Three."

Wait, she was actually serious? "No no no, please," he gabbled. "Jeannie I'm in trouble I think and I—"

"Two."

"*IwasattackedbyanalienatworkandIgotitonvideoandittriedtokillmebutitdidn'tandthenamarinedestroyedmyphonebutthevideo'sonmyharddrive* … help."

"What?"

He shook his head. "I know it sounds crazy, but please! It really happened, I haven't been to work since."

"No. Steve. I have no idea what you just said."

"Oh, sorry." He wondered if there was any way to tell her that wouldn't end in her hanging up. He took a deep, steadying breath. "Do you remember the alien attacks last year?"

"No, because I live entirely in my own head."

"You've never—"

"Like you," Jeannie interrupted pointedly.

"Jeannie! That's wholly undeserved, I—so you remember them?"

"Of course, Steven, who the hell forgets an alien attack? Now *why are you wasting my time?*"

"I think I might have been attacked by one of them. And I think I might have the only video evidence of them, outside the government." He paused to let that news sink in.

"You know, I might just give your local police department a ring, because you are either clearly extremely high, or—"

"What? Jeannie, do you have any idea how dangerous recreational ingestion of psychoactive compounds can be?"

"Yes. I *am* a police officer."

Bratta pinched the bridge of his nose. This was going far more poorly than he'd feared. But then, that tended to happen with a lot of his social interactions. "They … they were right in front of me, Jeannie. They wrecked my car, and I think … I don't know, they were angry. They came out of nowhere, everyone ran, I lost my glasses. I … I don't know what's going on, and you're the only person who can help me. Um, I think the future of humanity might depend on it."

There was silence, broken only by the sound of a chair scraping. "Steve, tell me you've learned to lie. Please."

Bratta found himself uncomfortably reminded of the circumstances that had lead to their divorce. How was he meant to respond to that? "No? I've, uh, always been able to lie? Most people can."

Jeannie must have exhaled quite forcefully, because the line blanked out to static for a second. "Alright, Steve. Just tell me what's going on."

An image of the alien's mottled parody of a face flashed before his eyes. He took a steadying breath. "Right. Well, four weeks ago, I was arriving at work. I couldn't find my ID and I hadn't had my coffee, but, well, that's probably not important. Anyway, I was just inside when a body fell out of the sky. A body. Abdomen all but destroyed, multiple lacerations, severe head trauma. Not good. That was when the alien showed up, on top of the compound wall near where the body had fallen. It looked around a bit, like … like a werewolf in the movies, honestly, and I started filming, because, well, it was an alien, so that was interesting. But then it attacked the crowd, where I was, so I obviously had to stop filming to run away, and one of them wrecked my car in the carpark and I kind of froze up and got some footage of it, but then a marine turned up and broke my phone but I'd been recording to my external hard drive anyway so I still have the recording and—"

"Steve! Stop talking, now."

He paused, confused. "Sorry?"

Jeannie's tone shifted, like she was talking to a child. "You're telling me this over an *unsecured line*?"

"You wanted to know...."

"I ... yes, this is important, but anyone could be listening!"

"I doubt they are. It's been four weeks."

"Steve," Jeannie groaned. "Look, remember that date we went on, where you" her voice turned mocking, "lasted half a second?"

Why was she making fun of him? Was ... was she talking about *sex*? Bratta stammered. "Jeannie it wasn't what you're making it sound like!" There had been a mechanical bull shaped like a giant wild haggis, a blasted over-sized rat —"Those things are *very* tricky to ride, I just anticipated it would go forward rather than back first, and—"

"I know, I know. I'm just never going to let you forget it." A low chuckle crackled across the line. "Meet me there on the anniversary of your, ah, performance."

All of this was completely uncalled for. What if someone was listening? Bratta's face burned. "I don't know what you mean."

"Steve. You need to meet me there. On the anniversary."

Was she trying to tell him something? He racked his brains, and glanced back at the calendar.

"But that's—"

"Yes."

He was still confused. "But it's not the … date—you mean, the date of the date, or the date-date?"

"Steve." Jeannie sounded like she might lose her temper. "Just … never mind. Ignore that, I forgot that subtlety isn't your thing. Listen. Pack your bags. You need to get off-planet. Now."

She hung up. He glanced at the calendar again, and finally realized why he'd been staring at it all morning.

Their anniversary.

And it was only a few days away.

He slowly packed his bag, unsure whether he'd made the right decision. She was a cop, and cops had guns, and ex-wives with guns on anniversaries was not a winning combination.

"What the hell have I gotten myself into?"

Chapter Five

Bridge
USS Midway
High orbit above Sanctuary
Omid Sector

Mattis watched as Z-space disappeared on the various monitors scattered all around the bridge, a thousand vibrant hues settling back into a vision of the real world.

"Z-space translation complete," said Lynch. "We are in orbit above Sanctuary."

Sanctuary was a bright blue world, similar to Earth but almost entirely comprised of water. Its days were short and hot, and what little land existed was rain-soaked and sun-scorched. Not exactly a pleasant place to live, but it had an abundance of fish and aquatic life, and accordingly, a thriving fishing industry. Where there was industry there were jobs, and where there were jobs, there were settlers.

"Very good," said Mattis. "And the jammer is still in effect?"

"Yes, Captain," said Modi. "All Z-space transmissions out of this world are being squelched; approximately forty-four seconds of recording have, unfortunately, been successfully broadcast."

"Forty-four seconds?" Lynch scrunched up his face. "Why can't you just say, approximately forty, or even better, approximately fifty, you damn robot? Does it really matter?"

"It matters to me," said Modi, his tone even.

Mattis raised his hand in a calming gesture, something he had seen his old XO, Commander Pitt, do. It seemed to work. "Let's focus on the mission at hand, gentlemen," said Mattis. The adoption of his former XO's mannerisms threw a cold blanket over an otherwise fairly lighthearted moment.

How often had Commander Pitt broken up these two from their bickering? Now that he was gone, did that responsibility fall entirely on him?

"Excellent," said Modi. "I concur."

"I concur," said Lynch, his tone bathed in sarcasm.

For senior Navy officers, wrangling them was sometimes like herding children. "Put a hole in the Z-space jammer," said Mattis, leaning forward in his seat. "And open a channel to the surface. This ... Marine Captain Mitch Ryan. I want to speak to him in person."

"Aye aye, sir," said Modi. "We're patching you in right now."

It took several minutes to establish the connection. When it did come through, the video was patchy and full of static. Seemed to be routed through the exact same camera the guy had used to film his so-called manifesto.

Through the digital dust he saw a man. Aged, with tanned skin and a strong jaw, grey streaks running through his thinning, dark hair. He carried an assault rifle slung in front of him, one of a style Mattis hadn't seen in decades.

Is this how people see me? A crazy old man, a relic from a battle long past, comically out of time?

No time to think about that. "Good evening," said Mattis. "Marine Captain Ryan, I presume?"

"You presume correctly, Admiral," said Ryan, clicking his heels together and coming to a swift attention. "It's good to see you again."

Mattis tilted his head. "We've met before?"

"A lifetime ago," said Ryan. "I was stationed on the *Midway* during the war. US Marine Corps."

So many servicemen had served upon a ship as old and storied as the *Midway* that claim was believable, but Mattis wanted the truth. Too many people pretended to be veterans—for benefits, for social prestige, to gain the edge in hostage negotiations. "That so. When's the Marine Corps birthday?"

"November 10th. 1775." The answer came instantly.

Something he could have looked up on the net, certainly, but there were other questions that those outside of the military would be hard pressed to answer. "What was your MOS?"

"2305," said Ryan, again instantly. "Explosive Ordnance Disposal. Because Total Badass isn't a proper job title."

That surprised him. "You were a minesweeper?"

"Yes sir," said Ryan. "We would pray every day to Bob Ross, the Patron Saint of EOD." He grinned like a jackal.

"Minesweeper's motto: there are no mistakes, just happy little accidents."

Mattis nodded slowly. The guy was who he said he was. "Very well, marine. Do you know who *I* am?"

"Yes sir, Admiral. Knew it the moment I heard your voice. Admiral Jack Mattis. The only guy who stood up to the Chinese and won. The only one who in this whole fucked-up galaxy actually believes us. Who understands what we're doing."

Mattis glowered. "Don't presume to know what I believe."

Slowly, whatever relief, joy, that was on Captain Ryan's face slowly faded away. "Sir," he said, "you *are* here to help us, aren't you?"

"Son," said Mattis, "I was *at* Freedom Station when it was attacked. I fought alongside the *Fuqing* and Captain Shao, and I was there when she died. I caught the first half of your little … manifesto. Regardless of whatever you suspect about the nature of that attack, the people you're holding are *not* in any way responsible. I'm here to secure their release."

Ryan's tone shifted. "That will prove difficult," he said. "I want the galaxy to see us end these rats on live TV." There was a long pause. "Seems like we're at opposite goals, Admiral."

"Seems so." Mattis squeezed his fist so tightly the knuckles cracked. "But it doesn't have to be this way, Ryan. Talk to me. We have a shared history. We can work this out."

"Sir, with respect, go piss up a rope." The connection ended.

Mattis slumped back in his chair.

"What an a-hole," said Lynch. "I think the good marine is two sandwiches short of a picnic."

"Aren't they all?" asked Modi.

Anger surged within him, but he smothered it under a professional mask. "Damn that idiot." Mattis stood out of his chair. "Get a shuttle ready, I'm going down there. Lynch, Modi, you're with me."

"Sir?" asked both of them, together.

"Modi, I need you because you're a genius. Maybe there's a way your skills can help resolve this peacefully."

"Okay," said Lynch, "but shouldn't I stay with the ship?"

"I need you for your tactical expertise," said Mattis. "In case this whole thing goes sideways."

Lynch grimaced. "You don't want marines for that?"

"Might be a needless provocation," said Mattis. "Besides. What could go wrong?"

Lynch didn't miss a beat. "Everything."

But Mattis was already out the door.

Chapter Six

Pilot's Ready Room
USS Midway
High orbit above Sanctuary
Omid Sector

Lieutenant Patricia "Guano" Corrick scratched the small piece of chalk across the large blackboard which had been set up to cover one whole wall of the pilot's ready room. A wall of shame where she wrote the same message over and over and over and over again.

I MUST NOT CRASH MY SHIP
I MUST NOT CRASH MY SHIP
I MUST NOT CRASH MY SHIP
I MUST NOT CRASH MY SHIP
I MUST NOT CRASH MY SHIP

It wasn't *her* fault, she mused, starting another line. The first time she had taken down multiple alien attack ships and the damage she had suffered was *entirely* legitimate. She had saved her gunner's life, Flatline, and that was good. Sure, that ship cost something like $120,000,000 but it wasn't like their CAG, Roadie, paid for it out of his own pocket. It was just … one of those things.

The second time was a little *less* justified. She'd been bounced by fighters from above and they'd taken out Joker. Her gunner had tried to eject, but no joy. Oops?

On reflection, she would definitely rather be here writing lines than the alternative.

I MUST NOT CRASH MY SHIP
I MUST NOT CRASH MY SHIP
I MUST NOT CRASH MY SHIP

This was literally the most boring thing she'd ever done. Which is probably why Roadie had assigned her to it with such relish. Boredom was the ultimate foe of the military serviceman. Groaning internally, she began to write again, fighting down a surge of anger. I MUST NO—

"Guano?"

The voice almost made her jump out of her skin. She dragged the chalk across the blackboard, leaving a large white streak. The noise made the hairs on the back of her neck stand up.

"What?!" she shouted, spinning around, chalk held out in front of her like a knife.

Roadie held up his hands. "Woah, easy," he said, frowning

slightly. "You okay?"

"I'm fine," said Guano, lowering her chalk and taking a deep breath. "You just … startled me."

"You been taking your meds?"

Up yours, she thought. "Yes. *And* the supplements. Gotta stay in tip-top shape, remember? Nothing like vitamin and essential amino acid supplements to satisfy a hungry fighter jock stomach."

"Oh stop complaining. We all take them. Orders from way up. They say it helps our reaction times."

Guano turned back to the board and wrote one more line. "I'll show you reaction times," she grumbled under her breath.

"Well," said Roadie, raising an eyebrow, "as enthralling as writing lines must be, I got a mission for you."

Her heart actually skipped in her chest. "You're shitting me, aren't you, sir?" Corrick leaned forward, unable to stop her mouth falling open eagerly. "Sir, Roadie, I swear, if you tell me you have a CAP for me, a new ship, I *swear* to you I might kiss you. I might."

Roadie scrunched up his face in disgust. "As much as I would hate that—" He jerked his thumb over his shoulder. "Get down to the hangar bay. The old man and the XO are going down to the surface. Gotta have someone fly the shuttle. Guess who."

Her ego deflated somewhat. She wanted to be back in a fighter. But at least it was *something.* "Because," she asked, "they need the best pilot for the job, right?"

"The *worst,*" corrected Roadie, a slight grin showing he was kidding. "At least the one with the worst history. I just figure that if we get them all killed in one fell swoop, I get to pick the next Captain. And I'll make sure they show more love to the air wing. Plus, you know, I'd get Lynch's room, and his quarters are *to die for.*"

Corrick poked out her tongue. "Nah, you want me because I'm the best," she said, waggling her finger.

"The best at *crashing.*"

Corrick snorted. If it were some other kind of mission, he might have just been ribbing her, but the Admiral… there was no way he genuinely thought this kind of stuff. You don't risk an Admiral's life by entrusting it to a flunkie. "What about Flatline?"

"Oh," said Roadie, almost as though it were an afterthought. "Well, our new fighters are being disassembled, and I thought some of the gunners could take a go at flying them. Just to break them in, you know?"

Corrick spluttered. "B-but my new ship—!"

"Relax," said Roadie, "he's going with you. I don't trust you with a shuttle on your own. Now go—the away party's waiting for you."

Grateful to be done with writing lines, Corrick tore out of the room, grabbing her flight suit off the rack as she went.

Roadie called after her. "Hey, Corrick?"

"Yeah?"

His face was serious. "Make sure that ship comes back in one piece. You're a great stick, I mean that, but there's only so many times I can explain to Admiral Mattis that the perpetual fuckup should keep being allowed back in the cockpit of multi-billion dollar spacecraft. Not. A. Scratch."

She bit her lip and nodded. "Not a scratch," she said, crossing her heart. "I promise."

Chapter Seven

Courtyard
Chinese Embassy
Sanctuary
Omid Sector

The shuttle touched down in an empty street opposite the Chinese embassy. Mattis stepped out, immediately greeted by a soft breeze tinged with ocean salt. The building had been freshly painted, a light brown with darker peaked roofs in the traditional Chinese style. A beautiful garden sat out the front, with two dozen flowering trees, a well kept layer of grass, and the bright red flag of the PRC flying above.

They always had an eye for style. The only thing out of place was the front gate; a fence flanked by ceramic dragons, its white metal bars twisted, forced open. Strange, because it wouldn't have been that hard to climb it. Not for a young man, anyway. But nobody who had fought in the war was young anymore.

Especially not him.

The streets surrounding the building had been evacuated, giving the whole area a desolate, abandoned look. The only hint it was artificial was the yellow and black striped barricades, beyond which were Chinese soldiers and American police.

Mattis beckoned one of the cops over.

"I'm Admiral Jack Mattis," he said. "Gimme a sitrep."

The cop, a tall, pale-skinned man stepped over the line, gun cradled in his hands. "Well," he said, eyes occasionally flicking to the building, "we got hostages on the top floor, with hostage-takers scattered around. We cut the power, but it looks like they have some kind of portable generator. They're heavily armed and they seem to know what they're doing. They move like military."

Great. Just great. Mattis waved the guy away and focused on the tall Chinese building. *What to do…*

"Okay," said Lynch, shaking his head as he stepped out of the shuttle behind Mattis, "you know you're out of your depth with this one, right? This is a hostage negotiation. This isn't like Friendship Station; some dang diplomatic party where everyone will be good to you. If we mess this up, those guys in there will probably shoot us."

"Probably," admitted Mattis, hands on his hips. "But I can't send some nineteen year old with a certificate into this. The war was hard, Lynch. It did hard things to these people. And I can help them because I understand them. These people fought with me."

"Yeah," said Lynch, his voice tinged in hesitation. "And now they're fighting *with* you, if you know what I mean."

He certainly did but there was no time to think about that now. "They're sick," he said. "And I want to help them."

"Sir?" said Modi, cautiously. "A vehicle is approaching."

Mattis turned to look. Coming down the abandoned, cordoned-off street was an armored personnel carrier, black and emblazoned with the star of the People's Republic of China.

The shuttle lifted off behind him, whining softly as it took to the air, and the APC pulled up in front of the embassy, blocking him with its body. The rear door opened.

"What the hell are you doing?" hissed a Chinese marine, poking her head out the back, her face partially obscured by a bulletproof visor on a black helmet. "This is a People's Republic matter—you need to come with me right now."

"Nope, said Mattis. "Not until I sort this out."

"An embassy is sovereign Chinese territory," said the marine, adjusting her helmet. "You can't go in there."

"But the street is US soil. You can't stop me while I'm *here* and not *there*." He stepped around the APC and moved up to the bent gate, straightening his back and putting on his best commander's voice. "Ryan! It's Admiral Mattis!" he shouted.

"Go away," came Ryan's voice from within. He was on the upper level.

"I just want to talk with you."

"Not sure you want to hear what I have to say right now, Admiral."

Mattis jabbed a finger to the APC. "You see them?" he called. "The armor on that APC is a composite matrix of laminated ceramic-steel-nickel alloy with underlaid reactive armor. It has an effective thickness of 1,600mm. When you busted down the gate and took over the embassy, did you drag any armor-piercing railguns along with you?"

Ryan said nothing.

"Come on," said Mattis. "We can talk about this. But I'm getting mighty sick of shouting."

"Like hell, you traitor." Ryan's voice picked up. "I thought you were going to be on *our* side!"

Mattis rolled his eyes.

"Sir," said Modi, behind him, "you should know, five marines just climbed out of the APC and into the sewers."

Chapter Eight

Dining room
Shuttlecraft Satine
Tonatiuh Sector

Bratta stared out the window at the receding inner worlds of the Tonatiuh Sector. It was an actual window, too, not just the usual camera and screen arrangement. The *Satine* was an expensive shuttle—far more expensive than he could afford—but she had been the first ticket off Zenith, and even a large bite out of his wallet was worth that.

A far more pressing concern than his dwindling cash reserves, however, was the view this angle gave of the rest of the passengers in the *Satine*'s restaurant. Adorned with tailored suits, expensive-looking dresses, and noses stuck high in the air, the logical part of Bratta's brain was fairly sure that the only attention he was getting from his fellow travelers (and there wasn't much of that) was thanks to his, well, less-than-boutique best clothes. A darker corner of his mind disagreed. Was that man in the dangerously-sharp tuxedo looking at him a little bit too closely? Had that woman in the plunging red dress been glancing his way too much? Was the old man in the other corner, the one with the goatee, really just looking at the painting above his table? Was he about to die? Or had he watched too many spy flicks?

Bratta pushed the food around on his plate, arranging it by alphabetical order according to its common name (color spectrum, classification, and similarity to the human genome had already been sorted) and tried to not look at any of the other passengers. He was fairly sure it wasn't the worst strategy for avoiding attention. *Just a bored guy in the corner, nothing interesting to see here. No governmental secrets being smuggled off-planet, no, keep moving, it's fine I swear.*

He was, of course, avoiding the problem. The problem with the aliens. Or … whatever they'd been.

They'd been bipedal, which was, well, coincidental. Interestingly so, perhaps. Bratta was fairly aware—on a conceptual level, at least—of the size of even the Milky Way. The odds of such a humanlike alien having evolved near enough to human civilization to reach them through Z-space were, while certainly within the realms of possibility, quite literally astronomical. A lack of obvious breathing apparatus on either specimen suggested that their respiratory systems required an earth-like atmosphere, which was another remarkable coincidence, although he hadn't exactly had a good enough look at either alien to confirm this situation. Then there was the actual structure of the creature—although the size and proportions were monstrously *off*, especially the great long arms, all the basic shapes had been there.

And yet, they had been anything but human. The rotting coloration had looked neither natural nor healthy; if not for the ruined teeth he might have postulated some skin-shedding process, but overall it looked like … necrosis, honestly. Then there was the strength of the creatures—and their durability. Most animals didn't pull off that kind of antics and walk away. The sheer *strain* they seemed to be able to shake off was terrifying. The scope of it all hit Bratta, and he swallowed, throat suddenly dry. He really had no idea what he was dealing with.

Except … maybe he did. Bratta shoved a chunk of buttered bread absently into his mouth as he scrolled through his phone's files. *No, surely not*, he thought as he flicked through years of particularly fascinating papers. *Those authors were crackpots, pedaling notions a step above pseudoscience.* The text slowed as he reached his undergrad years, and he kept an eye out for … it would have had "evolution" in the title, wouldn't it? *Still, it was pseudoscience that sounded like these aliens. Maybe there'll be something useful in their references?*

Or there might have been, if the paper had been on his phone. Damn. Well, that wasn't too much of a problem, he had everything on his external hard drive, he'd just have to wait until he was in his—

The sound of a child yelling broke apart his train of thought, causing Bratta to jump about a foot in the air. Around him, a few of his fellow restaurant-goers were similarly startled, but most of them reacted only by shaking their heads a little, and muttering, if at all. When Bratta's eyes found the source of the disturbance, he understood. Red Dress lady was standing over a boy of about ten years old in a suit—bow tie and everything—performing a strange duet with his steadily rising voice, as he pointed, red-faced, at his, uhhh, entrée, probably. They had Australian accents.

Bratta looked away, and noticed three sets of eyes on him once more. The old man with the goatee was definitely looking at him, eyebrow raised, and Tuxedo Guy had been joined by a friend two tables over in a turban. The old guy had a big chunk of his ear missing, like a dog had chewed it off, or even a wild haggis … perhaps some other kind of rodent? Either way, it had left a massive lump of scar tissue right on the side of the guy's head.

Bratta shuddered and stared back, trying to commit their faces to memory. Goatee looked surprisingly healthy for a man his age, actually, although yes, those were plastic surgery marks right there. Tuxedo Guy was plainer than his clothes, but he had a few red marks on his right eyelid. Bratta stopped. Those weren't just any marks, that was a signature rash of an irritated cybernetic eyesocket interface. He'd be able to see, well, everything. Paying for tech like that, the man must have been one of the richest people on the shuttle. And then Turban. Hmm. For one thing, the man was Caucasian, which made for an odd combination. Ooh, and for another, his fingers were ever-so-slightly yellowed. Nicotine staining. He was a heavy smoker.

Bratta was feeling quite Holmesian until he realized he was attracting more stares. Ah. He'd quite forgotten about that bread roll. And if he remembered correctly, it wasn't exactly good etiquette to sit around with half a bun hanging out of one's mouth.

On the plus side, he hadn't met up with Jeannie yet, so this was one social faux pas she'd never be able to insult him over.

Success?

He wolfed down the rest of his food, then bolted with almost equal speed for his room, where four walls and a porthole opening only to space would shield him from the rest of humanity.

On the *Satine*'s plush carpets, Bratta never even heard the footfalls coming up behind him. He only noticed the stun-stick pointed at him when its voltage was already coursing through his frame.

And he definitely never felt the hand rifling through his pockets, and plucking out his new phone, the Ume-chan anime girl sticker on its back filling his vision for a moment before everything went away.

Chapter Nine

Inside the Chinese Embassy
Sanctuary
Omid Sector

Ryan shifted away from the second floor window, careful to keep his head down. The damn reds would have snipers everywhere.

His hand was shaking. Hadn't done that since the war. Not even storming the building had gotten his fingers to tremble so. Yet now they did. The last time that had happened, the Chinese had established air support over Sanctuary, and with their newfound dominance, halted the American advance and reversed it. If the end of the war hadn't happened, every single one of them would all be dead; ground into paste by round-the-clock bombing.

He didn't like that it was back.

"Sir," said Gunnery Sergeant Kellie Castro, his

communications specialist, a middle-aged Cuban woman with a tablet in her hand, hair dyed bright pink to hide the greying. "We're still trying to get through the interference."

"Gunny, I need you to do better than try," said Ryan, snappishly. "There's a goddamn Chinese APC out there and they aren't coming over to talk."

"Yeah, well, they ain't exactly making things easy on me."

"Hearing a lot of excuses, Gunny," said Ryan. "Get through that goddamn jamming signal, oorah?"

"Oorah," she said, turning back to her tablet.

Ryan risked a glance out the window at the APC. It was a model he hadn't even seen before; an evolution of their previous types. Back in the day, they used to pop those things all the time. Attacking from below was their favorite trick. When the reds rolled into New Texas on Proxima Centauri Five, he and his men had used the sewer system to damage the vehicle's undersides. That's where the armor was thinnest. Even a moderate explosive from below would fuck up an APC.

His gaze lingered, looking to the street. Maybe they'd gotten lucky and a sewer grate was nearby.

There was one.

It was open.

"Dammit," he said, ducking back below the window. "Gunny. Gunny! Can you put me through to Mattis again?"

"Isn't he just outside?" asked Castro, not looking up from her work.

He didn't want the damn Chinese to hear. Or … did he?

"Mattis!" shouted Jack. "We know they're in the sewers! If those soldiers come even one foot past the boundaries of the embassy, we're going to detonate the bombs on every single fucking one of the prisoners, I swear to God!"

Castro looked up. "We have actual bombs? I thought all we had were grenades, and the SAM."

"You're right, of course. No bombs." Ryan smiled. "But *they* don't know that."

Chapter Ten

Shuttlecraft Satine
Tonatiuh Sector

Bratta wondered what had woken him.

He was comfortable, so that wasn't a problem. Curled up and … was that carpet tickling at his nostrils? Yes, that was definitely carpet. *What the…*? He'd never sleepwalked before.

He stretched out and *ow ow ow ow, no,* everything hurt. What was *wrong* with him? He cracked an eye open and saw a corridor. Voices, not bothering to keep quiet, echoed from the other end. There was … there was probably something wrong with that, wasn't there? He struggled to his feet and stared around. Empty, but yes, that was his room right there and—

His brain finally kicked into gear. Unconsciousness, muscular pain, particularly in—two areas of his back, he realized—serious disorientation and lack of coordination … well, more than usual. He'd probably been stunned, and drugged with … something. For good measure. Hopefully it would wear off soon; he didn't like not being able to think. That was why caffeine had been his friend so long. Being tired was the worst.

The voices grew louder.

Wait. This was weird. Weird drew attention. Attention was bad. He scrabbled through his pockets, fumbled—no, that was his work ID—ah! His room key! He waved it under the sensor and scrambled inside.

His room was a bit of a mess. Far messier than he'd left it, actually. He riffled for his phone. Came up with nothing.

A chill spread up Bratta's spine. Someone had robbed him, and he could think of only one reason a thief would target the most obviously poor passenger on this ship. He dove for his suitcase, clothes flying everywhere as he searched for…

His hard drive. There it was, the beautiful, beautiful machine. A little scratched and battered, but that was nothing new. Next target: datapad. The hard drive could, of course, connect to a regular computer as easily as it could a phone. What would have been the point, otherwise?

Bratta tapped his foot impatiently as he waited for the external hard drive to load. A quick search through his video files, and … yes, yes! There it was. His seated position folded, and he collapsed back onto the cabin's plush bed. It was safe, thank everything.

Of course, this meant his life was still under threat—assuming they figured out he'd kept a copy of the video. He shot upright and grabbed the datapad again. Mercifully, the *Satine* catered to just about every whim and desire a passenger could have, and that included in-flight communications over Z-space. A voice message would be too slow, but a text might work…

Steve Bratta: Hi Jeannie. On way, got mugged but they didn't steal everything. Help please?

Fifteen minutes later, he got a reply.

Jean Tafola: Not good. Send me vid right now. I have contact, she'll publish it. U will b safer.

Steve Bratta: How?

Jean Tafola: Cloud

Steve Bratta: But you were worried about security.

Jean Tafola: Speed more important. U r alive so they dont want u. Need 2 b public

Steve Bratta: Sent.

Jean Tafola: Received. C u soon, Steve.

Bratta frowned at the ceiling. He was still sore, but the wooziness was already clearing off—he should probably get some water, actually. That had been, well, anti-climactic, really. It was out of his hands now.

He pulled up another search, and quickly found the article he was after. He pushed his glasses up the bridge of his nose, and skimmed the title. "*Homo Insequens: On the Survival of the Human Race*".

Chapter Eleven

Outside the Chinese Embassy
Sanctuary
Omid Sector

"We know they're in the sewers! If those soldiers come even one foot past the boundaries of the embassy, we're going to detonate the bombs on every single fucking one of the prisoners, I swear to God!"

Mattis swore under his breath. The Chinese were good at lots of things—especially digital espionage—but actual stealth was not their strength. This wasn't going to end well.

"I would advise against that," shouted Mattis. Didn't that dumbass know that explosives going up in a building of that size would kill them too?

No answer.

"Damn," said Lynch, moving up beside him. "When do marines get all ornery like that, sir? When they retire from the

Corps, do marines have to hand in their brains along with their base pass?" Lynch blew out a low whistle. "Guess that's why they call 'em jarheads."

It was tempting to say he agreed—inter-service rivalries were a real thing—but Mattis knew better. It was something far deeper than that, far more human.

"As you take the throne to act, the throne acts upon you. These guys are … they're not crazy. They're marines, but that's not what's causing this. There's something else at play here. Something we don't understand."

"Yeah," snorted Lynch. "Like how these cut snakes believe that just because they storm an embassy building, they should get to negotiate from a position of strength. They have to know this won't end well for them."

The old Monty Python Black Knight negotiation strategy. It didn't matter how many times someone got hit, as long as they stood tall. "They just want their message to be heard," said Mattis, almost to himself. "And they're willing to do anything to make that happen."

"I'm warning you!" shouted Ryan from the embassy. "The tree of liberty must be refreshed from time to time with the blood of patriots and tyrants, and we got the fucking watering cans right here!"

"It's like that is it, huh?" shouted Mattis in return. He put his hand on one of the lion's heads, leaning up against it. "I'm telling you: there's another way through this. And that's by telling me the truth."

"You? You're on *their* side!"

"I'm on nobody's side!" roared Mattis. "I'm not even meant to be here, and you damn zealots are messing up a perfectly good, perfectly safe, perfectly boring patrol!"

"First he complains about it being boring," said Modi, his eyes fixated on the screen, "then he complains when it *stops* being boring…."

Mattis glared back at him. "I liked you a lot better when you were stuck in Engineering."

Modi didn't look up. "Admiral, it was your decision to promote Mister Lynch to the role of XO," he said. "I moved into Lynch's former role. Naturally."

"Dammit," said Lynch, eyes bugging out. "Are you trying to get *me* fired?"

"I'm simply saying that the Admiral's circumstances are entirely of his own making."

Mattis held up his hand for quiet. "Okay, fine. Fine. It's all my fault. Can we fix this so we can go back to the ship?"

Nobody seemed to disagree, so Mattis returned his attention to the embassy. "You like Jefferson, Captain Ryan? Well, here's one for you: honesty is the first chapter in the book of wisdom. Talk to me, Captain."

Again, no reply.

Modi had been remarkably quiet this whole time. Mattis slipped over to him. Modi was hunched over a tablet, watching the news.

"Has this made the media?" asked Mattis.

"Yes and no," said Modi, his tone curiously vague.

"What's that supposed to mean?"

"It means there's something more important that's stealing the spotlight," said Modi, tilting the tablet his way. "Your girlfriend just dropped one hell of a bombshell."

Chapter Twelve

Chuck Mattis's Office
Washington, D.C.
Earth

A short atmospheric craft ride back to his office later, and Chuck Mattis watched the video feed from Sanctuary with growing concern.

His new position gave him access to government feeds, and there were many eyes on the small, remote Chinese embassy in the Omid Sector. Normally this would be a matter for local police forces, but because the incident had involved the Chinese embassy and Chinese citizens, now it was in murky waters. Chinese law enforcement could only operate within their embassy, but the people involved were American citizens on an American world; communications between high level diplomats and their lawyers had been running non-stop. The whole thing was a bureaucratic clusterfuck.

Hopefully he wouldn't be dragged into it. Or dad…

A shuttle descended into view on his video feed. Probably American special services. Maybe U.S. Army Rangers, or Navy SEALS, or Air Force SSTs, or—

Or his fucking Dad, stepping out of the shuttle like he was going to storm the place himself. And, *of course*, he immediately starts shouting at the building. Fortunately the vidstream didn't have audio.

Chuck put his face in his hands. Why. Why was his Dad always getting involved in these things … right at the forefront of it all, too. The guy was a dinosaur. What was his ship even *doing* there after all…?

Angry, confused thoughts played in his head, but they were banished the moment he saw a squad of five Chinese marines slip out of the back of a recently-arrived APC, disappearing into the open sewer grate like sneaky communist weasels.

Well, now, this was just *great*. His father the crazy grandpa was going to get himself machine-gunned by crazier grandpas on live, intergalactic TV.

Chuck picked up the communicator and flicked through his numbers. He considered trying to call his father directly, but no doubt the old man wouldn't have taken his communicator with him to an embassy. Surely not. Maybe he could try the ship directly. Diplomatic channels had their perks. Maybe he could do this, or maybe…

As his thumb hovered over the *dial* button, one of his junior staffers, Ashley Fair, her face ashen, shoved a tablet in his face.

"Get that away," he said, scowling.

"Look," said Fair, insistently. "Martha Ramirez is on with a breaking story."

Reluctantly, Chuck took his eyes away from his Dad. "What can be more important than the embassy siege?"

Chapter Thirteen

Inside the Chinese Embassy
Sanctuary
Omid Sector

Ryan looked over Castro's shoulder at her tablet.

"You see," said Castro, pointing at the screen which showed a ghostly schematic of the sewer network with a handful of red dots moving through it, "the thermal sensors track the heat of those bastards pretty easily. The sewer lines are colder than the surface, so now we know they're in there their body heat is easy to track." She grinned at him. "Nice work, sir."

He didn't return her mirth. This was a problem. A big one. They had turned their thermal cameras downward which allowed them to see their enemies, but seeing them was only half the battle. "What kind of weapons do they have?"

"Not sure," said Castro. "The resolution on these systems

isn't that great. The modern ones are better." She hesitated, sensing that wasn't a good answer. "But, you know, probably rifles. Breaching charges. Grenades, probably."

Lots of probably. Lots of guesswork. "Can you increase the resolution?"

Castro shook her head. "Not with this equipment. The fidelity isn't there."

Damn. "A'right. Well, any idea where they'll come up?"

"I'm guessing," said Castro, "the embassy has some kind of emergency escape tunnel that leads into the sewers. Also useful if the place is stormed and needs to be recovered."

Well unfortunately for the Chinese, Ryan knew they were coming. "Keep an eye on them," he said. "When they get below the building, we'll prepare an ambush." A lightbulb flashed in his mind. "Wait … they're in the sewers, right?"

"Yeah," said Castro, raising an eyebrow curiously.

"Will a grenade fit down a toilet?"

Her whole face lit up. "You know, there's only one way to know."

He nodded energetically. "Flush a little surprise for our Chinese friends. *Don't* blow yourself up. I'll distract Mattis."

"Oorah," said Castro, standing and moving over to the bathroom, unbuttoning her grenade pouch.

Ryan crouched and shuffled over to the window. "Mattis!" he yelled. "You still out there?"

"Yes. Ryan, come on, there's no need to do this."

No need to do this. You can come peacefully. Words, words, words. "I know your men are underground," said Ryan. "Believe me, I got no desire to see bloodshed, but our message has to get out. Call them off."

"They're not my men," said Mattis, angrily. "They came out of a Chinese vehicle; I *can't* call them off, even if I wanted to." A slight pause. "You don't really believe that, do you? If so, I'm afraid I've gravely overestimated your mental capabilities."

You have misjudged me, Admiral Mattis, but not in the way you imagine. Ryan beckoned for one of his men, Sergeant Michael Carter, then pointed to a hostage. A young kid, no older than eighteen, with a shock of red hair. "Get that one," he said. "Bring him to me."

Carter grabbed the boy's hair and dragged him to Ryan.

"Stand up," said Ryan, pulling the kid up by his collar, up above the windowsill. "Let them see you."

"Ryan," called Mattis, urgency in his voice. "What are you doing?"

"Showing you I mean what I say." Ryan drew his sidearm and raised it above the lip of the window, pointing at the side of the kid's head. "I swear to God, Mattis, if you don't find some way of calling them off, I'm going to turn this kid's head into chunky salsa."

The kid started crying. Ryan smelt piss from the boy's shorts.

"Don't do it," shouted Mattis, his voice sounding so small from so far away. "Believe me, I'm no fans of the Chinese either, but this isn't the way! If you start killing the hostages they'll be forced to go in!"

"Wait," shouted Castro, scurrying over to his position, crouched low. "Sir, you should see this."

"You're supposed to be flushing grenades down the toilet," Ryan hissed.

"I know, but I saw this, and you need to see it too."

"What is it?" snapped Ryan. "I'm a little busy right now!"

She showed him the screen, playing a live news broadcast. "Captain, this just came across the news wire. Take a look."

Chapter Fourteen

Recording Studio One
GBC News Headquarters
New York City, New York
Earth

Moments before

Martha Ramirez adjusted her hair pin, using the screen ahead of her—a reflection of the live broadcast—as a mirror. The hair and makeup people never got her pins right. "Mic test, six one, six one."

"Sounding good," said Jerry, her audio guy. He gave a dopey thumbs up. "You're good to go, Martha."

Then her producers spoke up. "We're live in five, four, three…"

Okay. Time to do this story. She took a deep breath, steadied her nerves, and when her cue came, spoke up with as much courage as she could muster. Her cue light flashed.

"This just in: terror on the outer colonies," said Ramirez. A still frame from a video—a blurred image of a horrible creature, skin green and mottled, barely recognizable as human —flashed behind her. "This is Martha Ramirez with GBC News, joining you tonight with a very special report. A warning: this report contains footage which may be distressing."

The image of her dissolved, replaced by the video they had received. Where *exactly* it had come from her producers didn't say, but what it showed was compelling.

An image of a beast, its outline barely perceptible, the small camera's image washed out by direct light. The hand holding the camera was shaking so much the automatic image stabilization couldn't keep up; the beast was grainy, barely visible, but it was there.

The camera focused on it for barely a second. Then, screaming, and the camera jerked wildly. The bearer turned and ran, buffeted by a crowd of people running alongside them. Footsteps on the pavement and a man, presumably the cameraman, panting. The view was solely of asphalt, frantic sprinting, and then the view emerged into a car park, cameraman clearly panicking, searching for a vehicle. For an escape.

Then the beast leapt down onto a car, and for the first time, the viewers could see it clearly. A towering monster, a zombie-human, rotting and tattered, yet alive. Intelligent. Evil.

It was the fifth or sixth time she had seen it, and each time it had gotten harder, not easier, to sit through.

The recording paused.

"What happens next," she said, "is too graphic for us to show you. Shots fire, and soldiers wearing the uniforms of the US military destroy this … monster." Just as they'd rehearsed, the producer resumed play, but audio-only.

Gunfire. Screaming. And then: "Tangos eliminated." The sound of a reloading rifle. "Sir, give me that."

Ramirez took a deep breath as the live feed came back. "This GBC News exclusive video was shot on a classified military base at the edge of colonized space." She paused for effect, perfectly timed. "The recording shows combined American-accented speakers and Chinese speakers. GBC News inquiries into the location in this video have been met with resistance, even for the most basic information. It is the opinion of this news studio that there must be an examination into the truth. As you can no doubt imagine, we, like you, have so many questions."

The screen rewound to the first image of the creature, silhouetted in floodlight. "What is this creature? How did this creature escape? Is it related to the alien invasion from six months ago?" She paused for a beat. "Troublingly, the time-date stamp on the file we received was over a month old, raising the obvious question: why haven't we heard about this before?"

She looked down at the blank piece of paper in front of her—it was a prop, naturally—and then back up at the camera. "Obviously, something devastating has happened on this world. Even though our attempts to find out exactly *what* have been met with silence, further investigations have revealed that the whole of the Tonatiuh Sector is on full lockdown, with all ships appearing from Z-space being impounded and all transmissions out of that world being jammed. Is the world in question in that system, or another system altogether?

"It is clear our combined governments—the United States of America and the People's Republic of China, and possibly others—are keeping the truth from us. And not just in relation to this particularly incident on this particular planet. GBC News is laying down the gauntlet for all the civilized, rational governments in all the colonized worlds: tell us the truth. What is happening here?"

Bombshell, dropped. She gave the viewers several seconds to sink in. The next thing was the *true* wham moment of the whole broadcast, and she knew that once she said the words on her TelePrompter, she wouldn't be able to take them back. But it was time to let the galaxy start asking questions.

"There is more going on with this than we can possibly imagine," said Ramirez, "I'm sure of it."

Chapter Fifteen

Bob's Bar
Glasgow
Earth

Bratta shuffled his small suitcase closer to his feet and sniffled. Even though it was, unsurprisingly, cold and overcast in this particular corner of Earth, he didn't want to open his suitcase for a warmer jumper. Jeannie wasn't so much late as he was early, but the chill wasn't doing much to sweeten the thought. Nor was the neighborhood, for that matter. Bob's Bar had always been a bit seedy; in his day it had been a hole-in-the-wall where uni students could score a few cheap drinks—not that he'd actually studied in Glasgow, that was Jeannie—but now it was flanked by dark storefronts and a palpable air of neglect. As he was watching, a potato chip wrapper blew down the pavement—though he supposed here they'd be called crisps.

Through the slightly dingy glass behind him, the bar's infamous mechanical bull was visible, looking like nothing so much as an extraordinarily large rat with mismatching legs and a regrettable haircut. Other bars at least had the decency to sport terrifying riding bulls, eyes lit with a red glow. Bob's had just *had* to go for an unusually sized rodent, Scotland's national—and now, his ex-wife's personal—joke. Bratta glowered at the contraption. *You may have bested me in my youth, but—*

An engine cut through his thoughts, and a silver car rounded the corner. Through the windscreen, he could make out a woman's sensible brown hair and equally sensible coat.

The car purred to a stop in front of him.

"Steve Bratta, in the flesh. Didn't think I'd ever be seeing you again."

He tried to think up a clever reply.

"Well, you know, I *have* been working on an invisibility device." That was funny, right? Confident? Suave? He was pretty sure his colleagues would have laughed, at least.

"… Of course you have." Jeannie Tafola stepped out of the car. "Now get that suitcase in the back, we're going for a walk."

"I actually haven't," he said as he trundled the case towards the boot. "That was a joke."

Jeannie didn't answer.

"It was funny."

Still no response.

"Because I'm a geneticist, not a physicist?"

Nothing.

"And … it would be hilariously ridiculous for me to work

on such an advanced project untrained?"

The wind moaned between buildings.

Bratta gave up—her stoney face said she was in no mood.

Soon, the suitcase was tucked away, he had a much more appropriate jacket, and the car was parked in a side street.

"You're really leaving it here?" he ventured.

Jeannie raised her eyebrows. "Of course. I have a friend who patrols here; this place only gets nasty after dark."

"Alright, sure. Why do we have to be *here*, anyway?" His voiced pitched up a little at the end, but honestly, he felt some indignation was justified.

"It's secluded, it's fairly safe, and it's one of the last places anyone would run to. Also, it's funny. But, we have more important matters to discuss."

"Funny? I sprained my ankle falling off that thing!" he pointed through the bar's window. "It *hurt!*"

"And I still have the picture," Jeannie muttered just loud enough for him to hear. "Now, video."

He let memory be, for now. "Yes. Well, I saw when it was released; the shuttle I was on had a full Z-space communication suite."

"Really?" Jeannie's eyes widened. "You're still just a poorly paid scientist, right?"

"It was the first ship out from Zenith, and it wasn't cheap."

She whistled. "I'll bet."

"Was that reporter, Martha ... Ramirez? Was she your contact?" he asked.

"Yes. She's a good journalist, with a lot more integrity than most of the media. Did you see how the passengers on your shuttle reacted, Steve?"

He nodded. "I did at breakfast, in fact. There, uh … there were a lot of unhappy rich people making calls. Honestly, I thought they were just putting on a show at first, but I looked up our route, and I think it must have turned nine o'clock in America about then. Which means the news was on. Which means the news was interesting."

"Makes sense. No-one approached you in particular?"

He pulled a pen out of his jacket pocket and started fiddling with it. "I don't think so, no. And I was working on the assumption that sticking around to find out if someone would was a terrible idea."

"That was a surprisingly astute decision."

"Um, thanks?"

Jeannie ignored him, her gaze turned to the grey buildings as they walked by. "It's been like the start of a zombie apocalypse here on Earth. Minus the zombies. People are panicked—the planet's going to be out of canned goods and whatever looks like it could be used as a weapon, soon they'll all be in personal stockpiles—and the governments are denying anything's going on at all."

"The governments? Plural?"

"Yes. None of them are speaking up; even the US and China aren't blaming each other's spies for this."

"Wait, that's—"

"Terrifying?" She faced him. "Yes."

Bratta clicked his pen. He'd never really been that interested in politics, but even he knew how big that was. The thought was taking a little while to process. "Jeannie, what's going on here?"

Her expression went wry. "I was hoping you'd tell me."

"Well, I do have one rudimentary hypothesis as to the aliens' origin," he began, hesitantly.

Jeannie stopped in her tracks. "You do?"

"Er, just a paper I read when I was doing my undergrad. About genomics and the next steps of evolving the human race, being ready to deal with disaster, et cetera. It was very, very sci-fi. And the journal it was published in, *Genomics Yearly*, got shut down about two years after the article was published, actually. Accused of academic misconduct, letting people pay to publish then saying it was peer-reviewed. Not a good look. But, their theories have some merit, and—I know it sounds crazy—but I think it might be possible to … *make* those things."

"*Make* them? Unbelievable." She shook her head. "Steve, you do realize this is possibly the best lead anyone who isn't trying to cover this up *has*?"

"Wow. No."

Jeannie spun on her heel and marched back towards her car. "Come on. I have a few choice questions for your employers, and you're going to help me ask them."

He hesitated. "Uh, can you just … do that?"

She rolled her eyes, and pulled out her police officer's badge. "Pay is shit, but at least people answer me when I ask them questions."

"You mean, unless they invoke Miranda?"

"That only tells me they're guilty—makes my job easier. Get in the car, Bratta."

Chapter Sixteen

Senator Pitt's Office
Washington D.C.
Earth

Senator Peter Pitt didn't feel angry. He hadn't lost his temper, he wasn't a vengeful spirit, or possessing a thirst for blood. There was no rage in how he felt. His anger was cold, calculating, and entirely righteous.

Admiral Jack Mattis had killed his son.

Even now, months later, the very idea took time to sink into his head, to pass through his brain and lodge itself there. Any moment he expected Jeremy to call him, tell him it was all a dream, and they would discuss their days. They would enjoy a warm cup of coffee, or that delightful chai that Jeremy sometimes brought home, and they'd chat. Jeremy about his ship, and he about whatever BS blue-ribbon commission he was spearheading.

He'd fired Mattis's son. With relish and gusto. But that was a hollow victory. He'd actually felt worse afterwards, not better, as though he had prematurely cashed in his chips. Played his cards too early. Taking someone's job couldn't possibly compare to taking their life.

No more mistakes in the future. The next time Pitt put his cards on the table, he'd be doing it to win.

Until then he drifted around his office like a ghoul. Pitt had lost weight; exactly how much he couldn't say, but it was enough that his skin drew closer around his thin frame, erasing whatever muscle mass age hadn't already taken from him. His clothes reeked. His office was dusty. His body ached.

He could barely summon the strength to turn off the TV. Some breaking news story about something he couldn't begin to think or care about.

Then one word caught his attention and held it.

Alien.

Groaning like the living dead, Pitt slid into his chair, drawn to the broadcast with mute fascination. He watched the whole film clip. Again. And again. And *again.* The blurry, shaky footage taken by some panicked man on a distant world. The too-public reveal of their alien foe.

And all of the pieces slowly slid into place.

He knew what to do. Pitt took out his communicator and flicked through his contacts. P, Q, R, S…

Tvarika Seaton

Chantrell Segar

Caillen Selman

Spectre

There she was. No first name and no last. That little word

which held so much promise and so much risk. His contact in the government whose position, it seemed, was … vaguely defined. But she was usually able to help him.

For a cost.

He tapped the contact with no hesitation.

"This is Spectre," she said, with barely a ring being completed. Her voice was disguised by a voice-changer, as it always was. "I've been expecting you."

"I'm a patient man," said Pitt, his voice sounding almost alien to his ears. How long had it been since he spoke to someone? Too long. But it didn't matter. "I'm guessing you saw the broadcast."

"Most unfortunate," said Spectre. "We'll have to take action about this."

"I was hoping you were going to say that," said Pitt, his smile widening. "I know *just* the thing…."

Chapter Seventeen

Outside the Chinese Embassy
Sanctuary
Omid Sector

Well. The cat was out of the bag now. Mattis stared in bewilderment as the news feed cut over to some kind of expert or another; some talking head who would give their stupid uninformed opinion about what everyone had just seen.

Now he didn't need to keep the alien's nature a secret anymore. It actually felt … good. Like a weight had been lifted from him.

"What do you think, sir?" asked Modi.

"I think it might help us," said Mattis, turning his attention to the embassy once more. "Ryan, I hope you saw that. The galaxy is a big place—I know you have your concerns with the Chinese. You have questions about our government and the secrets it keeps. You aren't the only one interested in the answers to a lot of questions that, perhaps, I can help provide."

"What do you know about the video?" shouted Ryan.

"Not much," shouted Mattis in return. "But we can look into it together." A pause while he waited for an answer which didn't come. He tried something else. "You mentioned Friendship Station—I was there. I can talk to you about it, and listen. You're not the only one with a story to tell."

There was no answer, which could have been good or bad.

"Sir," asked Modi, "what are you trying to do?"

Mattis shook his head. "Exactly what I said. I want him to work with me on this. He's got a full crew of people in there: dedicated, loyal—they believe in him. Other people across the galaxy will too. I want him to say we're working on it so those people believe it. Hell, after he's done spending time in the brig for all this, he might even be able to help out directly."

"He may not want to do that," said Modi. "Especially if he does go to prison."

After eating prison meatloaf for a few months, or years, Ryan might change his tune. "For now," said Mattis, "let's get the hostages to safety."

He turned back to the embassy. "We're on the same side, you know," said Mattis, his throat hoarse from all this shouting. "You want what I want. I've fought these things; I know things about them. Things that I can't tell you. You know how it is, operational security and all that. But it looks like the media's fucked that all up, so maybe—just maybe—we can start to do something about it. Together." He wasn't sure exactly what he was promising. "But we're never going to get your voice out from within those walls. You have to come out and talk about this, or it's going to end in blood."

The kid's head disappeared from the window and Mattis breathed a sigh of relief. Okay. One thing down. He slowly, subconsciously, began patting the lion statue's head.

Lynch gave him a weird stare, his face all scrunched up. Mattis stopped patting.

"Is it true?" shouted Ryan, a hint of fear in his voice. "Admiral, the video, the newscast with that *thing*. Was it real?"

Mattis shrugged helplessly. "I didn't fake it, if that's what you're asking. I saw it at the same time you did." He gave a wry smile that, at the distance they were shouting to each other, he doubted Ryan could see. "Knowing Ramirez, though, I'd bet it's totally legitimate."

It was good to see her again, even if it was in this distant capacity. Ramirez … suddenly he felt like he wanted to see her a whole bunch more.

Why, you old fool? Why hadn't you gone and seen her all this time? Sure, the *Midway* was ordered on patrol, and that was a good enough reason to avoid seeing her. Maybe. The truth was, of course, a lot more simple.

She'd hinted that they might have a future together, and that scared him away.

"I dunno." Ryan's voice became so quiet he could barely hear it. The guy swore to himself, probably loud enough for everyone inside to hear but not those on the outside. "I don't know. That guy—that *thing* in the video—it looked Chinese."

"Lots of people look Chinese, Ryan. You're overthinking it." Mattis let it all sink in for a little bit, trying to banish the lingering thoughts of Ramirez out of his mind. There'd be time enough for that. Time enough later.

"Okay," he continued, his throat hoarse. "Just try to think this through. I can help you. You want to know the truth, well, I know things about these creatures. I fought them. And, well, now the whole damn galaxy knows that what attacked us wasn't the Chinese. Wasn't even human." More or less. The *full* truth would be too much for him, and too sensitive to literally shout in the street. "But Ryan, hear this: if you hurt anyone in there, even I won't be able to do anything. We can't work together if you resort to violence."

Ryan didn't answer right away.

"Ramirez didn't fake it," called Mattis. "Or at least, if she did, I'm not going to chase that rabbit. Word of advice: never pick a fight with someone who buys their ink by the barrel. If lawyers are sharks, reporters are piranhas."

Laughter drifted toward them, faint, but genuine.

"Okay," shouted Mattis. "Fun's over, marine. My throat's killing me, the sun's going down, and those PRC marines are probably getting sick of the sound of my yammering. I'm thirsty, my ship's sitting there rusting in space, and while I'm enjoying my XO and my chief of engineering actually not arguing for the first time in six months, I think it's time we wrapped this show up. Send out one of the hostages, and we'll talk specifics. C'mon."

There was a long pause. And then, finally, Ryan popped his head up over the window. "Righteo, sir," he said. "Lemme send out the kid. I think he pissed himself anyway."

Mattis nodded, unsure if he could see the gesture at that distance. "Good call. I'll be right here, and—"

He flinched as a gunshot blew out the window pane next to Ryan's head.

Chapter Eighteen

Inside the Chinese Embassy
Sanctuary
Omid Sector

"Good call. I'll be right here, and—"

The roar of a gunshot made his ears ring, followed instantly by shattering glass. Castro's head burst like a melon, painting the window frame with her blood.

Instantly his hands found his rifle and he swung it about, eyes tracking the source of the noise.

The biter had a tiny pistol in her hand, propped up on her elbows. How she found it was a mystery. How she freed her hands was a mystery. Her further intentions, though, were clear: she lined the still-smoking barrel up on him.

Years of training took over. Ryan squeezed the trigger of his rifle, spraying her down with a five shot burst, center of mass, blasting her back onto the ground. He put another two rounds into her head just to make sure.

"Castro?" Ryan risked a glance her way, and then immediately wished he hadn't. "Corpsman!"

Fitzgerald, their corpsman, ran over. His face fell the moment he saw her. "Shit. She's dead."

Dammit. Dammit!

"Ryan," called Mattis, that old fucking bastard. This was all his fault. "What's going on in there?"

"One of our hostages got hold of a gun," he said, staring at Castro's dead body. This was Mattis's fault. "Damn bitch shot one of my people. Now she's dead."

"You shot a hostage? You son of a—!"

"It wasn't like that!" roared Ryan. "She had a gun! She shot first, and she was going to do me too, it was self defense!"

"You don't get to bust into someone's house and claim self defense when they shoot back, Ryan!"

That was true enough. Nobody said anything. All his men looked at each other, then to him. Ryan touched Castro's shoulder, taking a breath. It was okay. It was *okay*. They could get through this. They would definitely serve hard time now but he'd take the most of the blame. He'd pulled the trigger, he'd organized the op, he'd been the leader—

A deafening roar threw dust into the air and the whole building shook.

Ryan grabbed Castro's thermal imager and waved it around like a lunatic. He saw the glow from the SAM's engine, the computers, the targeting antenna—

There. Five Chinese marines, coming in through the floor. They'd blown out the floor on the lower level. During all this, all this *shit* he had forgotten about the attack below. They had probably been there for some time, waiting for a gunshot, waiting for the signal to take them all down. Biter was probably a part of this—probably one of *them.*

Time to fight back.

"Take out their shuttle," said Ryan, to the nearest man.

"Aye sir!"

"Contact below," Ryan shouted over the ringing in his ears. "Five reds! Lock and load, marines, let's go, let's go, let's go!"

Chapter Nineteen

Shuttle Zulu-3
Lower Atmosphere of Sanctuary
Omid Sector

Corrick lifted up the shuttle away from the embassy through the lower atmosphere, passing through a thick cloud that was grey and bruised and full of moisture. She pulled the ship up, hovering inside the roiling cover, condensation forming on the ship's cockpit glass. She flicked on the autopilot.

"Flying shuttles sucks," she said, slumping back in her chair. "The damn thing handles like a pig in mud. With a broken leg. A pig with—" she waved her arms around. "I don't know. Another broken leg. Just because. I basically have to drag the controls around like they're made of lead, you know? Heavy and slow and fat and gross. I miss my fighter."

Flatline grunted.

She turned to him. "Hey, you've been awfully quiet this whole trip. Something on your mind?"

"Yeah," he said, entirely unhelpfully.

"What's that?" she asked, creasing her brow. "C'mon. Don't make me squeeze it out of you."

"Eh," said Flatline, shrugging.

Guano squinted. "What, you stop taking those friggin' supplements they're giving us? Going through vitamin withdrawal?" She shook her head. "Ever since the ejection you've been weird," she said, shuffling around in her seat so she faced him a bit more properly. That was one thing shuttles had over fighters: a lot more leg room.

"Me?" asked Flatline, blinking in surprise. "It's *you* that's the weirdo, Guano."

Now it was her turn to be taken aback. "What do you mean?" she asked. "I mean, we've barely said a word since the pickup. Roadie had me scrubbing the ready room, then writing all those damn lines—and now we don't even have a ship!"

"It's not the ejection," said Flatline, frustration creeping into his tone as though the source of it all was something she should have picked up on a lot sooner. "It's what happened *before* that. During the battles. When you went all … weird."

Guano hesitated. "Yeah."

"Yeah," said Flatline, staring straight ahead out the rain-streaked cockpit.

The two of them sat in silence for a bit, the only sounds the gentle sound of the wind outside and the soft beeping of their cockpit instruments.

"I don't really know what it is," said Guano, grinning and leaning over toward him, trying to lighten the mood. "But thanks for not reporting it. A mental health issue like that could get me crossed off the flight roster for good."

"Yeah," said Flatline, again, his tone humorless. "It definitely could."

She sat back down in her chair again. "It's not like that," she said, a tad more defensively than was necessary. "I just—it's not—" she shook her head. "I'm not crazy."

"Mmm. Spoken like someone who's *definitely* not crazy."

Guano grimaced. "I know how it sounds, but it's not a bad thing. It's just—" she paused, collecting her thoughts. "When I got really stressed, back in the fight, it was like a whole universe of possibilities opened up to me. It was like doing the best weed you could imagine, but instead of slowing *me* down, it slowed down everything *around* me; I felt like I was moving normally, doing everything just like I normally would, but the world was going at half speed, you know? It just made it so much easier to track enemy movements, give me time to think, casually plan out exactly what I was going to do."

"Maybe you were having a stroke," said Flatline, plainly. "You should get yourself checked out."

Guano laughed defensively and shook her head. "No way. If I gave Roadie any justification at all to get me crossed off the flight roster, he'd take it. I crashed two ships in as many days—that kind of thing looks pretty bad on your résumé. Last thing I need is a visit to the head-shrinks."

"Mental health's come a long way," said Flatline. "There's lots of different ways it could go. It might be just normal, you know? A perfectly normal, perfectly natural reaction to combat stress." A delicate way of saying Combat Stress Reaction. "But it might also be a clot in your brain that's slowly killing you."

Guano took a shallow breath. Suddenly, all the pieces clicked into place. "You told Roadie," she said, eyes widening. "You told him. That's why he won't let me fly. That's why he made me take you on this absolute milk-run. He doesn't trust me." Guano's tone soured. "And neither do you."

"He's worried about you," said Flatline, a tad defensively. "And so am I. What happened to you—Patricia, that's not normal."

Oooh. If he was calling her *Patricia* shit was serious. She straightened her back. "Lemme show you. I'll show you it's harmless."

Flatline grimaced, finally looking at her. "Maybe that's not a good idea."

"No," she said, firmly. "It is. I want you to see that it's not a clot in my brain, or me wigging out, or—anything. It's just a helpful state. Like a trance."

"Okay. Okay. So show me."

She shook her head. "Doesn't work that way. You gotta activate it."

"How?" Flatline snorted. "You got an on-switch or something?"

"Kind of," she said. "I don't really understand it myself, but if you stress me out enough, like put me in danger, it'll happen."

Flatline obviously considered. "Okay," he said. "How?"

Guano reached behind her, to the back of her seat, and withdrew the medkit stationed there. She pried it open and rummaged around inside, pulling out a box of painkillers. "Here," she said, handing them to Flatline. "Throw this at me."

He stared. "Just, like, throw it?"

"Yeah." She steeled herself, focusing on the box of pills. "When I'm in danger, it'll activate and I'll … I don't know. Ninja-swat the thing out of the air or something."

Squinting skeptically, Flatline twisted in his seat, coming to face her, and then pegged the box of pills right at her head.

It got her right in the left eye. "Ow! Fuck!"

"Sorry!" said Flatline, eyes widening. "You said to throw it!"

"I know, I know." Guano groaned and rubbed her face. "Dammit. That's going to bruise."

"It's not my fault," said Flatline.

"I know, I know. Piss." Guano sighed. "I dunno … it was supposed to turn on but it didn't."

Flatline shook his head. "First thing we do when we get back to the ship? I'm taking you to sickbay."

"I can't," she insisted. "I can't have them—"

"Because," said Flatline, stressing the words, "you obviously hit your head during some turbulence, and you, being a *sane* and *reasonable* pilot with a levelheaded and cautious approach to piloting, will definitely want to have a scan done of your head just to make sure that you're perfectly fit and healthy and ready to fly." He paused for emphasis. "Right?"

"Right," said Guano, rubbing her eye again. "Makes sense."

The console flashed, cutting off any more experimentation. "Okay," said Guano, "time to go get the Admiral and end this milk run."

"First thing," insisted Flatline. "First thing when we get back, you're going to go get yourself checked out."

"Yeah yeah," said Guano, flicking off the autopilot and

tilting the ship's nose down toward the surface. "I promise."

Chapter Twenty

Outside the Chinese Embassy
Sanctuary
Omid Sector

Five sets of boots stomped through the lower level of the embassy, flashing past windows. Mattis could see them, rifles raised, storming through the building.

"Wait!" he bellowed. "Stop! Stop!"

If they could hear him, they made no sign of it.

Shit.

The marines disappeared behind the front door. The defenders would want to secure the staircase up to the second floor. That was the natural choke point that also afforded the defenders high ground. With their height advantage, superiority of numbers, and well-disciplined cohesive force, it would be a hard fight.

Windows flashed as stun grenades went out, followed

immediately by a burst of automatic weapons fire from within. A half-dozen holes appeared in the walls, whistling over their heads.

Nothing more Mattis could do with words. He ducked behind the lion, crouching, hoping that its majestic raised paws would stop bullets. Or at least obscure him enough that he wouldn't be seen.

Lynch slid in beside him like a baseball hitter. "Well," he said, "that went well. I almost thought you had him until, you know, he started killing people."

Mattis glared at him. "Call the shuttle back. We have to get out of here."

"Already done."

Mattis cupped his hands around his mouth. "Modi! Wherever you are, find somewhere to hide until the shooting dies down!"

"I've obtained cover, sir," came the muffled reply. "And I'm preparing to secure our escape route."

Escape route? What the hell? Mattis risked a peek over the lion's paw. Modi was unbuttoning his holster. He'd brought a sidearm? Mattis hadn't even noticed. Then again, he hadn't even been looking.

"Put that damn thing away!" Lynch yelled, close enough to Mattis's head to make his ears hurt. "What are you planning on doing, storming the place by yourself, with that damn pea-shooter? You'll blow your own foot off!"

"You misunderstand me." Modi drew it and inserted a magazine. "And I'll be fine. I qualified with the standard M11 in basic."

"You haven't fired that thing since *basic*?" Lynch stared at

Mattis. "Brave as the first man who ate an oyster. He's going to die."

For once, Mattis actually agreed. "Modi, you can't do anything here. We need to get to our shuttle and get back to the ship, this is *way* out of our hands now. We've got ringside seats to a gun battle, and this is *not* why we're here."

"We're not meant to be here at all," hissed Lynch.

"We have to get out of here." Mattis risked another glance, right as a bullet snatched off the ground nearby, kicking up broken chunks of asphalt. "Sooner rather than later."

Modi returned fire, squeezing off a pair of shots at the building. They flew high, so high they almost missed the structure entirely. The rounds struck some small antenna on the roof, snapping it in half. He looked very pleased with himself.

"Stop that!" shouted Mattis.

"I *said* this was a bad idea," muttered Lynch. "I *said* Modi would blow his foot off."

"You never said that."

"I damn well should have," said Lynch, grumbling. "Modi! You're shooting at garbage!"

"Not garbage," said Modi, grinning from ear to ear. "The antenna's down."

"What?" shouted Lynch.

"The antenna! I recognized it; it's a Type 103 surface-to-air missile guidance antenna. They brought something to blow up our shuttle—they may have let us *down* here before all this, but they were definitely going to shoot us on the way back up to orbit—but not now! They can't target us!"

Modi's brain might get them all killed one day, but today it may have damn well saved their lives. The gunfire inside the embassy reached a crescendo. Right on cue, the shuttle returned, breaking through a low cloud, hissing faintly as it settled down on the street. It was time.

"My go-to policy right now," complained Lynch, loudly. "Is that if we're going anywhere, Modi's not allowed to come. He's a damn deer in the wilderness. Look at him, waving that thing around." He raised his voice. "Modi! Put that thing away!"

"Deer or no deer, we have to move." Mattis grit his teeth. "Modi! We are leaving—on three. One, two, *three*!"

The three of them broke cover, running toward the shuttle. Mattis wished he was a younger man, boots pounding on the street as bullets whizzed past them, *ping*ing off the hull of the shuttle. The ramp lowered.

From the sides of the shuttle, dozens of black-helmeted Chinese marines, their weapons raised, came running toward them. One of them snarled as he ran by. "You nearly squashed us, *Wáng bā*!" *Son of a dog*. How rude. Just like old times.

Mattis pushed past, struggling toward the open shuttle door, helping Lynch up the ramp.

"Come on, Modi!" he said, holding onto the ramp's hydraulic strut as another burst of gunfire splattered off the shuttle's hull. Blast that guy…

Modi fumbled with his pistol, ejecting the magazine and replacing it with a new one. He moved forward, through the last of the Chinese soldiers, putting a foot on the ramp.

Then he slumped forward, pitching face first onto the metal deck, a blood-red flower blossoming on his back.

Chapter Twenty-One

Inside the Chinese Embassy
Sanctuary
Omid Sector

Ryan ejected his magazine. "Loading!"

Hadn't hit any of them yet. None of his men had. But that was to be expected; the nature of close quarters combat was turning a lot of ammo into a lot of noise.

"Got you covered," said Fitzgerald, spraying a burst from his weapon over the lip of the stairway to the upper level, the bullets ricocheting off the tiles, smashing them to pieces.

Ryan reloaded, pulling the charging handle. He peeked over the edge.

Five marines fired. Their bullets screamed past his ears, hitting the ledge and embedding in the roof and floor beneath him. Fortunately the structure was strong enough to block whatever they were firing.

They were in position. Ryan pulled out a grenade, yanking out the pin. The lever flew up. One, two, three—he tossed it over the edge. "*Zhuā zhù!*" he shouted, mockingly. *Catch!* He'd picked up enough of their language during the war.

Their panicked cries below were music to his ears. "*Shǒuliúdàn*!" he heard. *Grenade! Grenade!* Ahh, music.

Boom. The shrapnel whizzed all around the stairway.

Maybe, just maybe, they could actually win this. Force the Chinese back into a stalemate. Pressure them until he could figure out a way around this … maybe they could slip out through the sewers. They were open and exposed now.

Ryan glanced over the edge. One marine lay sprawled out, his helmet blown off, face shredded. The other four were in a defensive prone. One had a riot shield, hiding behind it. The others cowered behind him, their hands over their heads, exposed body parts peppered with shrapnel. But the shield, and their armor, would have absorbed most of it. They were fine.

"Fitzgerald," said Ryan, turning to him, "get ready to—"

The man's shoulder exploded, arm flying off. Fitzgerald slumped forward, his shoulder a gaping wound. Then came the *crack* of a sniper's round.

No way to get to the sewers now. They were pinned down.

"Report," he said. "Sound off, marines!"

Six English-speaking voices came back to him. Everyone else was either dead or unable to answer.

Another explosion. The main door shook and bowed. Fortunately it was reinforced. Out through the ground floor windows, a veritable sea of black helmets clustered. Twenty at least. Maybe more. He gave them a sweep with his muzzle, catching one or two with a round, sending showers of sparks into the air as the bullets were deflected.

"There's more out the back," said one of his men, his tone suggesting the situation was dire.

The door shook again, bowing further. Soon it would buckle and surrender.

But they would not. Time for a blaze of glory. Ryan grinned so hard it hurt his face. Just like old times.

"Okay, time to wrap this dance up. Ladies, gentlemen; we're going to push through the marines downstairs and make for the breach into the sewers. Fresh mags in, dump your grenades before you go. Let's move!"

"Sir, yes sir!" came the chorus.

The sound of a half-dozen pins being withdrawn rang out. The snap of the levers. A flurry of grenades flew over the lip, raining down below.

No cries of alarm this time. They knew they were dead. Six blasts, and then the group moved down as one, with Ryan at its head.

A sniper's round darted past him, catching one of his fellows behind. He kept moving, past the main door, spraying fire out the windows. He saw the gap—the massive hole in the ground from which reeking sewer could be smelled over the gunpowder.

The main door gave way. Two Chinese marines rushed in, weapons cracking. Ryan shot back, hosing down the invaders at full-auto. The marines slumped forward.

He needed to reload. Ryan ejected his magazine and, before he could insert a new one, two more marines took the place of their fallen allies. Then two more behind them.

His five men became three in just a few bullets. He crouched behind a table, emptying his new magazine in short, controlled bursts. The Chinese shot back, firing through the walls, gunfire kicking papers into the air, bullets screaming off every surface, blasting into the fine wood and tearing up the carpets.

"Man down," shouted one of his marines, right before she caught a round in the gut, then two more through the chest.

He jammed in a new magazine, lining up on the Chinese.

A round thumped into his leg and he fell, weapon falling out of his hands. Pain blossomed on his thigh, his patriot's blood soaking into the fine carpet.

And then, briefly, there was only silence. It was over.

Almost.

He pulled out the last of his grenades. Just one left. This one wasn't kept in his grenade pouch like the others. No, this one was for just such an occasion as this.

In case he failed. He wouldn't spend the rest of his life in a Chinese prison.

Blaze of glory, indeed. He hooked his finger around the pin and pulled it out.

Five, four, three—

A gloved hand slapped the device out of his hand. The thing bounced and rolled across the floor, then it fell into the open hole, disappearing with a faint splash.

Boom. All of them were covered in rancid brown sewer water, ruining what was left of the room.

Then a black bag was shoved over his head, his hands were forced into handcuffs, and he was dragged away kicking and shouting.

Chapter Twenty-Two

Shuttle loading ramp
Outside the Chinese Embassy
Sanctuary
Omid Sector

Mattis grabbed Modi by the collar and dragged him up the loading ramp and onto the ship. The ramp raised, sealing off the ship from the outside world. All he could hear was the occasional muted thump of a round hitting the hull.

"Pilot," he roared, thumping his blood-soaked fist on the intercom. "Get us out of here right now."

"Can't," came the reply.

Mattis stared at the intercom panel. "Did you just say, *can it* to an Admiral?"

"Uhh, no, sir," said the pilot, her voice surprised. "I meant I simply *cannot* lift off at this time. It's not possible. The—"

"What's your name?" he asked, talking over her.

A slight pause. "Lieutenant Patricia Corrick," she said, "but uh, pilots call me Guano."

Corrick. That name rang a bell to him. "But you're a fighter pilot," he said. "I know you. You're the one who crashed your ship. Twice. The one who damaged the engines of that alien ship."

"That's right, sir," she said, an obvious tremor in her voice. "I'm flying the shuttle because, well, it's complicated sir, but —"

"Guano," he said, his voice pure ice. "Right now I don't care. Lieutenant Corrick, I am Admiral Mattis, the CO of the USS *Midway*. I'm ordering you to lift off right now, before I have you flying shuttles for the rest of your life."

Guano's voice came through the tiny speaker louder than expected. "I understand that, Admiral, but I'm telling you that I physically *cannot*. The Chinese marines attached a clamp to the landing skid. If I try and force us off, it'll tear off the lower half of the ship. That's the part you're standing on, in case you didn't realize." A slight pause. "There's a woman in an officer's uniform standing right in front of the cockpit. Guessing she wants to talk."

The Chinese did now? "Lower the ramp, Lieutenant," he said his tone stern. "I'm going out there."

Slowly, with a hiss, the ramp lowered. Mattis strode out into the raging gun battle, stray rounds flying all around him.

Just as their pilot had said, a yellow and black striped device was attached to their landing skid, chained to the APC. Beside it, a tall, officious looking woman wearing an officer's uniform with the trappings of the Chinese secret service stood, her arms folded, in front of their ship.

"Excuse me," said Mattis, grinding his teeth openly. "I'm hoping you have a *very* good reason for denying our ship liftoff after we—" a round pinged off the outside of the hull. "Assisted you."

She raised an eyebrow skeptically. "Yes," she said, her accent thick. "You definitely helped. Everything is much better now. You were warned to stay away."

"Honestly, I don't give a shit. This street is US soil, US jurisdiction. I could have the *Midway* nuke this city from orbit as long as I somehow missed your embassy. Furthermore, my chief engineer is wounded and possibly dying inside that vessel, and he needs medical attention." Mattis straightened his back, drawing himself up to his full height. "Understand this: if you do not release this shuttle right now, I swear to almighty God I will shoot you myself."

The woman turned to face him properly, a mocking smile on her lips. "You will, will you?"

Mattis yanked his communicator off his belt, turning a dial until it was on a military frequency. "Corrick, bring the ship's weapons around and aim them at this woman."

Silence, and then behind him, the faint groaning of moving metal. The woman took a step backward, holding up her hands, her face a mask of fear.

"Release my ship," he said, his tone even. "Or you will die."

The woman slowly, carefully reached down into her pocket and withdrew a magnetic card. She walked over to the clamp, swiped it, and the device fell away.

Mattis, without a word, turned and stormed back into the ship.

"Sir," said Guano, once he was aboard and the ramp closed once more, "you know this shuttle has no guns on it, right? I pointed the long range communications dish at her."

Brilliant. Mattis couldn't help but give a small little grin as the ship lifted off, gravity lurching slightly as the ship tilted upward, artificial gravity fighting with the real stuff.

"That'll do," he said, making his way over to Modi. He lay on the metal deck, bleeding heavily, his head resting in Lynch's lap. His tanned, olive skin was a whole shade lighter than it should have been, and his lips were white. Ghostly.

"Stay with us," said Lynch, his voice shaky, rummaging through a medkit, half its contents spilt on the floor. "You stupid dumb robot. What were you *thinking*, playing cowboy like that? I'm the Texan here, I'm the one who's supposed to, you know, have six shooters or whatever, and I'm the one who's supposed to be impulsive, stupid—"

"Keep pressure on that wound," said Mattis, taking a deep breath. The cramped shuttle interior smelled of blood. "Focus on saving him before you get all sentimental on us."

"Aye-aye," said Lynch, pressing tightly, both hands holding a compression bandage. He turned back to Modi. "I mean it, though, if you die, I will goddamn *kill* you. You hear me, Modi? I'll kick your ass. I swear it."

Mattis closed his eyes. He couldn't watch Modi like that, bleeding, without feeling helpless. Powerless to do anything about it. It was a distraction; a big one, and one he fought to shut out. He needed to focus. Clear his head.

But something didn't feel right about this. About everything that had happened. He didn't know who to trust; the SAM that the hostage-takers had acquired was some high grade equipment. Not the kind of thing one could just acquire, and not surplus from the last war, either. This was something new. Something dangerous. He couldn't take this to his CO; it had to go higher.

He needed to talk to the President.

"Sir," said Guano through the intercom, bumping him out of his thoughts. "We got a problem."

"What's that?"

"A Chinese warship completed its Z-space translation right above us," she said, "between Sanctuary and the *Midway*. They're blocking our way home, sir."

Chapter Twenty-Three

Shuttle Zulu-3
Upper Atmosphere of Sanctuary
Omid Sector

Dammit. Dammit. Dammit. A Chinese warship, kissing the uppermost parts of this damn planet's atmosphere, its huge bulk staring down at them, daring them to try and pass. They were being targeted by various radars. Ranging. Targeting. Surely they wouldn't open fire on an American shuttle in American space, would they?

Would they?

An alarm rang in her ears. Her communications were being jammed.

Very, very not good. If they wanted them dead, they would be dead—but they weren't exactly *friendly* either. Corrick slammed the throttle open, giving maximum power to the engines. For a fighter, this would be heavy G's and a full burn;

for a shuttle, it was … a slight push back in against her chair.

This thing had no armor worth mentioning except a thick heat shield to protect against reentry. No real maneuverability. No weapons.

"Corrick," said Flatline cautiously, "this would be a really good time for the weird-o thing to come out. You feeling stressed?"

"Plenty," she said, gritting her teeth and testing the rudder pedals with her feet. The ship continued to climb—painfully, slowly—and she checked what passed for the ship's radar. It had highlighted everything in green, even the Chinese ship. "But nothing yet. Don't worry. They won't shoot at us. We're Americans in American territory. There's just no way."

"We'll see," said Flatline, touching the ship's console panels, changing the identification of the Chinese ship to red. Hostile. Not that it mattered without any guns. "Corrick, they're launching fighters."

Well that was a *big* problem. The Chinese were making a liar of her by the second. "Are they coming our way?"

"You bet your ass."

Damn. Guano touched the passenger intercom. "Admiral Mattis, this is Guano. The Chinese ship is launching fighters and they are *not* looking happy to see us. They might not be aware that this is a VIP shuttle. I'm going to transmit our codes and try to talk them out of destroying us, but honestly, sir, I don't like our chances."

"Do what you need to do," came the terse reply from the back. He sounded distracted. Probably dealing with their wounded crewman. No sense bothering them anymore.

Guano flicked channels, broadcasting out in the open.

"Attention all, this is the United States Navy Shuttle *Zulu-3*. Be advised we are clearing planetary atmosphere at this time. We are unarmed."

No response. Not that she expected anything less with their comms out. It was worth a shot.

Flatline tapped on the screens. "I'm going to divert a bit of power to the ship's engines," he said, "taking it away from, well, whatever I can get. It won't be much but it'll help."

"Gimme what you got," said Guano, gritting her teeth as four Chinese fighters roared past their shuttle and executed sharp hook-turns in the thin atmosphere, pulling in behind them. Perfect gun-run position. "When they shoot, I'm going to hard over and see if we can turn their shots into glancing hits."

"Will that help?" asked Flatline, skeptically.

"It'll make me feel better." She drummed her foot on the rudder pedal. She was moments away from death. Why wasn't the strange hypnosis-thing activating? Where was the trance? The battle calm? Her heart pounded in her chest, racing a million miles a minute. Any second now the Chinese would be firing; they'd blow them to pieces and only extremely precise flying would get them out of it. Flying she could only achieve with the help of her special talent, whatever it was.

Come on, brain. Save me! Otherwise, you know, we both die. You live in my head too, and if my head is exploded, that's bad news for you. Any time now. Really. Any time.

Nothing. Trying to make herself more stressed only achieved, well, making herself more stressed.

Guess it was just her and the seat of her pants. Her eyes flicked to the rear view camera. The Chinese fighters were closing in on her—they were obviously struggling to fly as *slow* as their shuttle was, despite her flooring it. The shuttle's power-to-weight ratio, even at the edges of the world's atmosphere, was just too poor. The fighters, however—she could see the glimmer of their guns, the shine of the star off their cockpits. Any second, any second, any second—

A bright light flashed from one. She instantly jerked the control column hard over, jamming it into her leg. The shuttle lurched violently, although not nearly as violently as she wanted—the damn ship was designed to be stable. Comfortable. Not like a fighter that wanted to jerk and twist around.

Still, it was enough. A magnetic grappler flew past her cockpit, so close she could read the damn serial number. It wasn't deadly ordnance, but she wasn't exactly keen on getting snagged either. Expecting another shot, she flung the ship in the opposite direction, barely missing another magnetic grappler.

That was good. Two had fired and two had missed. They would have to wind back in the arms and that would take time. Too much time. They'd be back at the *Midway* by then; Guano could see the flashing lights of the ship in low orbit, coming around to meet them.

She just had to get there. Below her, the two fighters who had fired and missed fell away, dragged down by their long dangling cables. The other two—perhaps not expecting *both* of their companions to miss—overshot, soaring up past their cockpit.

If she had any guns, this would be a prime attack vector. As it was all she could do was glare at them angrily as their noses tipped and they spun around to face her, drifting backwards through space.

"Why don't they just shoot us?" she asked, glaring at the two ships impotently. "They have us dead to rights."

"Because," said Flatline ominously, "they want us alive. They probably think we're with the terrorists."

Explained the grapplers. Guano ground her teeth. "Well, I'm not looking forward to being 'guests' of the Chinese, so how about we shoot at them a little bit, huh?"

"How do you mean?" asked Flatline. "We don't have any guns."

"Not," Guano reached down and patted her sidearm pointedly. "*Strictly* true."

Flatline stared. "What, you think you can fight off a boarding party with *that*?"

"Oh, no," said Guano, taking a shallow breath. "You have a helmet, right?"

"Yeah, under my seat. You thinking of doing an EVA?"

Guano shook her head and pressed the emergency seal button, blocking the passenger compartment off from the cockpit. "No, I just promised Roadie I'd return this ship without a scratch, and you know me." She drew her pistol, aiming it through the cockpit canopy at the nearest Chinese fighter. "I can't keep a promise to save my life."

Flatline's eyes became wide as saucers. "Wait, you can't possibly—"

"Put our helmets on!" shouted Guano. "This is about to get wild!"

Flatline pulled on his helmet, then struggled to jam one over her own head, both helmets hissing as they sealed. "You damn idiot!"

She squeezed the trigger.

The round blew a hole in the cockpit canopy, streaking out across space and thumping into the nosecone of the Chinese fighter. Immediately, air began to howl as it was sucked out of the crack. She squeezed off two more shots—one missed, the other struck the fighter's wing—and the cockpit's air escaped faster.

She adjusted the helmet, making sure the seal was tight, as the atmosphere in the cockpit dropped. It was a risk, sure, but as she watched, the damaged Chinese fighter broke away, a thin wisp of smoke trailing from its wing. The other one, after a moment's hesitation, dove in to attack, guns flashing angrily.

Rounds impacted their ship, and alarms blared. Guano pulled the ship up, rolled over the fighter, exposing the shuttle's thick heat shield to the incoming fire, and flew toward the *Midway* as quickly as her slow, lumbering ship could manage.

The Chinese mothership could have fired on them, could have blown them out of space. But they didn't. Instead, one of the fighters flipped around and put another burst into her rear, striking one of her engines. She swore, kicking the rudder from side to side as the ship lurched, trying to avoid getting hit again.

"We lost an engine," said Flatline, his voice pitching up. "Damn!"

"Is the passenger compartment holed?" she asked.

A quick glance at his instruments, and Flatline shook his head. "No, but we're hit pretty good!"

She swung the dropship around, inertia carrying her toward the *Midway*, and she lined up her pistol again. She emptied her magazine. At that range, her little pistol had almost no chance of hitting, but apparently the gunfire—shot through their own windscreen—was enough to make the Chinese pilot have second thoughts. The fighter broke away, following their damaged companion back to the warship.

Slowly, aware her shuttle had been badly damaged, she turned back toward the *Midway*. They had a clear run home.

"You really are crazy, you know that?" said Flatline, but then he just laughed. Laughed like a jackal as the shuttle lazily soared toward the *Midway*, closing in on their mothership with frustrating slowness.

"Hey, they don't call me Guano for nothing," she said, as the last of the cockpit air drained out. The only air they had was in their flight suits. An emergency reserve, but more than enough to make it home. She holstered her pistol. "Shame about the windscreen though."

"They're cheap," said Flatline, with something almost approximating relief. "Don't worry about it. Believe me—I'll talk to Roadie and get everything fixed up."

She grinned and tapped in the autolander, coming up on the *Midway*'s hangar bay. She thumbed the intercom. "Attention passengers, we're arriving at the *Midway* momentarily. We understand you have a choice in crazy-arse pilots who will fly through fire to get you to and from your destination, and we're glad you've chosen us."

"Jackarse," muttered Flatline. "You're going to get us *both* fired at this rate."

Guano only grinned, but deep down, she was worried.

What had just happened?

Chapter Twenty-Four

Hains Point Picnic Area
South of the Thomas Jefferson Memorial
Washington, DC
Earth

Chuck sipped his still-warm coffee, cupping his drink with both hands and letting the warmth drive away the slight chill of the morning air as he leaned forward on the bench at the edge of Hains Point. The view was always amazing. The sun rose over the Potomac river, its light shining between the trees and casting long shadows across the park, like a giant's fingers reaching out to touch him.

Or strangle him.

A slight disturbance shifted the bench. Someone had sat down on the other side, directly behind him. Chuck sipped his coffee. "You're late."

"No, you're early," said Kyle O'Conner, long time friend

of his. His voice sounded tense. Stressed. "We shouldn't be seen speaking like this. The shorter time we spend together, the better."

"We're just two gentlemen enjoying public space," said Chuck. "And don't panic. Hains Point is the only place in this area without security cameras."

"Sure. That only leaves satellites, I guess. And security. And the secret service. Nothing to be concerned about *at all*."

Paranoia. Not good. Chuck decided to cut to the chase. "What have you got for me, Kyle?"

"Pitt still isn't happy with you. And he loathes your dad. I've never seen a man so angry—and so driven. It's not a hot rage, it's a cold simmer. And it's not going away."

He sipped his coffee again. "Who cares if he doesn't like me? He hates himself, why would he like anyone else?"

Kyle snorted. "Well, that may be so, but he *really* hates your Dad."

"Tell me something I don't know." Chuck considered. "Like about that video that's been doing the rounds. The one on the news."

"I can't talk about that," said Kyle, stiffly. "I still work for Pitt. That stuff—" He paused meaningfully. "Woah. That's *big* news."

"I didn't ask you here to chat about stuff I already know," said Chuck. "What about …" he searched his memory, for fragments of sentences picked up while he was working for Pitt. It seemed like a lifetime ago. "What about the Ark Project?"

Kyle hissed faintly. "I *really* shouldn't be talking about that. Besides, I don't know anything about it, no more than you, I bet."

That part was likely true, but there was a tremor in his voice that betrayed him. Kyle knew something about it. "C'mon."

"I'm serious," said Kyle. "Don't ask me about it. I can't answer."

"Well," said Chuck, "what *can* you tell me?"

Kyle hesitated, and then, as though choosing his words carefully, spoke. "You know, Chuck, from here you can see the Jefferson Memorial just through those trees."

Chuck didn't have to look to know. "No you can't. That's the golf course's clubhouse."

"And you know this because you've looked and seen it for yourself. But they're both white, tall, and if it wasn't for the trees, you couldn't tell the difference."

"You trying to tell me something?"

"I'm telling you that you're not seeing the whole picture here, and if you don't get in and look for yourself, you're going to be misled."

"Funny in the context of you giving me information."

A brief pause. Then Kyle spoke again. "Thomas Jefferson is pretty popular of late. That guy in the embassy siege quoted him. Funny you should choose to meet me here."

"It's a nice view," said Chuck.

Kyle stood up. "Whatever it is you're looking for, Chuck, let it go. Enjoy your family and your new job. There's nothing here."

Chuck drank the last of his coffee as Kyle walked away. The sun crested the tree-line and the dark fingers across the park retreated. He glanced over his shoulder. The white clubhouse was there, barely visible through the trees, just like Kyle had said.

I guess I'll have to look into this one myself.

Chapter Twenty-Five

Hangar Bay
USS Midway
High orbit above Sanctuary
Omid Sector

The shuttle skidded to a stop, the ramp dropping before the pressure had even finished equalizing. Space-suited medics ran toward the ship, grabbed Modi, placed him on a stretcher, and took him away.

He'd be fine. Mattis was sure of it.

Pretty sure.

He had no time to think about it now. Mattis stomped his way from the hangar bay to the bridge, hands clenched by his sides. All those months of boredom and frustration that he could do nothing finally boiled over.

The damn reds had tried to kidnap him.

They'd been attacked. The Chinese had tried to take him

alive. Kidnap him—for what purpose?

It didn't matter. For now, Mattis needed answers. Had to speak with the President. He marched all the way into the ready-room, Lynch in tow, and went to close the door.

"Captain?" asked Lynch, his Texan accent coming out, hands still covered in Modi's blood. "You sure you're going to be okay in there?"

"Yes," said Mattis. "I'll be fine. Hey, I want you to listen in on this call just—give me a minute." He closed the door.

When he was alone, finally on his ship again, Mattis took a deep breath and let it out slowly. Dammit. Everything had gone sideways.

When he was ready, he opened the door and let Lynch inside. Then he sat down at his fine oaken desk, pulled out his communicator, and patched in the special number to President Schuyler.

Having the President on speed dial had its perks.

Two rings. Three rings. Four. Then it connected. "This is President Schuyler's secretary."

"This is Admiral Jack Mattis of the USS *Midway*."

"Hold please." Although politely phrased, there was no way of interpreting her statement as a request. He could hear noise in the background. Murmured voices. Had he interrupted a meeting? What time was it on Earth? He hadn't even checked.

Tick, tock. Mattis waited. Finally he heard footsteps down the line, and then the ambient noises faded away.

"Admiral," said President Schuyler. She audibly sighed down the line. "Every time I take a call from you, Mattis, it's something awful. I'm starting to expect nothing but bad news from you. Disappoint me, please."

He almost made a snappy quip about being known for disappointing women, but he found he couldn't so soon after seeing Ramirez again. It was too true. Too real. Too raw. "I'm afraid I can't disappoint you this time, Madam President. We have a problem."

"You're telling me," said President Schuyler. "Have you seen the numbers on the latest poll? The blowback from the broadcast is eating me alive. Half the country is calling me a tyrannical warmonger, and the other half is calling me a lame-duck chickenhawk. Trying to re-frame this narrative is like pulling teeth. Gotta be tough on the aliens, but not *too* tough. Gotta move for war while calling for peace. Great. If I hear one more thing about—"

"Madam President," said Mattis, "I'm sure these are big problems for you, but they're more problems for your campaign managers, rather than you. What I have is a little more *important*."

"What's that, Jack?"

"The Chinese shot at me again."

Her sigh was long and loud. "Jack, I'm running on about four hours sleep a night for the last month. Just give it to me straight: what did you do?"

"Nothing," he said, and then corrected himself. "Well, okay. Not quite *nothing*. The embassy siege—I'm sure you saw it on the news—I stepped in the middle of it."

"I noticed. Why would you go and do a damn fool thing like that?" demanded Schuyler. In that moment she sounded just like a female version of Lynch. "That incident was a matter for local law enforcement."

Now it was his turn to get snippy. "Fleet Command ordered us to intervene," he protested. "It's not like I just *decided* to take a walk down there and sort it out."

"Great," said President Schuyler. "It means I gotta fire someone in *that* department instead."

At least he'd keep his job. That was something. "Madam," said Mattis, "This embassy thing has me thinking." It was difficult to express. He needed to be delicate. "In all their gun-toting craziness, I think the extremists might have a point."

"Mm hm," said President Schuyler. "That Chinese embassy security needs to be beefed up?"

"Not that. The alien creature in the newsfeed," he paused, needing confirmation, "it was one of *them*, wasn't it?"

"Yes," said President Schuyler, slightly defensively. "You know it was."

"I thought it looked kind of … Asian," he probed further.

Her voice turned sour. "Admiral, I thought you were over your Chinese paranoia."

He clicked his tongue. Her phrasing conjured to mind something Senator Pitt had said to him once. "Madam President, with respect, paranoia is a delusional fear that someone's out to get you. If it's justified, it's—"

"It's merely justified caution," said President Schuyler, bitterly. "You sound like Pitt. You two idiots are peas in a pod, you know that?"

Mattis chewed on the inside of his cheek. "I was kind of hoping you hadn't heard that particular little phrase of his."

"Well, when I heard it, he was talking about *you*." President Schuyler's voice turned sarcastic. "According to him, you've apparently been putting listening devices in his office, the navy has been hiring away his interns, and don't get me started on your son. The way he tells it, that boy is basically running the Illuminati now."

"Chuck has nothing to do with this." He folded his hands. "And I most definitely have *not* been bugging his office. Good God. Look, Madam President, I'm just saying the extremists, these … Forgotten. They're crazy, they're violent, but maybe what they're saying is true. Maybe there's more to this than is in the public eye."

"If there was," said President Schuyler, "you know I couldn't tell you. And you shouldn't be asking about these matters. Whatever point the Forgotten have, believe me, we have top people working on it."

That much he was sure of. "I know. Sorry. I'll let you get back to your meeting now."

"Thank you, Admiral." Without any further ado she hung up.

Mattis made sure the call was disconnected, then glanced up to Lynch. "What do you think?"

"Pretty sure there's more going on here than we were made privy to," said Lynch, nodding firmly for emphasis. "We should definitely do something, sir."

Mattis raised an eyebrow. "We can't do anything. We weren't ordered to look into this."

"But we weren't ordered *not* to." said Lynch, smirking slightly.

Mattis waggled his finger at Lynch. "I like the way you think, XO."

His communicator chirped. Internal ship's message. He put it on loudspeaker. "Go."

"Sir, this is the bridge. The Chinese ship just arrived in orbit. The Commanding Officer, Admiral Yim, is asking to speak to you."

The announcement caught Admiral Mattis completely off-guard.

Impossible.

"No," said Mattis, sitting back in his chair. "No. It can't be."

It took Lynch a moment, but eventually he understood too. "Isn't he dead?"

Chapter Twenty-Six

Senator Pitt's Office
Washington D.C.
Earth

Senator Pitt knew he was bargaining without a full understanding of the consequences of his actions, but he didn't care.

It was that important.

"So that's the deal," he said. He hoped it was enough for her. "I give you what you need, and you let me talk to the Deep State."

Spectre laughed down the line. The noise was odd, distorted through her voice changer, and although her tone was breathy and feminine, the fact that she was showing mirth terrified him. "You want to talk to the Deep State? What do you think you know about it, little man?"

"Enough," said Pitt, "and believe me—you don't get to be

in politics as long as I have without hearing *things*. There's another level to our government. Another layer. Beyond President Schuyler and the cabinet and the senate and the house. Above the opposition parties. Outside the control of the political appointees. They control the shit—the whole game. Doesn't matter who's in power, really, because they always end up serving the Deep State's interests. *That's* who I want to talk to."

"You're walking on dangerous territory," said Spectre, calmly. "The kind of people you're talking about—if they even truly exist—are not the kind of people who make fair deals. They take what they want and, if it suits them, they give you something back in return … or they might not. If that happens, there's no higher authority to plead to. No tribunals or appeal boards or due process. This is what the Germans call *realpolitik*; ruthlessly practical policies executed without consideration for ideology."

"I know what *realpolitik* is." Pitt ran his tongue over his teeth. "And I also know the risks."

Spectre was silent for a moment, the only noise a faint hissing on the line. "Allow me to ask you a question," she said.

"Shoot."

"How does this all end?"

Interesting question. Pitt tilted his head. "How do you mean?"

"All this. This crusade of yours against Admiral Mattis. Do you think they'll have a parade in your honor once you've taken him down? Erect a monument to your greatness, right next to Washington's? Will Miss Ramirez host a panel on her show entitled 'Senator Pitt was right all along'? What's your end game?"

"I don't have one," he said honestly. "I haven't thought that far ahead, nor do I care to."

"I see," said Spectre, slowly. "Revenge won't fix your problems, Senator. It won't fix the hole in your soul. It can't bring your son back."

"I know," said Pitt, a smile creeping across his face. "And yet, there *is* something that can, isn't there?"

More silence from Spectre.

"Tell me," said Pitt, "do you have any children?"

"No," she said. "I thank the good Lord for creating condoms and Darwin for giving me the good sense to use them."

"Then you couldn't possibly understand."

Spectre clicked her tongue, a strange noise coming through her voice changer. "Perhaps."

Pitt *knew* there was more going on with Spectre than she was prepared to let on, and knew that she was a modern-day genie; a mysterious creature able to grant wishes that some might consider impossible. It was worth asking. "Here's what I'm offering," he said, leaning forward. "I *know* you have the biotech to give me what I want. And I have the resources to give you what *you* want."

"And what is it," asked Spectre, "that you think I want?"

"You want to creep in the shadows. You want grunts to do your dirty work. Soldiers. Not enough to be an army, but untraceable. They have to be good at their jobs, but expendable enough that, if they just disappeared, nobody's going to be asking too many questions about them. No families crying in the street. No letter writing campaigns. The Earth would keep spinning and life would go on."

"Go on," said Spectre.

"I'm affiliated to a lot of causes. As a politician I have to be. I support various blocs and they support me. Some of these blocs are, shall we say, potentially useful to you and your causes."

"Why do you think we've helped you all this time?" asked Spectre, acridly. "Out of charity?"

"Of course not." Pitt took in a breath. "The thing on the news. That was you, wasn't it?"

Spectre said nothing.

"Right. Well, I'm guessing that after all the shooting's done, the Chinese aren't going to leave many survivors. You're going to want more people. Expendable, skilled people who are hard to come by. I can provide you with some. So here's the deal. I'll talk to some of the people at the VA. I'll get you twenty veterans—skilled people, experienced. Nobody'll miss them when they're gone."

"And what do you want in exchange for this resource?"

It sounded crazy even in his own head, but Pitt knew exactly what he wanted.

"I'll tell you when I get there."

Chapter Twenty-Seven

Bridge
USS Midway
High orbit above Sanctuary
Omid Sector

Drifting out of his ready room, Mattis refused to believe it. Yim was a common name amongst the Chinese people—surely there would be more than one admiral amongst them. Maybe it was just all a massive coincidence. Maybe the junior officer, whose voice he didn't recognize and so must be new to the crew, had made a mistake. Maybe he'd misheard.

Admiral Yim. Formerly Captain Yim. Killer of Mattis's brother.

Phillip had died during the Sino-American war. During a deep space engagement twenty years ago, a volley of Chinese torpedoes from Yim's ship had broken the *Saragossa*'s back, killing everyone aboard.

But Yim was dead too. Killed during the attack on Friendship Station.

As he opened the door to the bridge, revealing the corridor beyond full of Chinese marines, Mattis's eyes found Yim's eyes, and he knew there was no mistake.

There he was. In the flesh. Admiral Yim, with his baby face and his broad shoulders, completely unchanged from the last time Mattis had seen him, save a pronounced, jagged scar running down from the left side of his face and a black eye patch covering the same eye.

It was him.

"You," said Mattis, unable to form any other kind of sentence, anger bubbling within him. "How did you…"

"Reports of my demise have been greatly exaggerated," said Yim, half-smirking.

"No," said Mattis, firmly, "they haven't. You were on board Friendship Station when it blew. I saw you there, I saw the damn thing go up like an Independence Day fireworks show. We scanned for survivors, and there were none. There *couldn't* have been."

"You underestimate Chinese technology." Yim smiled, using only his mouth and not his eyes. "Our escape pods are decades more advanced than yours."

Mattis squinted at him. "Why didn't we detect the escape pod during the battle, then?"

"The transponder was damaged. Your low-grade American sensors probably couldn't detect life forms amongst all the debris. It's an understandable mistake."

Low grade American sensors? The best intelligence available suggested that American sensor capabilities far outstripped Chinese ones. "I don't believe you," said Mattis, flatly.

Yim gestured to his chest. "Is the fact that I am here not proof enough?"

"He's got a good point," grumbled Lynch behind him. "He stinks, but he ain't stinking enough to be a zombie, Admiral. And we ain't hallucinating."

It was a difficult point to accept, but try as he might, Mattis simply didn't—simply *couldn't*—believe that Yim had somehow survived. Yet the evidence was, quite literally staring him in the face.

"Okay," said Mattis, his tone absolutely painted with skepticism. "Sure. Why are you here?"

"Admiral Mattis," said Yim, "I need to speak to you in private."

Mattis practically laughed in his face. "After that fucking stunt you pulled out there? Absolutely *not*. You're lucky I don't have you arrested."

"Mattis," said Yim, his tone even, "there's more going on here than a simple misunderstanding."

"Misunderstanding?" His fists clenched by his side. "Is that what you call trying to kill me?"

Yim shook his head firmly. "I had no such intentions, and I can explain it in private. I promise."

Trust was a valuable commodity in Mattis's mind, and this ... this was a lot to ask. "This better be damn good," said Mattis, gesturing over his shoulder to his ready room. "Lynch, you've got the bridge."

"If we hear yelling," asked Lynch, "should we break down the door?"

Mattis just grimaced.

"I'll take that as a yes," said Lynch, glaring Yim's way.

Together, Mattis and Yim moved back into his ready room.

"So," said Mattis when they were alone, folding his hands in front of him. "Why'd you try to kill me? Make it quick."

Yim narrowed his eyes. "We were at war."

"No, not then you idiot. I meant ten minutes ago."

"Oh." Yim considered that. "Sorry. I was just thinking—that made no sense, we were never at arms against each other, it was your—"

Brother. Phillip Mattis, XO of the *Saragossa*, who died at the business end of Yim's guns.

Mattis scowled. "I still haven't forgiven you for that, you know that, right?"

"Of course," said Yim, plainly. "I don't expect you to. If our positions were the same, I doubt I could hold myself back." He pointed to Mattis's side. To his pistol. "You going to do something with that?"

"What?" Mattis shook his head. "What are you talking about?"

"Your ready room," said Yim, indicating the small office. "We're alone here. You could say I attacked you, tried to grab your gun but you were quicker. Nobody would question you."

Mattis's hand twitched by his side but he kept it still. "I won't do that. My brother deserves better."

"Are you sure?" asked Yim, casually reaching for his own gun. Slowly. Way, way too slowly. "This is your opportunity to get revenge for your brother. Think of Phillip Mattis, Jack. Think of how he died. Think of how I killed him. Think of the medal that destroying the USS *Saratoga* earned me."

Mattis grabbed the stock of his pistol. "Don't," he hissed. "What the hell are you thinking? Are you *trying* to get yourself shot? What are you *doing*?"

Yim met his gaze, evenly and stoically. His hand touched the hilt of his own pistol. "I am testing you."

Testing him *how*? Mattis squeezed the grip of his gun. "Don't do it," he said. "Don't."

A tense moment, silent, with both men's hands on their weapons.

Finally Mattis tore his hand away. "Dammit, Yim."

Yim folded his arms. The tension flowed out of the room. "My apologies. I needed to see if you would do it."

"Why?" demanded Mattis, baring his teeth. "Why would you do that? Why would you try and destroy my shuttle then come in here, into this room, and do something so fucking reckless?"

"Because if I'm going to trust you with what I know, I need to know that, even if you had an opportunity to turn on me, and an emotional state which would support it, and every justification in the world—you still wouldn't. Even if you wanted to, and even if you didn't believe me when I told you what I know." Yim inhaled, reaching up and touching his scar. "Because the information I have is … very unbelievable. But as unlikely as it is, it's true."

Whatever it was, it was so serious he would put his life in jeopardy. Mattis forced himself to calm down. To put thoughts of his brother out of his mind. "Why did you attack my shuttle?"

"We thought you were the extremists. Your ship was

detected taking off from the embassy. That's why we tried to capture it. We never expected it to be carrying US personnel, especially not *you*."

"Our pilot sent out transmissions—"

"We jammed those transmissions. It is our protocol."

"Okay," said Mattis, slowly. "I'll choose to believe that. For now."

"Thank you," said Yim, dipping his head. "Please accept my sincerest apologies in this matter."

Mattis didn't like it *at all*, and definitely did not want to accept that a simple apology could by their way out of what had happened, but he needed more information. "So with that out of the way, why are you here?"

Yim turned his back on Mattis, walking toward the desk in the corner of his room, arms still folded over his chest. "After I rode the escape pod from Friendship Station," he said, "I got picked up by my people. But they didn't return me to duty, take me back to Earth, or anything like what you'd expect. They threw me in a—" he looked over his shoulder, face twisted. "I wouldn't call it a prison. More like a hotel I wasn't allowed to leave. It looked nice, but it was rotten on the inside. Everyone was … foul. My captors were human beings, but they weren't people. Something about them was soulless. Empty. As though there was some chemical in the air that made them seem nice on the surface but underneath that, they were pure evil."

"Sounds like Canada," said Mattis.

"This isn't a joke. They kept me there for six months, being interrogated and debriefed over, and over, and over again by a group of people who were not the People's Liberation Army Navy. They weren't even Chinese intelligence. Or party officials. They seemed to be above them."

"Above the Chinese navy?" asked Mattis, confused. "As in, government officials?"

"As in, above the government. Above the *party*. And *nothing* is above the party. Something else. Something much more powerful."

That didn't make any sense. "You mean some other country?"

"This transcends countries," said Yim, his tone dark. "I think countries are a construct to them; something they use to create friction, something they use to pit us against each other, to let the people have something to identify with, cling to, while they pull the strings. They called themselves the Deep State."

A shadow government. Mattis had heard whispers of things like this—everyone had, at some point—but to hear Yim speak about it with such conviction, such genuine respect and fear in his voice, was sobering. "Go on."

"While I was at this ... place ... they asked me questions. Questions that didn't really relate to Friendship Station at all. Things about spies and genetic secrets and a lot of things I didn't understand. I told them I was a naval officer, not a scientist, but they didn't seem to care. They just kept asking over and over and over."

Mattis digested that, tapping his lower lip with a finger. His story was ... strange. Very strange. Nonsensical, even, but that actually made him trust Yim more.

A lie would have made much more sense. A lie would have been a carefully constructed narrative, designed to make him trust it.

Lies had to make sense. Reality, however, was under no such restriction.

"Okay," said Mattis evenly. "Let's assume that I believe you. Why did they let you go? Put you back into command?"

Yim gave a kind of non-committal shrug. "Probably a combination of things. Being a war hero was one. I still have powerful friends in the Chinese Politburo. Also, they probably realized I genuinely didn't know anything. At least, not anything they cared about. Despite this, I think they did it reluctantly—they put me on a work-heavy assignment way out on the border where I couldn't cause trouble."

Sounded familiar. Disturbingly so. Mattis hadn't been interrogated like Yim had been, but then again, maybe there were some legitimate differences in the way Chinese and American authorities operated. It made sense, sort of.

"Admiral," said Yim, "there are things going on that affect the whole galaxy. And I need your help putting the pieces in place."

"Okay," asked Mattis, "where do we go from here?"

"Depends," asked Yim, turning back to face him, finally. "What do you know about the Ark Project?"

Chapter Twenty-Eight

En Route to MaxGainz Branch Office
Glasgow
Earth

Bratta looked out of the car window at Glasgow's miserable sky.

"Jeannie, I *recorded a video.* I … look, I'm a *doctor*. I save the world by inventing a new type of vaccine or something, not with this—" he waved his arms around angrily. "Police- spy-journalism stuff."

Jeannie only seemed to half pay attention to him, her fingers drumming on the wheel as she drove."Well, maybe that's what they were trying to do."

"What? Journalism stuff?"

The tapping stopped. "Steve, cut the kid act. Maybe they were trying to create a new vaccine."

Bratta forced himself to look at her, face to face. Why did

arguments with her always have to be so hard? Even—especially—when she was wrong. "You don't know what you're talking about."

"You're right. And that's why we're on the way to the MaxGainz corporate office, to find out. You ask the right questions, I make sure they answer them."

He toyed with the zipper on his jacket. Four weeks ago he'd been going to work on a new planet like a normal human, with a bright future of brilliant scientific discoveries ahead of him. Three weeks ago he'd been hiding in his apartment on trauma leave, talking occasionally to his goldfish and the robot vacuum. The same held for two and one weeks ago, but that was fine. It had been … therapeutic, especially after he'd modified the robotic cleaner to sing. Well, actually, now that he thought about it that didn't sound healthy at all, but … that was in the past. Now, he was driving through Glasgow with his former wife, towards an office of a company he was technically right at this moment skipping out of working for, on the extremely questionable basis of "Jeannie decided it was the best lead so she's following it."

Not to mention the fact that what she seemed to have in mind sounded rather, well, *illegal.*

"Jeannie?"

"Yes?"

"How are you going to make them answer anything?"

She took her eyes off the traffic for a second to frown at him. "My work badge."

"But … you're a police officer."

"Well yes," she replied slowly. "That's why it works."

"Isn't that sort of illegal? Crooked?"

"*Crooked?*" she scoffed. "Steve, this is *literally my job*. I'm a police officer. We police things."

Technically correct. "But I mean, shouldn't you call this one in to the office, or … something? Aren't you worried about your professional integrity?"

She laughed. "I'm more worried about my planet. Besides, a lot of police paperwork is post-facto, and just remember: you can't make an omelet without breaking into the farm to check they aren't putting illegal additives in the chickens' food."

That was … an analogy. Perhaps not the best one. "Ok, Jeannie," he conceded, shrinking back into his seat. He didn't try to talk for the rest of the ride.

Far too quickly, they reached a blocky building with small windows. Light rain began to bead on the windscreen as they pulled into the half full carpark.

"So," Jeannie said as she crawled though the park. "Am I going to have to cover for you skipping work, or will they not be scanning faces at the office?"

Her tone was so conversational, Bratta took a moment to realize what exactly she'd said. "I … uh … well, they *might*." He thought about it for a second. "But, uh, if they're using my company photoshoot as a reference, then that probably shouldn't be an issue anyway."

Jeannie looked surprised.

"It's bad," he informed her, searching through his pockets.

He held out the ID. Jeannie glanced at it and slammed on the breaks.

"Wait. That's *awful*, Steve." She leaned in curiously, somehow fascinated by the depiction. "You look like a serial killer, smiling like that. How were you not carted off to a nut house? I've seen more genuine smiles on axe murderers. How. How did that even *pass* as an ID in the first place?"

He raised his hands helplessly.

Jeannie shrugged and slotted the car neatly into a vacant space. "Well, their loss, our gain, I guess. Get out, and let's go make some paper-pusher real uncomfortable."

Chapter Twenty-Nine

Captain's Ready Room
USS Midway
High orbit above Sanctuary
Omid Sector

The Ark Project. The same thing Senator Pitt had mentioned.

"I know it's gone," said Mattis, simply. "It was a genetic seed bank for humankind on Ganymede. It was the alien's first target. They blew the colony up from orbit. Whatever secrets were held there, they're long gone."

Yim nodded slowly. "I understand how you might think that."

The evasiveness was palpable. Mattis squinted. "You have something more for me, Yim?"

"I know there are more," he said, with confidence that spoke to the truth of his words. "Many more. The one on

Ganymede was the largest, by far, but there are others—smaller ones, backup storage locations that the Deep State will want to bring online as soon as they can, if they haven't already."

That tweaked his interest. "You mentioned that before. Deep State? What's that? A Chinese thing? American?"

Yim tensed up, visibly. "I honestly don't know. Probably both. It was a … *thing* I overheard after I was rescued. A whispered thing, spoken of only in the dark corners of this facility. They seemed to be a part of the Chinese Bureaucracy, but also part of something much more. The staff clamped down on my questions when I started asking about them, and after I got out, too. Something is off, here, and they don't want people asking questions about it."

More secrecy. More evasion of the truth.

"You mentioned backup locations. Any idea where these locations might be?" asked Mattis.

"I was hoping," said Yim, "that you could tell me."

Well damn. "How about you tell me what you know," said Mattis. "And I'll see if I have anything for you."

"Mmm." Yim nodded. "The genetic seed bank on Ganymede was modeled after one on Svalbard Island, up in the Arctic Ocean on Earth, built hundreds of years ago. That one was designed to safeguard humanity's food supply in case of global disaster. But *this* one was to safeguard *us*. Humans. Our DNA. It contained a broad, diverse record of our genetic history. It was designed to enable us to survive a disaster that would wipe most of us out, so we could use it to rebuild. There is a threshold of population, below which we simply would not have the genetic diversity to sustain the human race.

That's what the Ganymede seed bank was for—to recreate humanity if our numbers ever dropped too low."

"Right. Do you know why it was destroyed?"

"Not a clue," said Yim. "I can only assume the attackers wanted to eliminate our species—completely."

His conclusion, too. There *had* been one question Mattis wanted to ask, but he wasn't sure exactly how proper it was. He didn't want to push too hard, but … what the hell. Yim wanted *his* trust, right? "Actually," said Mattis, "maybe you can help me with something else. Shao's ship, the *Fuqing*. She was damaged, severely but not critically. We went to send over repair teams, and they scuttled themselves. Blowing themselves to atoms rather than risk us boarding. Why would they do that?"

Yim's eyes widened. "I have no idea. This is the first I've heard of it."

Mattis glowered, but he couldn't press Yim about that. "Then I suppose we'll never know." He then continued, half-joking, half-serious. "Not unless Shao got herself into an escape pod too and, similarly, miraculously avoided detection until her inevitable rescue. You didn't see her while you were in that place?"

"No. I did not."

Damn. Despite being enemies in the past, Mattis had found a quick bond with Shao. They thought alike and, despite their profound ideological differences, he had come to respect her as a warrior. The notion that Yim had survived where Shao had not seemed to be an injustice in the scheme of things, but one he could do nothing to change. Sometimes bad things just happened to good people.

Such was the nature of war.

"Very well," said Mattis, taking in a long, slow breath. "We should focus on our work."

To that Yim seemed to agree. "Yes, the Ark Project. But if it's gone, destroyed as you say … what more can we do?"

Mattis considered. "I honestly have no idea." It was a slightly grim, defeated confession, one made slightly worse by his demand that Yim tell him everything while he himself was not able to reciprocate. "The video that Ramirez broadcast," he said, carefully keeping his knowledge that the creatures seen within were not aliens, but humans from the future far away from his mind. "I can't help but feel that it's connected to this."

"It can't hurt to take a look," said Yim. "In life, I've found, the universe always gives you a signpost pointing where to go next; you just have to look for it."

"Interesting idea." Mattis nodded firmly. "Anything in particular we should look for?"

"We won't know," said Yim, "until we find it."

Circular Chinese logic. Mattis bit back his frustration. "It *might* actually be a good idea. Since the video was given directly to the media, and then they broadcast without editing, there's a chance there could still be some kind of hint as to its location. Might be a good place to start."

"That's what I was thinking," said Yim. "There might be more we can learn, too." He snorted playfully. "Unless we could ask Miss Ramirez to disclose the location."

That would be a mistake. Her last interview with Mattis had *not* gone well. More guilt welled up inside him. He shouldn't have let it go on this long; he should have spoken to her.

Focus on work. "If only we could," said Mattis.

"Why not simply ask your superiors? It was a military complex, was it not?"

"Like yourself, I'd prefer my superiors not to know my interest in this issue. Not yet, at least."

"Mmm." Yim considered again. "The video is raw and unedited. An intelligence nightmare. We should be able to get something from it if we're studious and careful."

It was about time an intelligence nightmare worked in their favor. Mattis tapped on his desk, lighting up the monitor that served as his port wall. A few more taps and he had access to the news feeds, and with a bit of searching, Ramirez's broadcast.

"Here," he said, "let's go over it."

So they did. Over and over and over. Mattis and Yim crawled through the video, frame by frame, trying to find something that might give them any indication or clue as to what they were looking for. Mattis mentally airbrushed out the alien creature, the marines, and anything that was a distraction. The flash of gunfire. Panicked people. The distant, unobservable skyline.

"This is pointless," grumbled Yim, the film paused over the giant, obnoxious coffee shop logo with its too-bright neon sign and Chinese lettering. "There's nothing here to indicate anything. We'll have to see if we can get intelligence on this. They can drag up sub-pixel content and look for things that might be smudged by frame interpolation."

"Maybe," said Mattis, stifling a yawn. "Maybe we just need a break."

"Not a bad idea." Yim stretched his arms up high. "A rest would be nice."

"I could go for a cigar," said Mattis, reaching into his breast pocket for a cigar. "You smoke?"

"No," said Yim, firmly. "I don't. Far too old for that."

"Smoking when you're old is the best," said Mattis. "Don't want to be too young, or it might kill you. But at our age, anything that's going to kill you would have already done so. What's the harm?"

With a reluctant sigh, Yim took the cigar, turning it over in his fingers. "Are you sure coffee wouldn't be better? I could really go for some *Yǒufú De Rénxìng*."

"Some what?"

"Coffee," said Yim, jabbing the cigar at the screen. At the giant logo with its Chinese writing. "That thing. *Blessed Humanity*."

Mattis shrugged. "Never seen that before in my life."

Yim laughed as though Mattis had made a joke, sticking the cigar between his teeth.

"What?" asked Mattis, confused.

"*Blessed Humanity* is a coffee company," said Yim, like he was talking to a child. Then he snapped his fingers. "Ah, of course you wouldn't have heard about it. It's only recently gotten permission to operate on two non-Chinese worlds—and Friendship Station of course, before it exploded. I made sure of it."

"Which worlds?" asked Mattis, eyes widening. Had the truth been staring them in the face?

"What?"

Mattis sat up straight, the lethargy banished. "You said the *Blessed Humanity* coffee company operated on only Chinese worlds, except two. The people in those pictures aren't Chinese, so: *which two worlds were they?*"

The light went on in Yim's head. "Zenith in the Tonatiuh Sector, and New London."

New London. What a shit-hole. "Okay," said Mattis. "New London is closer. Much closer. We'll go there first. And if we can't find anything, we'll go to Zenith."

"Worst one first, huh," said Yim, his tone grim. "I've heard stories of New London. I'd hoped never to visit."

"Why did *Blessed Humanity* set up a coffee shop there?" asked Mattis, curiously. "It's the last place I'd consider something like that."

Yim just smiled. "It was the only place they could get a permit for. New London's a backwater. They'll take just about any old Chinese company there."

"Right," said Mattis. It was strange to be working alongside Yim after all that had happened. Memories of his brother's face once again drifted back into his mind, but they were cut out by a chirp from his communicator.

"Admiral Mattis," said a voice, harried and angry. "It's Nurse Alonzo from sickbay. We need you down here. Now."

Modi.

"Get back to your ship," said Mattis, standing. "I have to take this."

Chapter Thirty

MaxGainz Branch Office
Glasgow
Earth

Bratta tagged along behind Jeannie as she strode into the reception area like she owned the place.

The receptionist, a well-dressed young man who looked fresh-faced enough for this to have been his first job, looked up and smiled. "Good afternoon, how may I help you?"

Jeannie fixed him with the look that Bratta had privately named *no I will not listen to reason no matter how convincing you may be, Steve.* "I'm here to speak to the manager."

The receptionist broke eye contact and looked at a screen in front of him. "Do you have an appointment, Miss…?"

"Officer Tafola. And no, we don't. Just a few questions for your manager." She flashed her badge.

The receptionist looked a little stunned. "Of course,

officer," he stammered. "Just let me check that he isn't in a meeting now … No, no, he's should be free to see you now. I'll … I'll let him know you're here, shall I?"

Jeannie nodded, entirely professional. "Thank you."

The room fell silent as the receptionist turned his attention back to the screen. Bratta spent the interval thinking about the work he should be doing—regenerating muscle tissue in mice with induced birth defects—because to think about what he was actually doing here was to invite disaster. Jeannie had a poker face, he had a poker … *fail.*

That always sounded so funny in his head.

Besides, the techniques he'd been briefed on *were* interesting, even if he'd never actually managed to work in their labs. He let his mind wander … the work he could have done with that kind of equipment, that sort of funding … he'd always been lucky, really, in his interests. It was definitely an advantage to be invested in the sort of research big drug companies wanted done. Much easier than being obsessed with, oh, a species of South American pygmy possum, or—

Jeannie cleared her throat.

"Ah, sorry," he jerked back to reality. "Coming."

She nodded and turned on her heel. That probably meant she wasn't going to be relying on him for directions, because, he realized with a sense of mild hope, he hadn't the foggiest where they might be going. Perhaps they would miraculously get lost and he wouldn't have to indulge in … corporate espionage? Fraud? Something illegal, anyway.

Five minutes later, they were knocking on an office door. Bratta swallowed.

"Come in."

It was the first voice Bratta had heard since arriving in Glasgow without some form of Scottish accent. Oddly, that was comforting—he supposed the reaction was a byproduct of working for some time in an international field. That, or Jeannie had ruined the accent for him forever. That hypothesis seemed plausible.

The subject of said hypothesis fixed him with a steely eye. "Keep it together, Steve," she muttered before opening the door.

They were faced with the sight of a blond man in a suit, seated behind a desk piled high with papers and several coffee mugs. Bratta found the sight quite relatable, although part of him was a little disappointed at the lack of any fluffy white cats or slowly rotating chairs, as far as *ominous villain lairs* went, a well-kept, expensive office suite was remarkably disappointing. Jeannie nodded to the man.

"May we take a seat, Mr. Stepka?"

The suited man nodded. "Of course, officer. I understand you have some questions for me?"

"Indeed we do." Jeannie didn't so much as bat an eye at the lie. "There are a few things we'd like to ask regarding potential illegal activities undertaken by your company."

Bratta's eyes nearly bugged out. She'd just come right out and *said it.*

A thousand possibilities flew through his head, and absolutely none of them good. The only one that he could find that would justify why she would come right out and basically accuse the guy of illegal activities … was that their own investigation was a little south of entirely legitimate.

Maybe Jeannie's superiors hadn't authorized it, or maybe

she hadn't even asked. She *was* still a policewoman, right?

He needed something, something to distract him. Chicken farm with illegal additives in the food. Bratta tried to focus on the greater good, despite a growing urge to squeak like a mouse. Fortunately, he remained quiet.

Mr. Stepka reached for his coffee mug. "Alright. I don't believe I know anything that could be of help, but please, ask away."

Jeannie folded her hands in her lap. "I assume you have seen the video?"

"I have," the manager replied. *The video.* There could only be one people were talking about. The memory of those *things* sent a brief shiver down his spine.

Keep it together, Bratta….

"And I assume," said Jeannie, "you further realize that this attack has been linked to a facility of your very own company?"

Stepka raised an eyebrow. "Where did you hear that from, Officer?"

Bratta gripped the armrest on his chair. *Please don't say me….*

"I have my sources," said Jeannie, unblinkingly. "Ones I keep close to my chest until I've finished my investigation."

Stepka locked gazes with her, for just a moment, and then seemed to relent. "I am indeed aware that our facility was targeted by an alien attack."

"Linked, Mr. Stepka, not targeted." Jeannie's voice was hard. "Our expert advice has identified these 'aliens' as displaying a disturbingly large number of characteristically human traits. Your company deals in human enhancement, particularly steroids and muscular growth. The creatures appeared to come from your company's building. Please explain these—*coincidences*."

Mr. Stepka set down the mug with an audible *clink*. "I'm genuinely not sure what there is to explain Officer Tafola. I suppose if you believe our company's products or research has aided in the—I can only assume, according to your theories—'creation' of these entities, perhaps it could then follow that the facility on Zenith was raided for the easy procurement of such resources? We, officer, are the victims here, not the perpetrators."

No. That was a lie. What the man was saying was reasonable enough, but … raiding parties didn't usually stop to try and kill one another. At least, he was pretty sure that wasn't how it was supposed to work. If only he had read that one text about sixteenth-century pirates he had been meaning to pry open for so long.…

Jeannie wasn't answering. His heartbeat skyrocketed. If it was down to him to save this situation, that would definitely be some form of cosmic mistake. He couldn't do it. Still, there was one thing that might save his hide: techno-babble. "Ah, excuse me Mr. Stepka," said Bratta, "but I … well, I don't think that's particularly feasible. Firstly, the observed behavior of the creatures was not consistent with the goal of a raid—if you remember, there was infighting reported at the end of the video, and the video never shows the subject carrying or otherwise transporting any sort of goods.

"Secondly, I, um, well…" He paused to gather his thoughts, his breath, and his courage. This was rather a lot of talking he hadn't meant to do. "I am something of a student of genetics and medicine myself. I'm aiding the good officer with her investigation. By sheer coincidence, I am quite familiar with facilities such as those your company would possess. So, while the kind of modifications we're talking about are as much in the theoretical stage as they are corporate secrets, so to speak, I believe your laboratories may be capable of producing such results, with the right minds guiding them."

He actually had no idea whether or not the labs were up to scratch, but it was *clearly* a great idea to take a leaf out of Jeannie's book.

The manager shifted his gaze to Bratta for the first time. *Oh no, Jeannie start talking, save me please.*

"Interesting points, Mr…?"

"Bratta. Ah, my name is Steve Bratta."

He probably shouldn't have told them his actual name. Especially since he was a former employee. Actually, had he even been fired yet? The last few weeks were a haze. He wanted to load a saved game and repeat this whole conversation, but it was done now, so there were only consequences and probably regret.

"Well, Mr. Bratta, you raise some valid but, as far as I can tell, unfounded concerns, wild speculation, and guesswork." Stepka gave a shark's smile. "Please, if you possess evidence of a more *concrete* nature, tell me now and I may actually be able to assist you. Otherwise, I would direct you to our legal department. They are far better equipped to have their time wasted with conspiracy theories than this office. Now, if there's nothing else…?"

Jeannie stood. "We've clearly helped each other as much as we can. Good afternoon, Mr Stepka."

They saw themselves out.

There was still a light drizzle in the carpark when they got there, which matched his mood pretty well. Jeannie's expression, on the other hand, would have matched thunderclaps. She was muttering under her breath as she walked toward the car.

"Sorry," said Bratta.

"Mmm?" Jeannie barely looked at him.

She sometimes got this way. "Sorry we didn't find anything," said Bratta, fiddling nervously with his keys. "I know that annoys you."

"Oh, no," said Jeannie, her expression unchanging. "I was just playing through things in my head. Shh, just let me think."

"Uhh, okay."

Jeannie unlocked the car, and as they drove out of the carpark, her knuckles were white on the steering wheel.

In his side mirror, Steve could see a long stream of lights behind him, refracted every which way in the rain droplets. More and more orbs were added to it as work traffic started to filter out of buildings. The car behind them had one light noticeably dimmer than the other, like a one-eyed pirate.

About ten minutes later, the car behind them still had one light noticeably dimmer than the other.

"Um..."

Jeannie glowered at the road. "What is it, Steve?"

"I think we have a tail."

Chapter Thirty-One

Infirmary
USS Midway
High orbit above Sanctuary
Omid Sector

With Yim returned to his ship, and the *Midway* in Lynch's perfectly capable hands, Mattis jogged down to the infirmary, his mind racing with a thousand possibilities. What had happened to Modi?

To his surprise, the guy was there waiting for him, sitting up on one of the benches in the waiting area, a nurse bandaging his shoulder. He had a sour expression on his face.

"Admiral Mattis," said Modi, his tone even and composed. "I'm surprised to see you here."

"Surprised I'd come and visit you?" Mattis's eyebrows shot up. "They said they needed me down here urgently."

"Indeed." Modi glared at the nurse beside him. The nurse

glared back. "There was some disagreement about the nature of my treatment. Voices were raised. The staff thought I could best be calmed with your presence, but the issue is now resolved. For now."

That man and his perfectionist nature. "Don't antagonize the medical staff, they know what they're doing."

"This isn't about me," said Modi, his expression souring just a tad. "This is about the butchers you call medical technicians—"

"I'm standing right here," said the nurse.

"And the various sharp pieces of metal that said medical technicians want to thrust into my veins and skin."

Mattis narrowed his eyes slightly. "They wanted to give you an injection?"

"We wanted to give him an injection," said the nurse.

"I," proclaimed Modi proudly, "do not like needles."

Mattis considered, walking up to the nurse and the thin syringe she still had in her hand. It was the smallest, thinnest needle he'd ever seen. "That's the thing?"

Modi grimaced. "Yes."

Slowly, Mattis let all the tension flow out of him. "Modi, take your medicine."

The nurse jabbed Modi in the upper arm.

"Hey!" protested Modi.

Mattis rolled his eyes.

"Anyway," said Modi, rubbing his shoulder ruefully. "Admiral, you have a whole ship to run, full of people who need your attention as well, and you are not a qualified trauma surgeon so your presence here doesn't seem to assist in any way."

Mattis managed a small smile, despite the almost-certainly-unintentional insult. "I know what you mean, but I just had to see if you were okay with my own eyes."

"Well," said Modi, his tone flat and emotionless as usual, "I do appreciate it. As it turns out, I'm much less badly injured than I initially appeared. The round went in and out, barely hit anything. Shock, however, played a significant role in my loss of consciousness."

The nurse nodded mutely as though agreeing, but also as though the act could, somehow, quicken the pace of time and get Modi out of the infirmary and out of her hair. "His arm will be in a sling for some time, but he'll be fine." She tapped his freshly bandaged shoulder. "There you go, sir. You can get going whenever you're comfortable."

Modi stood. Mattis helped him up.

"I'm fine, sir," said Modi, but Mattis noted how he took his arm anyway. "What happened after I, uh, had a little nap?"

"Well," said Mattis, "Yim's alive again."

"Oh," said Modi.

Mattis blinked. "You don't seem too surprised to hear that."

"I assume," said Modi, "that there's a perfectly good reason why he's alive when we thought he wasn't—not that he ever stopped being alive, mind, but more that we *perceived* him to be dead."

Mattis tried to keep up with his logic. "Right."

"So," continued Modi, without skipping a beat, "I remain confident that there's a perfectly reasonable explanation for the events which have transpired, and in due time, I am confident I shall learn it. In the mean time, Admiral, how can I assist you?"

"With your brain," said Mattis. "We're en route to New London. I'm going to take the lead on this one. I want you and Lynch with me. Take some painkillers, apply some bandages, and make sure you're ready to come down with us when we arrive."

Modi's eyes became saucers. "New London, sir? Are you sure there isn't an active war zone you'd rather visit instead?"

Mattis almost did a double take. Was that sarcasm? Modi? Perhaps he wasn't the robot Lynch was making him out to be. "Come on," said Mattis, smiling widely. "How bad can it possibly be?"

Chapter Thirty-Two

Cab 2094
Highway 11
New London
Omid Sector

The taxi driver swerved violently, a split second before nearly slamming into the rear of a frozen goods truck. The maneuver only exacerbated their problems; the car wobbled as it sped toward the thick steel railing that lined the edge of the road. Somehow, just before it hit, the car swung back into a lane, a cacophony of horns and angry shouts all around them.

"For God's sake," yelled Mattis, gripping the Jesus Handle with white knuckles, "slow down!"

"Can't slow down," said their driver, as calmly as if she were discussing the weather. "This area is gang territory." She swung the vehicle back into their original lane. To Mattis she seemed a ghostly, pale rider, with fading ginger hair and a cheap leather jacket. Strapped to her hip was a high caliber pistol with an extra five magazines. Inside her jacket was another pistol. A third one lay in the open glove compartment. Underneath her clothes, the woman was wearing body armor.

Body armor with two dents in it, and matching 10mm bullet holes in the jacket above.

Their taxi sped between two other cars, the white dividing lines of the highway running straight down the middle of their vehicle. They ducked and weaved around the traffic, sometimes dodging cars coming the other way.

"Admiral Mattis," shouted Modi from the back seat, "I must enquire; what is the purpose of attempting to get information if we are not alive to report it?"

"You're an Admiral?" said their driver, cracking a smile like a drug-addled jackal. "Yeah, friend, you *definitely* don't want me to slow down! If any of the local gangs find you they'll definitely want that ransom, and let's just say the going rate costs an arm and a leg, eh! Or maybe just a kidney!"

The taxi passed a flatbed truck full of cattle going the other way, so close that Lynch cowered away from the window, fearing a cow's head would smash through the side of the car. Lynch yelped something so quintessentially Texan, so incomprehensibly Southern, that Mattis genuinely couldn't understand it.

"Too right!" said their drive with a laugh, seemingly fluent in terrified-Lynch-isms.

He and Yim exchanged a look. The Chinese Admiral had lost all the color in his face, becoming almost as pale as their driver.

This wasn't how Mattis anticipated going out.

As the car careened through the streets he *knew*, deep down, that they should have come down with a marine escort. They should have come armed, with a strong military presence. He'd decided not to. Going under-cover, he'd thought, would be better. Safer. Less conspicuous.

Next time he would bring his own transport, an armored vehicle. Next time he'd bring a detachment of marines. Next time—

Thump. The car struck some kind of dark colored bird, the body exploding on the glass, smearing it with red juices and feathers. Their driver turned on the windscreen wipers. "Fucking ravens," she muttered. "Rats with wings."

The vehicle swerved and jerked, weaving in and out of the constant traffic, and then with the low screech of tires and a loud clatter, the car pulled up to a crooked stop in a filthy alleyway across the road from the *Blessed Humanity* coffee shop, the rear half of the car jutting out onto the road. The driver turned to Mattis, smiling widely and exposing her yellow, crooked teeth. "Ten euros, plus tip, mate."

In all his years of combat, Mattis had never felt anywhere near as unsafe as he did in that cab. Never had anyone he'd ever met been so undeserving of a tip. Yet, his eyes couldn't help but be drawn to the multiple firearms openly displayed on the woman's person.

With shaking hands Mattis gave her fifteen euros, and then he, Lynch, Modi, and Yim staggered out of the cramped, stinking cab and stepped out of the alley, blinking in the half-light of the smog-covered city. Grey buildings thrust to the skyline in all directions, lit up by bright neon signs and yellow-tinged floodlights, as though the bright colors could somehow bring some semblance of life and happiness to this smog-filled, intrusively brown world. The neon sign from the *Blessed Humanity* flickered briefly.

Tires screeched as their ride tore off, leaving them by the side of the road, all around them quiet save for the rumble of nearby traffic punctuated by the sound of what sounded like distant gunfire.

"You okay?" asked Yim.

Mattis stared daggers at him. "The taxi was your idea. Were you *trying* to get me killed?"

"What?" Yim's eyes widened. "No! I was in there, too, you know!"

"Well now," said Modi, even his voice displaying an uncharacteristic tremor, seemingly ignoring the argument between the two men. "How about a celebration, mmm?"

A celebration of their journey coming to an end with no deaths. "I could go for a coffee," said Mattis, straining to smile.

The four of them walked across the road. Mattis felt distinctly out of place in his muted, unobtrusive civilian clothes and single, small caliber pistol. Most people wore body armor of some description, many carried rifles slung across their backs—civilian models, although some were obviously heavily modified—and the style of clothing ranged from the punk to the obscene. In the short walk across the road to the coffee house Mattis saw more flamboyant and erratic outfits than he'd ever seen in his whole life. That mixed with the doomsday-level gear everyone was wearing made it all very disorienting. He wasn't entirely unconvinced he hadn't wandered into some kind of pride parade for doomsday-prepper bondage aficionados.

"Are all your worlds like this?" asked Yim, his voice

drenched in amazement. "This is very strange."

"No," said Mattis. "This is not normal in any sense."

The four of them walked up to the coffee shop. A beleaguered, scrawny Chinese kid with mopish, unkempt hair and a greasy uniform regarded them with sunken, dead eyes, standing behind a sheet of bulletproof glass with a dozen gunshot impacts in it. His expression lit up when he saw Admiral Yim.

"W-wait, I know you!" he shouted, jabbing a finger. "Hey! You! You're Admiral Yim, aren't you? You're here to take me back home, right?"

For once, Mattis wasn't the one being recognized in public. "Keep your voice down," hissed Mattis. "We just want to talk to your boss."

"Boss?" The kid shook his head. "That's me. Boss checked out and booked it months ago. I'm the only one left in this damn place, and I only stay because it means I get to keep all the money for myself. At least, until the stock runs out. You think I'd stick around if I had a ticket off-world?"

Damn.

"Mind if we take a look around?" asked Yim, then paused as he considered. "In exchange for a lift back to my ship. We can take you somewhere safer."

"Deal," said the kid, wiggling out of his apron. "Believe me, I'll be happy to see the back of this dump." The barista opened the side door, letting them all in. "I'm Sing. Friends call me Sing Sing. You know, after that New York prison? Got electrocuted once. That's what got me the nickname. Friends thought its was funny. Some friends, right?"

"Right," said Mattis, taking stock of the cramped

shopfront littered with open cardboard boxes, and with a dirty sleeping bag stuffed into one corner. Did the kid *live* here? "Let's search this place and find out what we can." He grinned at Yim. "Like you say, maybe the universe always gives you a sign, if you know how to look."

"What're you looking for?" asked Sing, clearly eager to please them. "Maybe I can help. You know, I know this place. And I know how to make a mean hazelnut latte with extra foam. Or maybe a caramel macchiato, that's some nice coffee and it'll definitely get your neurons firing. I mean, all I have left is the plunger to make stuff with, but believe me, I'm basically a wizard at that thing by now. Or a chai-chocolate, if you want? And, uh, if you ask nicely, I might have *extra flavors* under the counter, if you catch my meaning."

The best and only hope in their investigation was a barista who wanted nothing more than to buy a ticket out of his hell-hole using coffee laced with *stuff*. If the universe really *was* guiding their actions, it was doing so with a profound sense of irony. "Basically," said Mattis, "we're investigating that news report. The one with the alien attack. It had a coffee shop just like this one, and we were looking for leads. Specifically places, names, connections. That kind of thing. Anything you can tell me."

"No aliens 'round here," said the kid, his eyes widening slightly as he realized, presumably, he'd told them he had nothing to offer them. "B-but, I *can* tell you this: I overheard the old boss talking. The only reason *Blessed Humanity* was allowed to operate was because they had a partnership with an American company. MaxGainz. They make steroids. Lot of their workers used to come here, before the gangs moved in.

Lot of 'em."

Interesting, but not that useful.

"Sorry sir," said Modi. "It looks like we nearly got killed in a cab for nothing. I think this expedition is a failure."

Maybe, maybe not. "You could call it a failure, but I prefer the term 'learning experience.'"

Sing looked uncomfortable. "You're still taking me with you, right?"

"Yes," said Yim, distractedly. "We will."

"Maybe that company is a front for something," said Mattis, considering. "Steroids are basically bioengineered these days, grown entirely in a lab. It's not unreasonable that they might use that as a cover for other genetic research."

Sing looked around. "Genetic research? In a tiny dump likes this?"

That was a good point. Mattis tried not to focus on the smell emanating from the open boxes, nor thinking about how long Sing might have been sleeping here. No wonder he was so eager to leave. "Are all the stores this big?"

Sing nodded. "Mostly. I mean, if you wanted information, you'd have to go to the corporate office on Earth. But good luck getting information out of *Blessed* corporate—you'd be better off asking MaxGainz."

"MaxGainz have an office on Earth?"

"Most companies do," he said. "For tax reasons. Tax havens. If you stay on Earth, pay less."

Seemed like a good enough reason as any.

Yim's communicator beeped, followed almost instantly by Mattis's. And Lynch's. And Modi's.

Mattis picked his up, cautiously.

"Sir?" said a young-ish sounding officer. "This is the Bridge."

"We're a little busy down here," said Mattis.

"So are we," said the officer. "A ship has just finished a Z-space translation. They say they're the Forgotten."

More of those assholes. Lynch looked pale, glancing forlornly at the road. He hadn't said a word since they got out of the cab. "Should I call a taxi, sir?"

Mattis scowled. "Screw taxis. If I'm going to die down here it's not getting T-boned by some lunatic. Get the shuttle to come pick us up directly. We gotta get back to the ship before another veteran with a chip on his shoulder starts a war."

Chapter Thirty-Three

The streets of Glasgow
Earth
Sol System

Bratta glanced at the wing mirror. The mismatched lights glistened behind them. "Jeeeaannie?"

She didn't take her eyes off the road. "I'm doing everything I can, Steve."

He looked around. Even he could tell his eyes were slightly wild. "You *slowed down?*"

"Yes, I did. Shush."

"Shush? We are being tailed! Jeannie, in the last twenty-four hours I've fled off-world, been mugged, and interrogated my own boss! This is getting to be a bit much!"

"You should try police work some time. Have I told you about the time I got shot?"

Bratta glowered. Yes, okay, she usually had a story to one-up his experiences, but did she have to keep bringing that up every *single* time they got into an argument? "Technically," he said, "your body armor got shot."

Jeannie pulled into a different lane without indicating, and his heart leapt straight into his throat. This was why people had self-driving cars, this was why people had self-driving cars, this was why people had self-driving cars and *he was actually going to die*. Horns blared around them. "Are we going to have this argument again?"

"No," said Bratta. "I just want you to drive like a normal person, and also, while we're at it, shake this tail!"

"I'm not even sure we have one," said Jeannie, "but we'll know soon enough. If they follow us after *that*."

Bratta twisted in his seat and stared out the rear window. As the chaos began to settle, the odd pair of headlights was nowhere to be seen. He slumped back into the chair. "That was …" he took a deep breath. "That was *really* illegal, Jeannie."

"You keep using that word. I don't think it means as much as you'd like it to mean in this situation."

She was so calm it was unnerving. "You're not *worried?*"

Jeannie flicked her eyes to the rear-vision mirror. "Not yet. If it shows up behind us again, then I'll consider being worried. There's a lot of traffic. Could be a coincidence. Rule number one about losing a tail: The key is to be unpredictable. Slow down, speed up, make ridiculous, obvious mistakes. If they make ridiculous, obvious mistakes too, you know they're following you."

He turned back again. Nothing. "Why are you so bloody calm about all this?"

"No point in being bothered by what you can't be sure is

there." Her voice was low, even. Calm, like someone talking to a spooked cat. He found he didn't particularly appreciate the gesture. "I drive better when I'm not panicking, Steven." She slowly turned the wheel around a corner, sarcasm seeping into her voice. "Funny that."

"I—well, that's obvious, I suppose."

"Yup."

Silence between the two of them. Bratta knew what that meant. He had annoyed her. "It's funny," he said, trying to strike up conversation again. He'd found this sometimes worked. "How you know so much about an ancient psychology. Driving, that is."

She raised her eyebrows and craned to look in his wing mirror. "Driving isn't exactly ancient yet."

"I was using hyperbole, Jeannie. It happens to people when they're about to be attacked for playing super-spy. It's an incredibly strange coincidence, really, you know?"

She didn't seem to think his joke was particularly amusing. That wasn't too insulting though, neither did he. "Well, there is good news," she said. "If we do get attacked, we're right, *and* we're the good guys."

"What?"

The car in front of them braked suddenly. His heart hammered. What if they were being caught in a trap? It would have taken a really good driver, but a pincer maneuver would probably be possible in these conditions. His mind raced with a thousand possibilities.

"Well," Jeannie shrugged. Perversely, she seemed to have relaxed tenfold since he'd raised the possibility of them being under attack. "They're expending resources to stop us. That means something we said—in fact, I'm willing to bet something *you* said—hit Stepka hard. We're on the right track. As for the good guy bit, have you watched any blockbusters lately? Random conspiracy theorists harassing hard-working staff is bad. Cops following their guts over regulations and plucky scientists—that's you—investigating corruption in their own company, and then being attacked by our corporate overlords for it? That's good. Heck, if—"

She broke off, eyes fixed on the rear-view mirror.

"They're back."

Damn it all. Bratta had just gotten his heart rate under control....

"Well," said Jeannie, "I'm normally on the other side of this, but buckle up, Steve. Here goes nothing."

Chapter Thirty-Four

Outside the Blessed Humanity *coffee shop*
New London
Omid Sector

The shuttle roared as it hovered overhead, engines blasting up dust and filth in all directions, scattering it all in a blast radius away from the ship. It lowered itself down through the air, resting in the middle of the street, blocking both lanes of traffic. Another one descended further down the street, bearing the flag of the People's Republic of China. Yim's shuttle.

Mattis, flanked by Modi and Lynch, walked toward the lowered ramp of their craft, ignoring the beeping and shouts all around him. He worried for a moment if someone was going to shoot at them, but as he stepped onto the metal of the deck, he knew why they restricted themselves to hurling verbal abuse.

Next time, marines. Armored vehicles. *Definitely.*

Yim got aboard his shuttle with Sing in tow. Mattis was glad that Yim hadn't made his promise idly. Strangely this little moment, more than everything they had gone through so far, comforted him.

It meant he could trust Yim.

Maybe.

Lynch flipped the planet the bird as the loading ramp raised itself up and sealed closed.

"What a shit hole," said Lynch, his tone half angry, half bitter. The shuttle lifted off, rumbling as it drifted up through the atmosphere. "Hope we don't have to go back there again."

Mattis smiled grimly. "Well, you know. The *Midway* still has sixty-four nuclear missiles, armed and prepped. Delivery in two minutes or less, or your next one's free. Would definitely clean up the city."

For a second, Lynch almost seemed to be considering it. "Nearly got killed by a damn taxi driver," he murmured to himself.

Mattis bit his lower lip as he watched his XO's face mulling over the possibility. "Lynch, you know we can't *actually* nuke the —"

"I know."

"And you know I was joking, yeah?"

"I know," said Lynch, staring out the window at the retreating lights of the city down below. "Ahh, but a man can dream."

Mattis honestly couldn't say he wasn't thinking it, too, but Lynch seemed to take the joke a little *too* seriously. "I'll pencil in nuking New London from orbit when we're done with this mess," he said. "For now, we should look into what these idiotic extremist assholes want."

"Aye aye," said Lynch, somewhat reluctantly, then with a firm nod. "Yeah. Okay. Let's do this."

Mattis took out his earpiece from his pocket and clipped it on. "Lieutenant Corrick, was it?"

"No sir," said the pilot, a man. "Guano—uhh, I mean, Lieutenant Corrick promised the CAG that she wouldn't damage the last shuttle. And she damaged the last shuttle. I assume she's being roasted alive right now, Admiral."

He resolved to instruct Major Yousuf to go easy on her. Shooting out their own cockpit was crazy, but it had prevented a major diplomatic incident. "Okay," he said. "Get us home. Meanwhile, fire up the long range antenna, I wanna talk to my ship."

"Aye sir," said the pilot.

His ear-piece chimed. "*Midway*," called Mattis. "Tell me about this incoming ship."

"Admiral, we're still gathering information about it," said the officer. This was why he liked having Lynch on the bridge, he would have already had everything ready to report by now. But at the same time, the guy couldn't be both on the bridge *and* down on the surface with him. "But it looks like it's a smallish size troop carrier. An older, outdated model."

Older and outdated sure described those angry veterans. And himself, probably, in the eyes of the public, but he put those thoughts out of his mind. No time for feeling sorry for himself. "What's it doing?" he asked. "Is it engaging anything?"

"Negative," said the bridge officer. "In fact, it seems to be unarmed. It's docked with the orbital defense grid."

Every colonized world had a satellite defense grid. Earth's

was Goalkeeper, the most massive and well-funded of them all, but even a little world like this one would have something formidable defending it. Mattis cursed quietly to himself. It was only designed to defend the planet from external threats—a ship flagged as American would be allowed to dock.

"Launch fighters," he ordered. "Engage and destroy that troop carrier. Stop them from taking command of the platform. Don't engage it directly, however—if we hit that platform, it'll shoot back."

"Sir, it might be too late for that. The orbital platform is launching drones to engage us." The guy on the other end of the line was shocked. "They can't have taken it that quickly. It's about as likely as winning the lottery."

Damn robots. The Forgotten had worked fast; too fast, in his opinion. Maybe they had a guy in the inside. Maybe they were exploiting a known bug in the system. Either way, it didn't matter. They had to be stopped. "*Someone* wins the lottery," said Mattis. "Every week. *Midway*, engage and destroy those drones. We'll be docking with you shortly. Prepare to receive us."

"Yes sir." The link closed.

The shuttle began to duck and weave, artificial gravity fighting with inertia. Mattis strode over to a passenger seat, folded it down, and strapped in.

"I'm gonna puke," said Lynch, looking green as he fumbled with his straps.

"I'd recommend not doing that," said Modi, firmly secured, his hands resting on his knees.

The motion made even Mattis a little ill. "You're coping well," said Mattis to Modi.

"Why are you even a *little* bit surprised?" asked Lynch,

running his hands through his hair. "You know he's basically an android. Maybe that's more literal than I thought—*urrgh*."

"Androids," said Modi, seemingly able to hold a perfect poker face, "can act without emotional barriers, without filters. I notice things you fleshlings miss. Such as where the medkits are. They include anti-motion sickness pills." He pointed. "Between your legs, Commander."

Lynch growled angrily, reaching down and grabbing the small plastic container clipped between his thighs. "You're really starting to tick me off, Modi. I don't know if it's this ship bucking like a bull or your smug goddamn face that's making me wanna hurl."

Modi smiled, probably for the first time in months. "Boop beep. Our kind don't know the meaning of annoy."

Mattis couldn't help but guffaw at Lynch's discomfort. "Okay, okay," he said, waving a hand. "Settle down you two. Lynch, take your pill." He took a breath to steady himself. "When we get back to the *Midway*, we have to get ready to move."

"Aye aye," said Modi.

From outside the tiny window on the cramped shuttle, the *Midway* loomed closer, hangar bay doors wide open.

A ship leapt into view, an old model boarding craft, its entire front a giant magnetic grappler. It swung to the side, smashing into their craft.

Alarms blared. The shuttle rolled over, jerking as the pilot fought to right themselves. The hangar bay, once a welcoming beacon of safety, became a terrible danger.

Shit shit shit shit shit—

Mattis held on tight as the shuttle slammed onto the deck,

screeching as it slid across the metal landing strip, throwing up sparks. Lynch was thrown from his seat, disappearing into the isle.

With a loud *crash* the ship came to a stop half way down the landing bay. For a second there was eerie silence, broken only by Modi leaned forward, groaning and clutching his wounded shoulder.

The boarding craft flew into the hangar bay beside them, narrowly avoiding the closing hangar bay doors. It latched onto the far wall of the hangar bay, throwing out sparks as it began to cut into the inner hull.

Tricky. The enemy had piggybacked on their transponder signal, bypassing the *Midway's* point defense systems and anti-boarding countermeasures. Clever bastards. Their next step was all too clear.

Mattis groggily touched his earpiece. "Attention *Midway*, we've been boarded."

Chapter Thirty-Five

Pilot's Ready Room
USS Midway
High Orbit Above New London
Omid Sector

"Come on, sir," said Guano, whining a little. "It's a windscreen. Windscreens are cheap."

Roadie looked like he was about to go thermonuclear. "You *promised* me," he said, through gritted teeth. "You promised me you'd bring that shuttle back in one piece—"

"It *is* in one piece," she protested, "I mean, more or less. Basically. Sure, it's got a few holes in the windscreen—"

"I don't care about the windscreen!" roared Roadie. "You lost a whole engine!"

"Only one," said Guano, holding up her hands, palms upward. "It still has three left. It's fine. I flew it back, didn't I?"

"What about the heat shield?" hissed Roadie, blinking so

rapidly she thought he might be having a stroke. "The whole thing will have to be inspected. If there's a crack, that's *not* easy or cheap to repair."

She winced. "That heat shield has to be serviced regularly anyway, and—and it was probably due soon. Or something."

"Corrick," growled Roadie. "Dammit…"

He was using her real name—shit, this guy was really mad. Guano gave up and threw her hands in the air. "I didn't *ask* to get bounced by four fighters in the upper atmosphere of that shithole," she said, "that's the *worst* place for a shuttlecraft to be doing a dogfight. It's got drag, gravity, and worst of all, no weapons. What was I supposed to do? Surrender the ship and let the Chinese take Mattis and Lynch?"

To that, seemingly, Roadie had no answer. Slowly, slowly, the anger seemed to fade out of him. "I guess not," he said, simply.

"I know you're under pressure because of this," said Guano, reassuringly. "But believe me … Mattis is going to be pretty damn happy you saved his hide back there. Modi was shot, and *I* was the one who got him back to the infirmary as fast as I did, and *you* were the one who picked me as the pilot. So really, all the credit goes to you."

Roadie mulled that over, looking away from her for a moment, his hand on his chin. "I guess you're right," he said.

Guano smiled a half-moon. "So everything's cool, right?"

He shot her a furious death-glare. "No, it's not, you jackass!" But then he calmed again, taking a deep breath. Something came across his face … a genuine sadness. "I can't keep protecting you for ever, Corrick. These incidents—they look *bad*."

She knew he knew, but didn't say anything.

Finally Roadie shook his head. "Doesn't matter. You got a get-out-of-jail-free card with this one, you hear me? One time only. And only because you saved Mattis."

"Right," she said, thumping her fist into her hand triumphantly. "You got it, boss."

Roadie groaned. "Don't call me that."

"Okay, chief."

"No."

"Okay, glorious master."

"That is … a *lot* worse. Now shut the fuck up."

She had more, drawn from her inexhaustible supply of banter, but a bright blue light flashed in all four corners of the room. The intruder alert.

The two of them exchanged a wide-eyed look. "Did we pick up a stray?" she asked. "Or is this another damn drill?"

Roadie clipped on an earpiece, listening for a moment. "No drill," he said, his tone grave. "And it sounds like multiple strays, at least." He nodded to her, the anger from their argument moments ago evaporating as quickly as it had arrived. "Get to the hangar."

"We're launching?" asked Guano, hopefully.

"No," said Roadie, simply. "Our battle isn't outside. It's *inside.* There are intruders in the main hangar bay, and we gotta stop them."

Guano grit her teeth. "That's the marines' job," she complained. "I'm a pilot, not a soldier, with or without vitamin supplements!"

"Do you see any damn marines here?" A distant, dull explosion emphasized his point. "Get ready to defend the fighters. When reinforcements arrive, we can stand down. All we have to do is hold out until then."

Guano clipped on her helmet and stepped toward the airlock leading to the hangar bay, pistol in hand.

One day I'll get to fly a fighter again … but until then, I guess I gotta shoot bad guys the old-fashioned way.

Chapter Thirty-Six

Hangar Bay
USS Midway
High Orbit Above New London
Omid Sector

Mattis unstrapped and pushed himself up to his feet. The ship had settled evenly on the flat deck, but he swore it had a slight list to it, as though the small vessel had dug into the landing deck—*his* landing deck—and was now almost imperceptibly tilted.

"Modi," he said, "let's get out of here."

"Coming," said Modi, blood trickling from his lip. "I think I tore my stitches."

"That's your fault, coming down to a place like New London after getting shot so recently."

Modi stood up, rubbing his shoulder mournfully. "You ordered me to, Admiral."

"You know being an Admiral just means anything I say is a suggestion." Mattis searched for Lynch. "Hey, Lynch, you okay?"

Lynch's head appeared above one of the seats, squinting as though seeing through a harsh light. "Feels like a bronco bull kicked me in the brain-pan."

Mattis offered his hand. "Can you walk?"

"Yeah, I'm fine, just whacked my noggin pretty good." Lynch touched his hairline and his hand came away covered in blood. "At least, I think I'm fine."

"Going to have to be," said Mattis, glancing to Modi. "I have some good news for you, Commander: this time you get to take your pistol out and, God willing, actually try and shoot a living person."

Modi seemed somewhat less thrilled than Mattis thought he'd be, but he drew his pistol resolutely. "With you, sir."

Lynch stood, somewhat wobbly on his feet, but he too drew his pistol. "Aye aye, sir."

"Pilot?" asked Mattis, over his shoulder. "Hey! Pilot, you coming with us?"

No answer. Mattis moved to the front of the ship, stepping into the front cockpit of the shuttle.

The ship had impaled itself on the nosecone of one of the fighters, the tip of it spearing through the pilot's chair. The young man inside had died instantly—there was nothing that he could do, or could have done.

He made his way back into the passenger compartment. "Pilot's not coming," he said, fighting to keep his tone even.

"Fucking … shit," said Lynch.

"That is unfortunate," said Modi.

With the hangar bay doors closed and the landing bay re-pressurized it was safe for them to exit. Mattis took the lead, pistol cupped comfortably in both hands, Modi and Lynch behind him. Through the windows of the enemy troop carrier he could see Forgotten soldiers pouring into his ship.

"Mattis to bridge," he said, touching his earpiece. "Dispatch marines to the hangar bay. Looks like the intruders are cutting their way into the lavatory near the pilot's ready room."

"What a *shitty* entrance point," said Lynch. A stern glance from Mattis took the levity from him. "Sorry, sir."

Mattis waited for his answer. Static in his ear and no acknowledgement. He made his way over to the airlock that lead into the rest of the ship and opened it.

They stepped in, closed the outer door, opened the inner door, and were immediately greeted with a raging gun battle.

The *Midway*'s marines had occupied the far end of a long corridor leading to a fork. The Forgotten had filled the pilot's lavatory and had drilled holes in the door for firing ports. The airlock opened directly into the middle of the corridor, between the two sides who were bathing it in automatic fire. The gunshots echoed in the cramped quarters, bullets ricocheted off the bulkheads and deck, bouncing around until they finally got stuck somewhere.

Modi calmly reached out and closed the door. "Not that way," he said.

"Yeah, did you figure that one out on your own?" asked Lynch. "I was just going to skip across the battle, have a nice little merry gander—"

"I would advise against that. Despite your attempts to

conceal your obvious head injury, I am aware of your condition and concerned for your well-being.

"Cut the crap." Mattis checked the safety on his pistol. "Problem is, out there is the hangar bay. I'm guessing the *Midway* is going to want to decompress that bay, just because, you know, those assholes are pinned down right next to the wall, so if the *Midway* can get a fighter in there we can take out the bulkhead with a missile. Flush them out into space. That would neatly take care of all of them."

"That's what I'd do," said Lynch.

Mattis glanced to Modi, twisting around to see him in the cramped airlock. "We have to get you to Engineering. Lock it down as best you can and wait for the marines to come flush out the garbage."

"Aye aye," said Modi, his expression flat and unreadable. "Once the rain clears up, I'll get right to it."

Mattis touched the open button again, and found himself face-to-face with a team of his marines.

"Sir," said one, her face obscured by a thin slit of a heavily armoured combat space suit. A round bounced off her shoulder plate. "We need to get you out of here."

Mattis nodded. "No argument from me."

"Excellent." The marine completely ignored the incoming fire that plinked off her armor, holding up a white-tipped grenade. "We'll pop smoke, and you three make your way down the corridor. The three of us will provide covering fire and hard cover."

"Hard cover?"

The marine tapped her breastplate. "They don't call us the Rhinos for nothing, sir. Intruders didn't bring heavy weapons, so they basically can't hurt us. Once you're safe, we'll engage them."

The use of their armored bulk as physical cover was a novel idea to him, but it made sense. This was, after all, why the ship had marines; specialists in murder-time and surviving the same. "Do it."

Instantly the three hooked arms, like football players, a wall of flesh and steel that blocked the corridors. Six pins clattered to the deck, and smoke poured from the grenades in their hands. The gunfire intensified, rounds bouncing off their armored suits as the corridor filled with green smoke.

The marines started a grim march toward their enemies, boots thumping on the deck in sync.

"Ready?" said Mattis. "On three. One, two—"

"Don't get shot again," said Lynch to Modi, grinning maniacally.

"Three!"

The three of them bolted out of the airlock, running down the corridor and toward the fork. Modi went right, toward Engineering, while Lynch and Mattis went left. When they were clear, heavy, stomping boots walked down the corridor toward the pilot's ready room, punctuated by the sounds of automatic gunfire.

"Remind me to give the Rhinos a raise," he said, "but only if they promise to stop singing. None of them can carry a tune worth crap."

"I think," said Lynch, "that's part of their *thing*. Singing, being thick skinned, horny—you know. It's their motto."

"What's the motto?" asked Mattis.

"Nothing, whats-a-motto with you?" Lynch grinned like

an idiot. His head injury may have been more serious than they thought.

"I should have left you in the airlock." Mattis pinched the tip of his nose. "Let's get to the bridge before I kill you. Or myself. I dunno, I was just going to play it by ear, but there was going to be a lot of killing." The gunfire receded down the corridor as the Rhinos advanced. "Maybe we don't need those armored goons after all, we'll just flush out the boarders with your dad-jokes."

"Aye aye," said Lynch, strolling down the corridor toward the bridge. "I'll make my way to the intercom. I'll think of a funny joke on the way. Very funny. Promise."

Mattis fell into step with Lynch, flanked by a pair of marines who, mercifully, only wore the standard combat armor. How many of those Rhinos did they have on board, anyway? Couldn't have been more than the three.

"Sir," said a voice in his earpiece, barely audible through the static. "We have an issue."

"Send it."

"The boarders escaped the ready room lavatory," he said, "they're headed down corridor G11."

G11—the one parallel to their own.

Straight to the bridge.

Chapter Thirty-Seven

Bridge
CNS Luyang III
High Orbit Above New London
Omid Sector

Admiral Yim definitely should have picked up a cup of coffee in New London. They were *right there* at his favorite coffee shop, why hadn't he? The kid they had picked up, he was onboard now. Maybe they could get him to brew them up something. Yim's mouth watered just thinking about that smooth, warm, caramel-y flavor—

The *Luyang III* shook slightly as a wave of incoming fire washed over the hull. No time to think about coffee.

"Status on the American satellites?" he asked.

"Their weapons are still powered down," said Xiao. "But they appear to have launched combat drones." He snorted dismissively. "Don't know why they bothered. Our J-84's have much greater acceleration. The maneuvers are a success; we're able to hit and run before their weapons can get a lock."

"Good," said Yim. "Remember, those are drones: no pilots. No diplomatic incidents. Shoot them all down—no hesitation."

Xiao smiled. "You got it, sir. Gun batteries are also engaging, and we're spinning up the point defense cannons. Our pilots report that they're enjoying their target practice very much."

Drones were excellent at certain things, but they were predictable. The Chinese intelligence nerds had figured out through some arcane wizardry that the American space-combat drones had a fatal flaw in their target acquisition software. It was complicated and, not being a pilot, he couldn't describe the exact natures of the maneuvers needed to confuse them, but his understanding was that by approaching the drones at high speed, engaging with guns, then retreating at a similarly high speed made them switch targets. Perform this maneuver with too many craft too quickly and the system became overwhelmed, constantly shifting between targets and never committing to any of them.

Risky, but apparently successful.

Their communications officer spoke up. "Sir," said Ting. "We are receiving an incoming transmission, top priority."

It was tempting to just ignore it—nobody would question the commander of a navy vessel not picking up the phone during a heated battle no matter who it was—but Yim knew better. "Put it through," he said.

"Admiral Yim," said a voice in his head. The sound came through a vibration in the side of his skull, an implant inside his skin that his ears translated into speech; a nifty piece of Chinese technology the Americans probably didn't even realize he had. He recognized the voice instantly—General Lok Tsai. The Chief of Joint Staff for the entire military of the People's Republic of China. The big wig. "How are you doing?"

Such a strange question. Yim smiled slightly, despite the complete impossibility that Tsai could see the gesture, and whispered his response as quietly as he could. "Blowing up billions of dollars of American property with absolutely no repercussions or political fallout? It's just like old times, and I love it." He leaned forward, putting his chin on top of his folded hands. "Just don't ruin the moment and tell me I have to stop."

"Well," said General Tsai, "you know how these things are. Target the drones, the automated platforms, and the rebel ships, but don't fire on the Americans whatever you do."

The use of the word rebel—*Pànnì* in Chinese—was interesting. Yim knew they were some kind of disgruntled veterans or something, but of course Chinese intelligence would probably assume the worst and tell themselves that the Forgotten were full-blown rebels. They had always been paranoid about that kind of thing for themselves and their own colonies—probably because most of the Intelligence spent their time looking inward instead of outward. Projection was a real thing.

"Don't worry, General," whispered Yim. "I'll try to keep collateral damage to the Americans to a minimum." He glanced at his various monitors. The boarding ships were swarming Mattis's ship. Little leeches attaching themselves but, instead of draining blood, injecting dark poison.

There wasn't much he could do. Firing on them directly would be difficult—especially in light of his just-made promise —and inserting Chinese marines would just make things worse. A lot worse.

He and Mattis had gotten along well on the surface of New London, but the truth was, Yim had killed Mattis's brother. It might have been decades past in a war long fought, but there was no way he was forgetting that fact any time soon.

"Okay," said General Tsai. "Play nice with the Americans for now. but know that you may be called upon to defend the Motherland."

Would he? They had almost—almost!—made some kind of breakthrough with the Americans. Almost had one whole incident where the two nations didn't end up shooting at each other … and now it had come to this.

They would understand, of course. Yim had the American government's full permission to break as much stuff as the Forgotten had taken, but, it seemed, his government would stymie any attempt at a lasting peace between the two.

"Of course," whispered Yim, somewhat more angrily than he could reasonably conceal. "General, I must return to the battle."

"Swift hunting, Admiral Yim," said General Tsai, and closed the link.

What a bastard. Was he trying to cause war between the two nations?

Yim tried, unsuccessfully, to put the conversation with Tsai out of his head and focus on the battle. He couldn't. It stuck in there like glue, taunting him with how close they had come to a bit of peace, a little bit of teamwork which, he hoped, they hadn't almost immediately squandered.

On his various screens, he watched a breaching craft slip into the *Midway*'s hangar bay.

Damn thing was so small, it must have evaded notice somehow. How, exactly, he wasn't sure—possibly a composite material that would absorb radar, possibly some other much more mundane solution—but it didn't matter. That was a problem for the Americans.

"*Luyang III* to *Midway*," said Yim, "I'm sure you're aware you've got a parasite craft. Let me know if you want help dislodging it."

No response, but that was normal given the circumstances.

"Sir," said Xiao, "two—no, make that, *three* of the American satellites have been activated."

Now things were starting to heat up. The defense satellites were similar in style to the Goalkeeper system defending Earth. But they had been powered down—who had flicked the switch? "Were they activated by the *Midway*?" he asked.

"No," said Xiao, "by the Forgotten. They're preparing to fire on us."

Chapter Thirty-Eight

Corridor G10
USS Midway
High Orbit Above New London
Omid Sector

"Okay," said Mattis, holding his pistol in both hands as he, Lynch, and two marines power-walked down the corridor. "The intruders are traveling down corridor G11. That's parallel left of our position. Both of these corridors lead toward the bridge, but halfway to the bridge they join up and run side by side, divided only by a line of paint on the floor. Then the corridor turns inward to the core of the ship, to the bridge."

"Right," said Lynch. "If they reach that choke point first, they can cut us off."

"Actually," said Mattis, unable to fight back a wide smile. "If we wait there, we can plug them in the back as they move past. They have to. It'll give us the element of surprise."

"It's a bad plan," said one of the marines, furrowing his brow. "Trained marines will watch all corners. They probably even know where we are, and they might be getting ready to do the same thing to us."

He hadn't considered that. Once again he was reminded to leave the soldiering to the soldiers. "Good point. Let's just go faster."

The four of them broke into a jog. To the right, they passed store room after store room, each holding various supplies. Food. Medical. A water tank.

"Wish we had some of those Rhinos," said Lynch.

"No you don't, Commander," said the marine, jogging down the corridor, his rifle raised. "They can't move like this. Barely more than a walking pace. Plus, they're *real* dumb, sir. It takes a special kind of person to want to crew something that's *designed* to get shot at—much less enjoy it."

Another good point. They passed a section of hull that was all wall. Up ahead, Mattis could see the intersection of the corridors where G10 and G11 met. "Well," he said, "the mental stability of our elite counter-boarding units aside, we should be coming up on the fork now, and—" A cramp shot up his left leg and he stopped.

"Sir?" asked Lynch, moving up to him. The marines ahead stopped.

"It's fine," he said, gritting his teeth and rubbing his leg. "It's just me being old, is all, one second and—"

A blast blew out the bulkhead to his right, fragments peppering the left side of the wall and chewing up the metal—right where they would have been standing if they hadn't suddenly stopped. Old age had its benefits, he supposed. The blast knocked him off his feet, the sound of everything was swallowed by a profound ringing in his ears. Smoke poured out everywhere—purple smoke, as though from smoke grenades.

"Contact!" roared the marine, barely audible over the ringing. He fired down the corridor at something Mattis couldn't see. "Dammit, they got here first!"

The Forgotten had moved fast. Real fast. Mattis had been slowed down by his age and a cramp in his leg that never would have happened when he was younger, but the Forgotten weren't exactly spring chickens either; most of them were veterans of the same conflict, had the same grey hair he had. The same aches and pains.

It was the Battle of the Grandpas.

Mattis shook his head, trying to clear out the ringing. He pushed himself up onto his elbows. Everything felt lighter, as though the blast had damaged the artificial gravity. Or maybe that was just the damage to his ears.

"—gotta go!" shouted Lynch, right behind him. "The hull's been breached! Those bastards blew out the emergency valves!"

The explosion hadn't been directed toward them. It had been directed away out to the outer hull where a shaped charge had blasted a fist-sized gap in the metal. As his hearing came back, he could hear the howling of air as the corridor decompressed, the wailing of alarms, and the hissing of the emergency doors sliding down to seal off that section to keep the ship's precious air in.

Adrenaline kicked him back onto his feet, along with some manhandling from Lynch. With the marines firing wildly the four of them sprinted down the corridor toward the rapidly descending airlock door. His cramp was forgotten.

Down, down, down came the door, dropping rapidly. Too rapidly. Gunfire was hissing all around him, bullets screaming off the walls, and the rushing air threatened to pull him off his feet.

Both marines darted through the door. Lynch ducked the descending wall of metal, but Mattis was taller. He slid forward like a batter sliding onto home base, barely missing having his head sliced off as the emergency bulkhead sealed itself ten centimeters away from his head.

"Jaysus H.," said Lynch, his face white. "You love cutting things close, don't you Jack?"

"Just enough is good enough," said Mattis, panting softly, his bones aching. He hadn't run like that in years. Pushing himself back up to his feet, Mattis looked through the thin window. On the other side, people wearing a mixture of civilian and military spacesuits from various services—Space Navy, Terrestrial Navy, Marines, Atmospheric Force, and even one from the Coast Guard—hurried toward the heavy steel decompression door with glowing oxy-torches that burned like angry little stars. Behind them, a team of five people carried heavy bits of some kind of machinery in both hands.

"Time to go," said Mattis. "We gotta get to the bridge. They won't be able to cut through the armored casemate there with anything people can carry by hand."

"Right," said Lynch, and the four of them started toward the bridge, jogging once more.

"Sir?" asked one of the marines, his helmet projecting a small image in front of his head. A view from one of the security cameras in the corridor they had just left. "The intruders. It looks like they're constructing something."

"What kind of something?" asked Mattis as the troupe rounded the last bend to the bridge. The huge steel wall that was the armored casemate of the bridge was half open, ready to be sealed at a moment's notice. They were obviously expected.

"A laser drill," said the marine. "I think."

"Maybe they just want to give us a light show," said Lynch.

Unlikely. But how the hell did veterans get their hands on this kind of equipment? It nagged at him, just like the SAM from the Chinese embassy. That kind of hardware you couldn't just *buy*. It had to be supplied by a government. Yim's people, maybe?

Or his own?

"Can that thing crack the casemate?" asked Mattis. Now was not the time for idle speculation.

"Probably," said Lynch. "We'd have to ask Modi."

The four of them slipped past the armored door and, with the groan of stressed metal, it slowly began to seal closed. Then, beyond, a simple door, just for neatness sake. They stepped through and onto the bridge.

"Officer on deck," said someone. The two marines standing by the door came to attention.

"At ease," said Mattis. "Close the casemate. Get the Rhinos in here to clean out the trash. Lynch?"

"Aye aye," said Lynch, moving over to his station, clipping on an earpiece. "On it."

Mattis let him do the work, settling into the captain's chair. "Report."

"Looks like the intruders are cutting through the first

door," said Lynch, who then touched his ear. "Modi! You awkward bastard, I need to ask you a favor. Can you look up the specs for mining lasers?" A brief pause. "No, I don't know what damn type of laser! Hang on, I'll send you a picture."

Mattis couldn't help but smile, despite the faint vibration in the deckplate that signaled some kind of powerful energy displacement. If they got through the armored shield, there would be a firefight on the bridge, something he definitely wanted to avoid.

"Suits on," he said, reaching below the chair for the helmet and fragile emergency suit stowed there. "We might have company real soon."

Chapter Thirty-Nine

Bridge
USS Midway
High Orbit Above New London
Omid Sector

The decompression door between corridor G11 and the bridge didn't hold long. Mattis didn't expect it to. It was tough and reinforced, yes, but it only designed to keep air in. In fact, to facilitate rescues, it was specifically engineered to be easily cut through.

However, the armored casemate was another story. It was designed to be utterly impregnable; under normal circumstances if there was a hole in the casemate then the ship had probably sustained so much damage that the whole thing was lost. It would hold for a time. Minutes, definitely. Hours, maybe.

Enough.

"Lynch," said Mattis, shuffling and getting comfortable on his captain's chair. "What does Modi say?"

"A bunch of jibber jabber. I swear the robot's off his meds." said Lynch, grumbling softly. "But mostly that the casemate is tougher than a bull's hide. The Forgotten will not get through it for at least half an hour, assuming they're using standard drilling lasers."

"Something tells me we don't have that kind of luck." It was always foolish to assume one's enemies would be operating at a disadvantage. Hope, yes. Expect, no. "Assuming the absolute best equipment and ideal conditions, how soon could they get through it if they *really* wanted to?"

Lynch relayed the question. "Five minutes," he said. "Although it could be closer to eleven."

That was a fairly large variance in potential capabilities. Mattis began clipping his suit on. Either way, no sense in not being prepared. "How far away are those Rhinos?"

"They're coming," said Lynch, "but they're moving slow. They should be here in twelve to thirteen minutes, assuming nothing slows them down."

Twelve minutes. So a potential two or three minute battle. That would be difficult. They had two marines assigned to guard duty, plus the two they had dragged along with them. The marines had rifles, combat armor, and the works. However, he and the rest of the bridge crew only had their sidearms.

It would have to do. Mattis clipped on his helmet and ensured the seal was tight. "All hands, prepare to repel boarders."

Everyone checked in. The marines and the bridge crew

including Lynch all had their suits on and sealed. Only the marines had armor, so for everyone else a single puncture would probably be their death, but such was the nature of combat.

"Sir," said Lynch, his voice crackling slightly over the radio, even though he was standing right next to him. "Commander Modi reports that there is a firefight outside engineering. They've sealed the doors."

The doors to engineering were strong, designed to contain minor breaches from the ship's reactors, but they were nowhere near as strong as the bridge casemate. Did the attackers down at engineering also have a huge laser? Maybe they did, maybe they didn't.

Mattis touched his helmet. "Mattis to Modi."

"Modi here," came his perfectly calm, Indian-accented voice. "What can I do for you, Admiral?"

"Heard you got a bunch of rowdy gatecrashers trying to force their way into your party, Commander."

"I don't know what kind of parties you attend, Admiral, but engineering work is serious business. Diagnostics, reports —endless reports—and a lot of fixing broken things."

Lynch cut in on the line. "So you finally admit you're a space janitor? After all these years?"

"Space janitor?" Modi's voice hardened. "Mister Lynch, I assure you—"

Mattis cut them both off. "Intruders, now. Bickering, later."

"Yes sir." Modi's composure returned. "Six armed people are attempting to break down the door to engineering. We are suited and ready to resist any attempt to secure this ship's engines."

Having seen Modi shoot he was reluctant to consider his assertion to be anything other than bluster. No doubt his fellow engineers couldn't shoot much better. Things were looking grim.

Through the small window in the door, he could see the armored casemate start to glow faintly in the center, a little yellow tinge as the Forgotten's laser began to burrow into the metal, heating it. Soon it would break through, creating a tiny pinhole in the shield, then begin to cut—slowly, inexorably, until a breach was formed.

Until then, a stalemate. Neither side could engage each other. Nothing to do but sit there, casually bouncing his gun in his hand.

The radio crackled in his ears. "This is Admiral Yim."

Mattis grimaced slightly, checking the safety on his pistol. "Talk to me, Admiral. Give me good news."

"I'm afraid not," said Yim. "The Forgotten have occupied three of the orbital defense platforms."

Mattis swore loudly, forgetting to mute the connection.

"My thoughts exactly," said Yim. "The danger to your ship, and to my ship, is now both internal and external."

This was true. But no crew could effectively fight an external foe while also battling an internal insurgency. The danger had escalated dramatically.

"We'll do our best," said Mattis. "Gotta clear the inside of the ship before we can focus on the outside."

"Be quick," said Yim, and closed the connection.

Mattis pulled back the slide on his pistol and chambered a round. "Let's do this quickly, so we can actually get to the *real* fighting."

Chapter Forty

Hangar Bay
USS Midway
High Orbit Above New London
Omid Sector

Guano crouched behind a Warbird, using the magnetic skid clamp as cover. She swept the hangar bay, taking in the oxygen from her mask. She couldn't see anyone. The hangar bay was still decompressed—outside was a vacuum. Everything was as it should be. Planes lined up, munitions neatly stacked. Everything save the crashed shuttle. It lay to one side, ramp extended, passenger compartment empty.

"See that?" she said into her radio. "That was one ship I didn't crash."

"That's four for Guano, one for not-Guano," said Roadie.

"What?!" Guano glared at him, his face invisible behind his reflective visor. "I only crashed *three*. And one of those ships is fine. Probably."

"Only three," echoed Roadie, his pistol up high. "You say it like it's a good thing."

"Three's less than four," said Guano. A spark drifted in front of her helmet and she pulled back, confused. Another spark drifted down, and another. With a start she realized what was happening.

Someone was shooting at her. Vacuum made the gunshots silent.

"Shit!" she ducked down behind the magnetic clamp. It was thick and metal, basically bulletproof. "Someone's firing!"

"Where?"

"Don't know!"

She risked a peak above the rim of the clamp but had to duck back down almost immediately. No sign of anyone.

"I see the prick," said Roadie. "I see him. Behind the crashed shuttle."

Guano popped her head up again, and then she saw them. Two figures, crouched behind the wreck, only a thin sliver of their bodies visible. Their weapons flashed silently. She ducked again.

Hey, so, battle-crazy-calm-thing? Second time. Now would be good. I kind of need you—this is not what I'm good at!

Nothing. She just felt her own heart beating in her chest, accompanied by the hissing of her suit as it filtered the CO2 out of her own personal tiny atmosphere and replaced it with oxygen.

"Loading," said Roadie. "Cover me, Guano."

Of course he'd been shooting. In the silence she'd forgotten. Guano gripped her pistol tight and popped up again, aligning her sights to the thin sliver of man she could see. Her gun flashed twice, then twice again, rounds bouncing off the hull of the shuttle or impacting on the far side of the hangar bay.

Her enemy shot back with a spray of automatic fire. She was forced back into cover. They were outgunned, outmanned—where the hell was Flatline? It didn't matter. She only had the ammo left in her pistol and one spare mag. Roadie had used his spare. They needed another option.

"Roadie?"

"Yeah?"

"We gotta get to the shuttle."

Roadie said nothing for a second. "Say again, Guano? it sounds like you said we needed to get *to* the shuttle. You know, that place where the bad guys are."

"That's right," she said. "That hull armor is strong enough to stop small arms. We can move it to block the exit from the hangar bay, stop any reinforcements from getting aboard—worst case scenario, we can hide there, or even maneuver the thing around to squash anyone we don't like."

Roadie growled in her ear. "The hull is strong enough, but as you *so aptly* demonstrated, the cockpit canopy isn't. And you guessed it, we'll need to be *in* the cockpit in order to pilot that thing. Plus, it's twenty-five meters away over a completely open landing strip! This is a bad call, Guano."

"No, no, it's a good call. I can make it." She peaked above the magnetic clamp, then ducked back down. "Look, I have—" she checked the side of her pistol, to the display readout there. "Eight rounds left, and one spare mag. If I toss you my spare mag, and I shoot while I move, I can make it. I can make it."

"We're fighting in void," said Roadie. "If you get hit—you're dead. Your suit will decompress and I won't be able to get your stupid ass back to the airlock in anywhere near enough time. Assuming they don't just shoot me too."

Yup. That was definitely a risk. "Roadie, we don't have time to debate this. We'll fight this in the true American fashion: by throwing US taxpayer's money at the problem. They'll take one for the team, as always. I am going to break cover and run in five, four—"

"No, Guano, no!"

"Three, two, one—" She leapt up, pistol in both hands. The two intruders were behind cover. Guano tried to break into a sprint, but ended up moving with a swift awkward waddle. Space suits were restrictive, in both movement and field of view. All she could see was a steel framed window that bounced and jostled as she ran, waving her pistol around like a lunatic.

The intruders appeared. She fired wildly, not even close to hitting them. Roadie hit one—or maybe she did, it was hard to tell—the intruder's spacesuit erupting in a spray of white gas and red blood, then slumping on the metal deck.

She expected to be shot at any moment, but then she realized the remaining intruder wasn't even looking at her. He was looking *past* her, to Roadie. His rifle flashed.

"Get down!" she shouted, stopping and lining up her pistol. One shot, two shot, three—and the third round went straight through the guy's helmet, blasting him back down to the deck.

Silence.

"Hey Roadie," asked Guano, somewhat fearfully. "You

okay?"

"Yeah," he said, breathing labored. "I got shot."

Shit. "You okay?"

"I said, I got shot! No, I'm *not* okay! Shit!"

"How bad?" she asked.

There was a brief pause. "Not bad," said Roadie. "I think it clipped my thigh. I'm leaking atmosphere but not too bad. I think my, um, blood clotted when it hit vacuum and basically sealed the hole. It hurts like hell though."

"Okay," said Guano, taking a deep breath. "You just hold tight now, okay? Come over to the shuttle, and I'll fire it up. We'll block the entrance into the ship, stop any more reinforcements from coming in."

She saw him limping across the deck; he was wrong about the clotted blood sealing the hole—white gasses were escaping from a hole in his leg. Guano waddled her way over to the shuttle, her boots clanking on the metal as she climbed up the ramp.

Based on the debris strewn around the passenger compartment—and the conspicuous blood trail leading down the loading ramp—the shuttle had seen better days. Fortunately, the presence of standby power indicated that it would still fly. She stepped into the cockpit.

"Damn," she whispered, eyes falling upon the dead pilot, impaled on the nosecone of a Warbird. "I found Stealth. He didn't make it."

"Shit," said Roadie. "Wait, they just left him in there?"

Guano bit the inside of her cheek. "Not like they had much choice," she said. "He's kind of … stuck."

"Well, un-stick him. I'm almost aboard. And hurry the hell

up—I see another boarding craft coming in."

Another ship with more intruders. She had to hurry. Guano couldn't possibly push a Warbird by hand, nor could she move the shuttle, but she *could* try and cut off the nosecone holding Stealth into his chair. Shuttles had shears to cut people out of their restraints in the event of a crash. She rummaged around in the container behind the copilot's seat, digging out the heavy metal shears.

"Sorry, Stealth," she said, ramming the tip of the shears onto the metal nosecone. She started to cut around, until finally the tip fell off. She pulled him forward, until the sharp tip was out of the chair, then gently pushed his body into the copilot's seat.

Corrick gingerly sat down in the bloodstained pilot's seat, her back sinking into the hole in the rear of the seat. She tried not to think about the mangled seat and powered up the shuttle. Apart from a decompression alarm—duh—everything else came up okay.

Roadie moved into the cockpit with her. "What was the Admiral thinking, going down to that shithole with Lynch and Modi?" he asked, shaking his head inside his suit. "Same as with the embassy siege. That's why we have marines—the CO shouldn't be down there."

"I dunno," said Guano, trying to keep her mind off Stealth's blood congealing on the back of her suit, and the dead body just a meter away. "Captaining a warship by day, shooting people by night. Pew pew. I think it's pretty awesome."

"Well that's how I *know* it's a terrible idea."

She laughed, appreciating the distraction, and lifted the

shuttle up. "We'll have to jam the shuttle's nose in the doorway out of the hangar bay to the ship to block it fully," she said. "We'll raise up the loading ramp and seal it."

"Do it," said Roadie.

Sparks began flying off the hull of the shuttle—even without sound, she could tell they were being fired at. Guano spun the ship around, aimed the nose toward the airlock that led into the rest of the ship, and jammed the throttle open. The shuttle lurched forward, crunched against the airlock and lodged itself in, crumpling the nose even further. A press of a button sealed the rear loading ramp. Done.

The shuttle was a cork blocking entrance into the rest of the ship. More gunshots bounced off the rear of the shuttle but, as she predicted, the hull was simply too thick.

Only then did she realize they were stuck in the shuttle with a dozen angry invaders on the other side of the hull.

"Okay," she said, turning to Roadie, "what now?"

"Wait, you didn't have an exit strategy?"

"I was coming up with this shit on the fly!" Guano groaned.

"Clearly."

She looked around the cockpit, eyes darting back and forth to any piece of equipment, emergency controls, big red magic buttons—*anything* that would help them get out. "Just got to think …"

"Hey Guano?" asked Roadie, glancing at his oxygen meter. "How much air do you have?"

"Hopefully enough to last before they get us out," she said, grimly. Then a dark thought occurred. "They … do know we're in here, right?"

Chapter Forty-One

The streets of Glasgow
Earth

Bratta gripped the sides of his seat, which logically—especially in the rush hour congestion—did nothing, but at least made him feel better. Jeannie scoffed, but she didn't spare him any further attention.

"Relax, Steve, this isn't going to be easy for them."

"What? How so?"

"Visibility is low. The roads are difficult to drive, and there are plenty of cars around us that look like ours. They lost us for a while back there. If we'd been near a turnoff, we might have made clean away already."

He hoped she had a point.

"Shouldn't you, you know, be going a little faster? If we're trying to get away and all?"

Jeannie snorted. "I arrest speeders for a living. Only thing we're going to do by speeding is get pulled over, or, in these conditions, cause an accident. No," she paused to jerk the gearstick—which seemed to be an actual gearstick, not the usual automatic affair. How old *was* this car? The engine sputtered and stalled, to an outpouring of disapproval from the other drivers. "The trick is to drive like a complete fool. It's hard to chase an idiot when you have to anticipate their every move *and* they're causing traffic jams." She pretended to fumble with the keys, then she turned to him, smiling like the Cheshire cat, as the car fired back to life. "Want to swap seats? We'll have time."

Bratta peered through the window, and saw the next set of traffic lights a *long* way ahead. She had a point.

Behind him, he could see the car with the mismatched lights, just sitting there. Patient. Silent. Waiting for the kill, or whatever they were planning. And the only thing between him and his fate was *joking* about it. He shuffled more deeply into his jacket.

"At least you have a new car," he said, because talking was better than thinking. "Your old monstrosity would have been visible for miles."

When they'd been married, Jeannie had owned an ostentatious and overly-treasured truck to facilitate her dreaded camping and hiking trips. The vehicle had been his chariot to many midge-filled, muddy memories.

"New car?" She hopped across two lanes. Their tail dropped back a few cars, unable to cut into their lane. Bratta held down a giggle. Perhaps they'd win this, after all. "The Wee Beastie's over in Edinburgh, where she lives. I came over on the train—this is my parents' ride."

"Your—your *parents'* car?" And he'd thought the day couldn't get any worse.

"I get to read on the train, and Mum and Dad don't mind me borrowing this thing while I'm here."

She had a point, at least about the reading thing, although if she'd just slow down a tad that would make him feel a lot better … but, at least a car like this was heavy, so if they had an accident, they'd be a fair bit safer. Still, that didn't really make the situation any better. "Your parents are scary when they're angry, Jeannie."

"It runs in the family—damn, they've caught up again."

Bratta turned just in time to see the mismatched headlights slot in behind them. He whimpered a little.

Jeannie hummed a little. "You make a good point."

He looked at her. "How? I wasn't talking, how can I have made a point?"

The traffic lights were coming up. Jeannie indicated, but didn't turn the wheel. "Your misery speaks for itself. This is turning out to be a pain."

"Do you … do you have a better solution?"

"Sure. We turn the tables on them. They might know why they want to tail us; we definitely don't."

"What? But the point is we *don't* want to talk to them because they probably want to attack us. Or worse!"

Jeannie shook her head. "No, we don't want *them* to talk to *us*. But if we're asking the questions …"

Bratta stared out at the low clouds. "How? Jeannie, I'm not exactly scary, you know? And I don't think they're going to play by the rules."

"Just trust me, Steve," Jeannie said, putting on a sudden

burst of speed to catch the orange light. "We'll be fine."

Their tail lost them at the lights, stuck behind a red. A minute later, they caught up again, just as they were exiting onto a smaller road. They dropped back a few cars during a lane merge. They advanced on them even as the streets started getting smaller and less predictable. Whoever was behind that wheel, Bratta thought, they either had extremely good eyes, or an excellent memory.

Jeannie went the wrong way down a one-way street, and their pursuers missed the turn.

"Perfect."

"Really? How?" Bratta asked, glancing at the end of the lane, where a perpendicular street led from the main street to their hiding place. "You've trapped us!"

"No," Jeannie replied. "I've trapped them." She turned the car into a narrow side-alley. It was a dead end, wide enough to turn around in, but nothing more. "This is a residential area—see those garages? They'll think we're running, or that we have a safe house. Now, get out and hide."

It was now freezing outside, and while his jacket could stave off the light rain well enough, his trousers could not. Jeannie pointed behind him, to a corner angled back from the alley's entrance. "Over there. No need to do anything fancy, just stay still and don't make any noise."

He nodded and made his way over to the damp corner, and tried to not let his teeth chatter too loudly.

Rain beaded on top of his head and ran down his forehead, falling over his eyes.

Droplets landed on his glasses; now he couldn't see.

On the other side of the alley, Jeannie kept one hand

tucked into her jacket, unmoving.

They waited.

Tires crunched on gravel, getting closer. A single headlight painted the garage behind them. Bratta shivered, and not just from the weather.

The tires stopped. Then the sound of the engine died.

A door slammed, accompanied by a male voice saying something in thick Glaswegian. From the tone, Bratta assumed he was swearing, which hardly did much to assuage his fears. *Come on,* he told himself, *a month ago you were facing down aliens. You can deal with one Glaswegian.*

Actually, that category included Jeannie, so no. No, he could not.

Footsteps sounded, growing nearer and nearer. A burly man in a black leather jacket appeared in his peripheral vision, and Bratta stopped breathing. There was a blur of movement from Jeannie's side of the alley, and then—

"Put your hands up, sir!"

Holy *coprolite* his ex-wife was scary.

Their tail must have thought so too, because his eyes—even from here—widened. He looked over and saw Bratta.

No, no, no. This was a non-ideal situation.

The man glanced at Jeannie, met her steely eyes, and charged. At Bratta.

Chapter Forty-Two

Orbital Defense Platform J4
High Orbit Above New London
Omid Sector

US Army Captain Jessica Mao adjusted the connections on her prosthetic hand, the fleshy fingers on her right fiddling with the metallic ones on her left.

The sensation of touch came back as the dodgy prosthetic jerked back to life, her steel fingers flexing experimentally. Hopefully it would hold for the rest of the mission.

"Ma'am," said Petty Officer Third Class Leonard Alexander Jacobs, his chubby face lighting up. "We're in."

It was just her and him. It felt strange to be a Major working with a single Petty Officer, but such was the nature of the impromptu, thrown-together units. She'd asked for four men. They'd given her one. That was fine. They'd accomplished the mission—the Forgotten made do with what they had. And very effectively, too, it seemed. Despite her misgivings.

Now they owned an orbital armored box that pooped missiles.

"Good work," said Mao, putting her hands on her hips and facing the small camera they had set up. "Ready to open the connection."

"All good here," said Jacobs, giving a firm thumbs up. "Should we hail the Americans or the Chinese?"

That decision was hers—mission planning had specified she was to hail whichever ship responded first—but that discretion meant she was also free to resolve some of her own, personal, grudges. "Hail the Chinese ship."

Jacobs worked over his keyboard, fingers tapping on keys. An old-style keyboard being typed on by an old-style man. Apparently this guy, despite his age, wasn't even a Sino-American war veteran. He was something else—a survivor of the destruction of Capella Station.

Mao knew it had something to do with the alien attack but beyond that she honestly didn't really care. She was more concerned with *why* Jacobs had been picked to work alongside her. It didn't make any sense—Capella Station was way, way out in the sticks. The guy must have been a fuck-up.

But the camera's light came on and Mao had no time to think about all that.

"This is US Army Major Jessica Mao to Chinese vessel," she said, her voice steel and anger. "Request permission to speak to CNS *Luyang III* actual."

There was a delay—longer than she was anticipating, presumably to account for translations and relays—and then a firm, crisply accented voice came over the line. "This is Admiral Yim."

Mao smirked out of the corner of her mouth. "It's a *pleasure* to finally get to speak to you," she said, drumming her prosthetic fingers on her fleshy arm. "How does it feel to work for the people who destroyed Friendship Station?"

"Major Mao," said Yim, a slight tinge of sarcasm painting his voice. "I can assure you that I had *no* part in destroying the very station as I was standing on it when its reactors went critical. And yes, I was there. Got the scar to prove it."

"Got my own scars," said Mao, pointedly folding her prosthetic arm in front of her, the servos whining slightly as her fingers settled. "I'm not blaming you personally for what happened. I blame your government. You were the ones who worked to destroy it—to blast a symbol of cooperation into atoms. You couldn't stand it, could you? The Chinese flag flying alongside the American one."

Yim's voice hardened. "Do you have any proof at all of what you're saying?"

"Look to the world at your feet," said Mao. "Look to New London. The galaxy needs to wake up to your evil; this world was once a jewel, a hub of trade and commerce and culture. The people there were rich, prosperous, happy—I know, because I grew up there during the war. And what happened when the war ended? An influx of Chinese. Because we made peace, Chinese immigrants poured into the place like locusts, eating up the jobs, buying up the local industries and employing only their own people, brought in off-world to work for a pittance per hour, strip-mining our wealth and leaving nothing for the people who made it."

"I'm sure," said Admiral Yim, evenly, "the exhaustion of the tungsten mines, leading to an end to the mining boom, and the simultaneous influx of narcotics from New London's moons had absolutely nothing to do with your world's misery. While I don't doubt that unscrupulous Chinese businessmen played a part in what happened, it's difficult to accept, either personally or as a representative of my government, that this is *all* our fault."

"Typical Chinese," said Mao, curling back her upper lip. "Always trying to deflect blame. Those kind of games are in your blood."

"Funny," said Yim. "If I'm not mistaken, Mao is a Chinese surname."

Oh he *didn't*. "I'm a tenth generation American," spat Mao. "I'm as fucking American as apple pie on a foggy Boston morning."

"And the land upon which you were born, the nationality on your birth certificate, this changed your blood content?" Yim chuckled down the line. "Talking to you is like arguing with Swish cheese. Your argument stinks and it's full of holes."

Mao squeezed her fists so hard the motors in her prosthetic whined in protest. "I'll give you full of holes," she said through clenched teeth. "Admiral Yim, now hear this: you have ten minutes to initiate Z-space translation out of this system and *never* return, or we will turn these orbital stations around, aim towards the surface, and we will glass the whole fucking planet and all its moons."

Yim was quiet for a few seconds. Stunned into silence, possibly. "You would destroy your own world?" he asked, his tone befuddled. "For what end?"

"Chinese overran the city," said Mao, simply. "There are so many of them that, to be perfectly honest with you Admiral, it is no longer our world. They arrived, they bred, they outnumbered us. They voted to become independent, and then to ally with China politically, economically, and socially. Now whatever claim we hold to that planet is essentially just a title." She sneered, scrunching up her face in anger, meaning every single word of it. "And I'll see it burn before I let the likes of you plant your flag there and turn the de facto takeover into a legitimate one."

"We have no such plans—"

"Lies!" shouted Mao, fighting to keep her composure.

"It's your own planet," said Yim. "Your homeworld. It's yours, it's under U.S. jurisdiction, I can't make it any more clear to you that—"

Lies, all lies. "You're as bad as the politicians," said Mao. "You're all the same. Corrupt, arrogant, conquering. Lemme tell you something: corruption spreads like a systemic infection. Ancient humans used to use hot pokers to seal their wounds, burn out the puss and the blood and, by inflicting pain and harm, ultimately promote healing from the ashes."

Yim snorted across their connection, half dismissively, half amused. "Such drama. You realize that's a myth, right? I mean, they absolutely *did* do that, but the process of cauterization actually increased the vector for infection by causing further tissue damage and creating a more hospitable environment for bacterial growth. You couldn't possibly have picked a worse metaphor if you *tried*."

Mao glared at the camera. "Nine minutes, fifty seconds, Admiral."

"I'm aware," said Yim.

Out of the corner of her eye, she could see Jacobs waving his hand. "Enemy fighters incoming," he hissed, quietly. "Chinese!"

She squinted at the camera. "Call off your attack, or New London burns. Call me back when you make up your mind." She terminated the link.

"Are you really going to do it?" asked Jacobs.

"Yep," said Mao. "He was pissing me off."

The two sat in silence for a brief moment. Finally, Mao spoke.

"Load and arm all missile tubes and prepare for orbital bombardment," she said, taking in a low, steady breath. "And prep a pair of missiles for the good Chinese Admiral. Maybe he'll be more sympathetic if he's feeling the pain firsthand."

Chapter Forty-Three

Bridge
USS Midway
High Orbit Above New London
Omid Sector

A fierce orange glow burned in the center of the armored casemate like a slowly spreading flower, dull red at the edges and bright yellow in the middle. The core of it was white hot. It must have been at least a thousand degrees or more. That laser was doing impressive work—good thing he had assumed they had the best equipment available. Because they did.

"Modi," he asked into his helmet's radio, "how's that gun battle going down in engineering?"

"The gunfire seems to be abating," said Modi, his tone carrying the faintest traces of relief. "I am no longer concerned."

Mattis stared at the growing glow on the casement. "I'm

glad that makes one of us."

"Although," said Modi, on reflection, "it is possible that the attackers have defeated the defenders and are preparing to breach engineering. My demise may be imminent, for all I know."

"Barring that, what do you think has happened?"

"Unsure," said Modi. "No sign of the Rhinos, then?"

That was a good question, well asked. "Hold on, I'll find out." Mattis changed frequency. "USS *Midway* actual to Rhinos. Report status."

"Uh," said a confused voice, "sorry, Admiral, we're on our way. One of our suits experienced a malfunction. ETA has been increased by four minutes."

Four minutes. Almost anything could happen in four minutes, including the casement giving way. "Better double time it," he said, "the bridge casemate is getting mighty hot."

"We're on it sir," said the Rhino. "We just need a little more time."

"That's exactly what we don't have," said Mattis.

He wanted to say more, to encourage the Rhino along a bit further, but his helmet chirped. An incoming transmission. His helmet projected the caller's ID on the side: Unknown Chinese Vessel. The call was being routed directly to him.

"Admiral Yim, I presume?"

"You are correct," said Yim, his tone dour. "But I have bad news. The satellites the Forgotten have commandeered—they do not intend to use them on us. They are, instead, determined to use them on the civilian population below, on New London."

Mattis's blood ran cold. "But almost a million people live

there," he said. "The whole planet's population lives in one big settlement. If they fire those weapons—"

"It'll be a bloodbath." Yim's tone was resolute. "Admiral, I'm calling you to ask you in plain terms, do you think we can destroy all three stations before they open fire?"

That would be extremely difficult. Each of the platforms was heavily armored *and* heavily armed. It was no Goalkeeper, but it was close. "That will not be possible," said Mattis.

"Sir," said Lynch, pointing to the casemate. "They're almost through."

Modi called him again. "Admiral, my second supposition was right. They are setting breaching charges at the doors."

Too many things happening at once. Mattis focused and shut out the distractions, patching Modi, Lynch, and Yim into the same channel with a touch of his wrist. "Playtime is over, gentlemen. It's time we finished this. I'd hoped to spare the platforms—I'm sure Fleet Command would have loved me for it—but unfortunately sometimes, these things just simply can't be done."

"Ready to engage the platforms directly," said Yim, "when you give the word."

He took a deep breath. The shimmering heat of a laser shone through a pinpoint crack in the casemate, drawing a dangerous line of death across the bridge. Fortunately, they had all prepared for this.

"No time for that," said Lynch, "and it's too great a risk to fire on them directly. You know what you have to do, sir."

He did, but it was difficult. His intellect was begging him to trust Yim, but his emotions—that part of him that remembered his brother, remembered his face and his laugh and his smile—simply couldn't.

Fortunately, in the titanic battle that was as brief as it was painful, his intellect won out.

"Admiral Yim," said Mattis, dragging the words out of himself as though he were pulling a drowning man from a tar pit, "I have something that may allow us to disable all those platforms at once. The command override codes for the station." The laser began to drift across the bridge as the Forgotten cut into the casemate, slowly drawing an invisible beam of doom through the room. "But I'm afraid I'm going to have to give them to *you* to upload. We're a little busy here."

Chapter Forty-Four

Bridge
CNS Luyang III
High Orbit Above New London
Omid Sector

Admiral Yim watched with satisfaction as the codes came through. A 2048-bit key. Exactly what he expected, given standard encryption algorithms. The maths was a bit beyond him, but he knew it represented two enormously large prime numbers. It seemed, at first glance, that a number 2048 digits long comprising only 1s and 0s should be easy for a computer to guess given enough time, but his military training had taught him better. It was deceptively simple. There were only 2^2048 potential key pairs it could be. How hard would it be to guess the right one?

Most people couldn't even comprehend how large 2^2048 even *was*. He certainly struggled. As the ship's computers worked through processing the keys and getting them ready for transmission, he indulged a little of his curiosity.

He bought up the calculator and tapped the numbers into his console.

>function.convert(sciNote, decimal)

Input=2^2048

Result=323170060713110073007148766886699519604441 0266971548403213034542752465513886789089319720141152 2913463688717960921898019494119559150490921095088152 3864482831206308773673009960917501977503896521067960 5763838406756827679221864261975616183809433847617047 0581645852036305042887575891541065808607552399123930 3855219143333896683424206849747865645694948561760353 2632205807780565933102619270846031415025859286417711 6725943603718461857357598351152301645904403697613233 2872312271256847108202097251571017269313234696785425 8065669793504599726835299863821552516638943733554360 2135433229604645318478604952148193555853611059596230 656

Six hundred seventeen decimal digits, said his computer. A very large number indeed. Substantially more than even the largest estimation of the number of atoms in the universe, which capped out a meager eighty-three decimal digits. Chinese Intelligence could put every computer in the galaxy to work on this problem—could turn every atom of every single thing into a computer working on this problem—and still never solve it in a single human's lifetime.

He was bought out of his musings by a vibration on his sub-dermal implant. Another communication from General Lok Tsai. He tapped his throat to answer it, dropping his voice back to a whisper. "*Luyang III* here."

"Well, Admiral Yim," the man said, practically smiling down the line. "I don't believe it. Access codes to a genuine American military installation. You truly are one of a kind."

He knew? And so soon? That caused Yim's eyebrows to shoot up toward the ceiling. "General, with the greatest respect, you're learning about this about one minute after I did. How is that even possible?"

"Oh, Admiral," said Tsai, enigmatically, "we have our ways of knowing things."

Yim glowered. "Is the *Luyang III* not my ship, General?"

"It's the *people's* ship," General Tsai reminded him gently. "You are merely placed in command of it by the grace of their appointed protectors." His tone hardened ever so slightly. "A grace which can be rescinded at any time."

"Well, when you threaten me so lovingly, how can I possibly complain?" Yim grimaced to himself and reached up to touch his neck again, to end the call.

"Wait," said Tsai. Could he *physically see* Yim? That was an unsettling thought. "Send through the codes. I want to see that station shut down for myself."

Tsai had no right to that, but Yim didn't want to argue the point. "Send through the codes, now," he said to Xiao, barely able to hide his disgust. "Let's end this thing once and for all."

Chapter Forty-Five

Bridge
USS Midway
High Orbit Above New London
Omid Sector

The laser cut a one-foot hole in the casemate. A hunk of metal, almost square, fell out with a loud *clang.*

Mattis expected the air to rush out of the hole, and shooting to start. He had his gun in hand. The marines had their guns in hand. Lynch, crouched behind his console, had his gun in hand.

Instead of explosive decompression or gunfire, a sign came through the hole, hand written, the edges singed as they brushed the sides of the hot metal.

On it, only one thing written: *194 mhz.*

Obliging them, Mattis adjusted his radio. "194 mhz," he echoed.

The voice of an unseen man came through, thickly accented. British, maybe? "Admiral Mattis. This is Flight Lieutenant Khawlah Bagram. Your casemate is down. It's time for you to turn your ship over to us."

Flight Lieutenant? What kind of a rank was that? "You're British?" he asked. Maybe he could use the memory of Captain Salt to get some leverage.

"Australian," said the man.

The Australians had played a role in the Sino-American war, a fact that had totally slipped his mind. Ironic then that Bagram's contribution had been *forgotten*. His group had been well named.

"Regretfully," said Mattis, trying to push the uncomfortable moment of truth out of his mind, "I cannot and will not be surrendering the *Midway* to you."

"Your bargaining posture leaves something to be desired," said Bagram. "You're trapped in there. I'll repeat: we have breached the casemate."

Mattis regarded the still-glowing metal with a skeptical eye. "That much metal is going to take a long time to cool, and unless you can squeeze through a one-foot gap without touching the sides, you're going to cook yourselves trying to get in. Our consoles and the inner door will protect us from grenades, our suits protect us from gasses and decompression, and if you can shoot us, we can shoot you. The only difference between us is: we have a whole ship full of crew who are working their way toward defeating you and your other boarding parties. Pretty soon you'll be fighting on two fronts." He smirked to himself. "We're not trapped in here because of you. You're trapped out there because of us."

"So full of confidence," said Bagram, and a deafening roar blasted the weakened, still yellow-hot metal of the casemate into the bridge.

Fragments and globs of half-molten metal sprayed inside, splashing off almost every surface. Globs and shards struck his suit, the internal computers activating various alarms. The ringing in his ears returned, worse than before. If he didn't have *some* form of hearing damage before, he did now. That, however, was a matter for later. Nothing he could do about it now.

With a forced casualness, Mattis brushed the semi-molten metal off his suit. Lynch had fared better behind cover, but one of their marines wasn't moving, laying face down, wisps of smoke rising from the edges of his armor. He had been so much closer….

The Forgotten walked in through the bent, warped ruin of the casemate, their boots hissing as they stepped on red and yellow fragments. They had automatic weapons held comfortably in their hands.

"One last chance," shouted the middle guy—Bagram—his face concealed behind the reflective visor he wore. "Mattis, you don't have to die here today."

If that massive explosion had done nothing to them—granted, they were on the other side of it, but still—Mattis's pea shooter wouldn't get past their suits. Lynch was similarly armed. They'd lost a marine already, making it six versus two. And the way the Forgotten walked, the way their carried themselves, suggested that they knew how to use their weapons.

Mattis stood up from behind cover. "So," he said, doing

absolutely nothing more than stalling for time until the Rhinos got there, "let's talk."

Bagram nodded to him, his expression unreadable behind the reflective visor. "A wise choice, Mattis. There's no need for more of your men to die."

"Yes, well, I'd prefer to avoid further bloodshed if possible —but I won't surrender my ship."

"So you won't surrender," said Bagram, shrugging, "but you won't fight either. I think that's a de facto surrender, you know, like it or not."

Definitely more *not* than *like*. Mattis tried to stall for more time. "I'm suggesting a truce. There's no need for *anyone* more to die here, on either side." He pointed to Bagram's wrist, to the glowing, lit-up communicator there. "Go on. Call your satellites. You'll find them shut down."

"Mmm, are you trying to play us, Admiral? Stringing us out while the cavalry comes?"

Mattis pointed again. "Ask them," he insisted.

Bagram touched the small device, cutting the commlink to Mattis and the others, speaking quietly to his fellows. The rest of them, on both sides, stood around awkwardly, guns pointed at each other.

It was good. Regardless of how the communications went, every second the intruders waited was another second the Rhinos got closer. Unless they'd gotten lost or something. Where the hell were they?

"They're shut down," asked Mattis, "aren't they?"

Bagram said nothing. Which said everything.

"Look," he said, "I'm not exactly known for my love of the People's Republic. And I have questions too, questions about Friendship Station, questions about a *lot* of things, but you gotta believe me when I tell you: attacking US vessels, and pissing off the Chinese at the same time—this isn't how either of us are going to find answers."

"And what do you suggest we do, Admiral?" They still called him that, despite everything. Military to the end.

Mattis slowly sheathed his pistol. It was useless anyway. "A few things," he said. "First of all, lemme talk to your leaders. Officers who are in charge. I know you mean well, but I don't want to make any promises I can't keep, and I don't want you to promise me anything you can't deliver. Especially something that I later come to rely upon or assume is true. I'll talk to them, hear what they have to say, and see what I can do."

"Really?" Bagram leaned forward slightly. "You'd listen to us about all the back pay we're owed, and the useless Veterans Affairs people who won't cover our medical costs? Or even our funeral allowances when we finally kick the bucket?"

For some reason, the denial of a funerary allowance struck home to him. He'd only just months prior laid Commander Pitt to rest, and the notion that his funeral might not have been covered because of some bean counters trying to wiggle their way out of their responsibilities made him more angry than he should have been at that moment.

"I'd certainly listen," said Mattis. "I know the VA's office isn't exactly popular with vets, but … I'm one of you. I fought in the same war. I know what you're feeling. But it should come from someone with authority, someone who speaks for all of you."

That *really* seemed to grab him. "You'd talk to our CO? Hear his grievances?"

"I would."

Bagram considered. "How do I know you aren't just trying to get a leg up so you can kill us?"

Mattis pointed over their shoulders. "Because," he said, "I could just have my highly sociopathic anti-boarder marines standing behind you kill you and not have to worry about any of this."

Bagram and the intruders all shuffled around. Two Rhinos stood at the end of the hallway, flanking the Forgotten, heavy weapons trained on the intruders.

"Say the word, sir," said the lead Rhino, sweeping the bridge with the gleaming barrels of her weapon. "I'm real cranky after all that walking."

Mattis knew that if she fired that thing in the enclosed space of the bridge there would likely be casualties on both sides, but there was no sense in letting Bagram know that. "Not yet," he said. "We're just having a friendly chat right now, is all, but if we could lower the amount of firearms present that would be real neat. And all of you need to keep your hands where we can see them."

The Forgotten slowly put their weapons on the deck and put their hands on their heads.

"Despite the fortuitous arrival of my reinforcements, I want you to know this doesn't change my position at all. I still want to talk to your leader, whoever he is, and hear out what he has to say. Without preconditions." Mattis rested his hand on his hip. "It's a good deal for you. Worst case, you get a lift back to wherever your boss is hiding out. Hell—your men on the satellites can come too, assuming they didn't kill anyone in the taking of them and they didn't do anything that'll make the

Chinese want to detain them, either. Which they shouldn't because, legally speaking, as long as Yim can convince his superiors that this is an internal US matter, that's how I'm going to treat it."

With the metaphorical shoe on the other foot, Bagram was clearly more reluctant to trust him. "How do I know you aren't trying to find his location so you can kill him?"

Mattis shrugged. "Honestly, you don't."

"Honesty counts for a lot," said Bagram, "but something more concrete would be better."

"Your bargaining posture," said Mattis, grinning slightly to himself, "leaves a lot to be desired."

Bagram hesitated. "I understand. Just ... promise me you'll go see him."

Mattis straightened his back. "I'm a man of my word. Now hear this: I can promise you I'll do my best to get to your CO and talk to him, genuinely hear his grievance,s and then do what I can to address them. But I can't promise results, and I can't promise he'll talk to me in the first place. Only that I'll listen."

Bagram nodded. "Right. Then I'll tell you."

Chapter Forty-Six

Money Tree Lotto Office
Georgetown, Maryland
United States
Earth

Kyle O'Connor was having a *really* good day. Winning the lottery will do that. He'd played most of his life, now and then, but this was the first time he'd won *anything*. He smirked. *So much for luck of the Irish.*

He hadn't scored division 1, not by a long shot, but it was enough that he would have a real nice year this year. Maybe pay off the car. Or a chunk of the house. His mind raced with the possibilities.

$888,416.94. The cents both confused and amused him; somewhere, someone had decided that the payout would include exactly ninety-four cents. Why ninety-four? Why not ninety-five or ninety-six? Couldn't they afford the six cents it would take to round to a dollar?

Whatever. The main thing was collecting his earnings. That was why he had come to the Money Tree Lotto building downtown—a squat, gaudy building perched on a corner in the bustling business district. The double doors were narrow glass sheets, strangely uninviting. Maybe they didn't really want people to collect their winnings after all.

That made sense.

Kyle stepped up to the doors and waited for them to open. They didn't. He tapped his foot on the ground impatiently. Maybe the storefront wasn't open today … maybe he was too early. Nine in the morning couldn't possibly be *too* early, though, could it?

The first inklings that, perhaps, there wasn't any money waiting for him at all began to seep in. He did usually buy a ticket, most weeks, but he sometimes didn't. But this winning ticket was, apparently, from over a year ago, and this was the first he'd heard of it. How sure were they that the winner was definitely him? It might be some other Kyle O'Conner. There were bound to be dozens of them in Georgetown alone, probably more….

As he stood there, pondering the mathematical chance that this was all just a mistake on behalf of the lotto company, he felt a hand gently touch his shoulder.

Some guy had appeared beside him. An older man, probably in his late forties, with a one-week shadow on his face, black growth speckled with white. His whole left ear was mostly gone, just a lump of scar tissue that couldn't possibly pick up any sound, gnawed and damaged like some kind of beast had chewed it off. His clothes were nondescript and plain, and even though he had a kind face—despite the ear—there was something *odd* about him; something *off*. Something false, as though the whole thing were a carefully crafted act.

"Mister O'Conner?" asked the stranger.

"That's me," said Kyle, a little more guarded than he intended to. "Are you here to give me my money?"

The stranger just smiled. "No," he confessed. "I'm just here to talk to you." The man held out his hand. "I'm John Smith."

John Smith? *Really*? That seemed suspicious to him; such a generic, empty name—he may as well have called himself *John Doe*.

Kyle took the offered hand, giving it a firm shake. "I'm Kyle O'Conner," he said.

"I know."

Of course. The man had greeted him by name. "Uhh … yes. So, what can I do for you, Mister Smith?"

Smith reached into his pocket. For a split-second Kyle thought he might be drawing a gun—the streets were unusually quiet here, lacking their normal bustle—but instead, the man withdrew a communicator. A slightly older model with an anime sticker on it. "Do you recognize this device?"

"I don't," said Kyle, shrugging. A faint amount of relief managed to sneak into his mind. Maybe this wasn't about him after all. "What about it?"

A slight pause. "Walk with me, will you?" asked Smith, and something in his tone—just something about the way he phrased it—compelled Kyle to do so.

So he did. The two men fell into step, walking away from the Money Tree Lotto Office which, Kyle began to suspect, was deliberately closed.

"I wanted to talk to you for a little while," said Smith, folding his hands behind his back. "About a certain matter."

A certain matter … Kyle's heart clenched. "To what are you referring?" he asked, forcing his voice to be as calm, collected, and nerve-free as he could.

"I'm aware you spoke to Chuck Pitt," said Smith, his tone light as if discussing a change in weather. "I don't mind that—it's a free country, people are allowed to talk to one another—I just want to know what you talked about."

"Just … things," Kyle said, evasively. "How did you know about that?"

"It's my job to know," said Smith, plainly.

Well. This wasn't good. This wasn't good at all. "So," asked Kyle. "What about that communicator? I don't want to buy it."

"And I don't want to sell it. I liberated it from a Doctor Steve Bratta some time ago," said Smith. "Steve Bratta. Do you know that name?"

"Nope."

"What about Admiral Jack Mattis?"

Kyle squinted. "Chuck's father? I've never met him."

"Mmm." Smith returned the communicator to his pocket. "I feel, Mister O'Conner, that you didn't adequately answer my question from earlier. You and Chuck Mattis: what did you discuss?"

Kyle frowned darkly. "I'm not telling you that," he said, a wellspring of anger surging up in him. "I don't know who you are. I don't owe you the time of day, let alone anything more. Now piss off."

Smith seemed unaffected by the shift in tone. "This is a

national security matter," he said, continuing to walk as though nothing were wrong. "There are very curious, very driven people asking questions about you and Chuck and what your involvement in all of their affairs may be. They have charged me with finding the answers." Smith smiled at him, a strange, empty smile. "I am firmly of the opinion that the best answers are those given freely. I do not wish to resort to *unpleasantness*, Mister O'Conner, and I would prefer that you answer my question without any further attempts at delay or misdirection."

It was tempting—*so* tempting!—to just tell this guy to fuck off and leave him alone. He was weird, creepy, and John Smith was the worst fake name *ever* ... but there was something about the man's tone, about the way he phrased things, that was layered with implied threats, and despite the thick coat wrapped around him Kyle felt distinctly cold. Some part of him understood that this man, although seemingly kind and gentle, had a profound darkness to him that was best left unexplored.

"We barely talked about anything," said Kyle, honestly. "He asked me about the Ark Project. I told him that I couldn't answer that question because, well, I *couldn't*, and I told him to just leave the whole thing alone and get on with his life."

"Is that all?" asked Smith, softly. "Did you mention anything else?"

"Uhh." Kyle searched his memory. "I mentioned Senator Pitt still hates him and his dad. He asked about the video, the one that leaked, about the alien attack—"

"Oh, yes," said Smith. "Tell me about that. What did you say to him?"

"Nothing," said Kyle. "Neither of us had anything to do with that."

Smith said nothing for a brief moment. "Did he give you anything? Or you, him? A file, perhaps? A link to something backed up on the net?"

"No," asked Kyle. "Nothing at all like that."

Smith regarded him for a moment, and then nodded. "I believe you. I'll look elsewhere for what I seek, then." He took a shallow breath, stopped, and then turned and began walking away. "Enjoy your day." He started to turn away, before adding, "and, needless to say, we never talked. Goodbye, Mister O'Conner."

It felt strange to be dismissed so readily, but Kyle just wanted the weird, unsettling conversation to be over. There was one other thing though….

"Wait," Kyle called, "so, I didn't really win the lotto?"

"Oh Kyle," said Smith, smiling ever so slightly over his shoulder. "You aren't that lucky."

Chapter Forty-Seven

Orbital Defense Platform J4
High Orbit Above New London
Omid Sector

Jessica Mao selected the dead center of New London.

"Are you sure you want to do this?" asked Jacobs, for the third or forth time so far. Piece of chicken shit.

"Yes," she said simply. "Target these coordinates. Fire all the missiles at once; no sense in waiting. The more we send as one big salvo, the less likely they are to get intercepted."

"Lots of people are going to die," said Jacobs, whining softly. "I thought this was supposed to be a bluff."

Jesus Christ. He knew what he was signing on for, didn't he? "The thing about a bluff, Jacobs, is that it's meaningless if you aren't willing to follow through with it."

He said nothing. He wasn't happy, obviously, but Mao didn't care. As long as he did his job, there would be no problems.

"Loading complete," announced Jacobs. "Target coordinates locked in."

No time like the present. Time to burn that miserable hellhole to ashes, just like she'd been training for. "Firing," she said, tapping a key on the console.

A faint hiss reverberated around the orbital defense platform as it powered up, and then—almost too suddenly—the light flickered out, the power draining from every system. Her feet lifted off the ground as the artificial gravity went out.

She and Jacobs were left on a floating hunk of metal, spinning slowly above a world she had tried to destroy.

"Shit," she said, as she caught sight of the Chinese ship drawing closer to her platform.

"Shit," said Jacobs, his eyes fixated on the screen. They met hers. "We're going to be okay, right?" he said, voice cracking. "I didn't survive Capella for *this*!"

"We're going to be fine," said Mao, watching the Chinese ship draw closer. "We're going to be fine."

She spoke with a confidence she didn't feel.

Chapter Forty-Eight

Bridge
USS Midway
High Orbit Above New London
Omid Sector

"So," said Mattis, removing his helmet with a faint hiss. "Let's talk."

"Okay," said Bagram, still obviously nervous at the heavily-armed Rhinos guarding him and his men. Their weapons lay in a pile in the corner of the bridge, their hands in binders. Engineering had secured themselves, and all over the ship Forgotten boarding parties had been secured in a similar fashion.

Too bad about the casemate though. It was integrated into the ship; repairing it would be difficult. Modi would have his work cut out for him.

But that was a job for the future. Mattis took a deep

breath. "So. Places. Names. If I'm going to meet a guy, I'm going to want his name at the very least."

"His name?" Bagram's reluctance was clear. Mattis could understand. If the Forgotten were a nation, this would probably be considered high treason. And revolutionary groups—or at least, armed groups with an agenda—tended to be a little less than perfect sticklers for the rules. "I dunno …"

If Mattis couldn't convince the leader to lay down arms, and the US Government wouldn't offer him asylum and amnesty, Bagram's life would be short and painful. "Look," he said, "a good lawyer knows the law but a great lawyer knows the judge. The word of a US Admiral, especially one with the media presence I have, counts for a lot." At least, he hoped it did. "If you give me what I want, I'll do my utmost to make sure you're protected."

"John Armitage," said Bagram at length. "At least, that's the name he goes by. I don't know if it's his real name—nobody does. There's even some suggestion that there are multiple people who simply assume the name whenever its convenient—there are more Forgotten than you think. Tens of thousands of them …" Bagram hesitated, shaking his head. "But that doesn't matter. If you want to speak to the leader of the Forgotten, you want to speak to John Armitage."

Right. John Armitage, who might or might not be one person or several. Useful intel, if incomplete. "And where can I do that?"

"It's …" he took a deep breath. "It's an asteroid. Way out in the belt of a distant star—Kepler-1011. A dead star without any other kind of name. It has a single planet, Kepler-1011b. Unsuitable for settlement. There's a tiny automated mining colony there. No people. But the star has an asteroid belt… and one of the 'roids' name is Chrysalis." Bagram was warming up now. "There's basically not much there. A few small industries; a mining facility, a few smelters, a bunch of odds-and-ends type companies. Pegasus Security are out there too, bunch of thugs with badges if you ask me … what else … the rest is mostly black-market shit, some casinos, whore houses, whatever you want, really. Oh, and the HQ of some genetics company is there, too. Probably one of the more legitimate operations around."

Genetics company. Interesting. "Okay," said Mattis. "Keep talking."

Bagram rubbed his know. "You should know this place ain't like most other places in the galaxy. Chrysalis is a semi-popular civilian destination. Don't know why it is when it's so far out, don't much *care* to know. All I know is, they employ a lot of veterans, and they pay pretty well, so our kind tend to gravitate toward there."

It always rankled him that the veterans of the Sino-American war had fewer job opportunities than even regular civilians. Military personnel sometimes left the service with a trade, but for many, that skill was "shooting people in the head." The civilian market for that was vanishingly small and the perception of veterans' mental health wasn't good. But a genetics lab in the middle of absolute nowhere? Why would any company hire a former soldier when they could hire someone who didn't have years of advanced training with heavy weapons?

Fortunately Mattis hadn't ever been in that situation—he'd stayed in the service, and he'd been able to, but there were many who hadn't. No surprise then, that they would go where they work was.

"Right," said Mattis. "Anything else we should know about this place?"

Now Bagram *truly* hesitated, obviously torn between two loyalties.

"C'mon," said Mattis. "If there's something I gotta know I gotta know about it."

"There are … defensive mines," said Bagram, finally. "A small minefield in the belt. Gravity mines, high yield little bastards. They generate an artificial gravity pulse—1000 g differential over a space of just a few kilometers, lasting less than half a second—which, if you were anywhere nearby, would turn everyone inside this tin can into goo."

Such technology would not be possible for a smaller 'roid to manufacture. "How did they get their hands on something like that?"

"The minefield is left over from the Sino-American war. The Chinese laid it, but now the Chrysalis folk control it. And it's been good to them; the mines are programmed to allow civilian traffic through, and military traffic only if you have the passcode or someone transmits it for you. Since the minefield got laid, that little rock's become some kind of Libertarian's paradise; the only law there is what you make, which is kind of why some companies are drawn to the place. I mean, who's going to sail through a damn *active minefield* to enforce Occupational Health and Safety regulations?"

Mattis digested that. "Do they have visitors? What do they think of outsiders?"

"There are regular shuttles coming in from all over the

galaxy. Money is money, and trade is great, but if you sail in there in a gunship and they don't like you? *Crunch.*"

Crunch was bad. "How do we get past it?"

"Well," said Bagram, considering, "they use an optical recognition system to ID incoming craft. It's primitive, but the system gets almost nothing that isn't an automated mining drone so it works well enough. The whole system is basically a bunch of high-res thermal cameras slaved together to make a 3D model of the ship, which is compared to 3D models of the authorized ships. If you're authorized, no worries. If you're not, squish."

Crunch or squish, neither were good options. "Well," said Mattis, "the *Midway* is pretty distinctive. No way we could disguise it as an uncrewed drone, or civilian shuttle."

"No way you *should* do that," said Bagram. "The minefield is only in the belt. If you complete your translation a little way out from Kepler-1011b's orbit, you could probably get a signal to them. They might alter the minefield to let you in. Or …"

"Or?"

"Or, you know, *not.* The only way you'd know is if you ventured inside."

Well. What a pain. "Okay," he said. "There is one more thing."

"Okay?"

This part might be difficult to explain. "As much as I'd like to consider us square, there *is* the unfortunate matter of you and your men boarding and attacking our ship. You seriously damaged this ship and you caused a *major* international incident. Plus you threatened to fire on an inhabited world, putting millions of lives at risk."

"We were just bluffing—"

Mattis held up his hand. "You made the threat. Bluff or no. That's one for your lawyers to explain, and they will. I'm afraid I will have to turn you over to the authorities on New London, and I can't say you won't be spending a very long time in prison indeed. This isn't something you can simply get away with. But I will make sure to note your cooperation in my log, and I will try to see your inevitable sentences minimized, or at least, your conditions improved. No promises, but I'll see what I can do."

Bagram nodded. "Prison beats unemployment."

"Let me discuss this with my XO," he said, "and we'll work on a plan. For now, though, thank you."

He stepped away, beckoning Lynch up to him. When they were comfortably out of earshot, he clicked his tongue. "You heard that?"

Lynch nodded. "Never been in a minefield," he said, whimsically. "It could be fun."

Mattis grimaced. "Yeah, well, getting stretched into paste in under a second isn't exactly how I anticipated going out. Think Modi can help us with this one?"

Lynch whistled. "Probably not. Gravity mines were old tech—you'd know more about them than he would, I'd wager."

"I know enough to stay the *hell* away. Gravity mines are big and extraordinarily dense. They're easy to detect at long distances, which makes them pretty useless to use offensively. They're only really good for area denial such as this."

"We could shoot at them, then, from a distance? If they're easy to detect, we should be able to pick them off one by one."

That wouldn't work. "We want this Armitage's

cooperation," said Mattis. "If the first thing we do is start shooting at their only defense, I doubt that would endear us to him."

"We don't know it's their only defense," Lynch cautioned.

That was true. "Guess we'll have to rely on their generosity and whatever insane solution Modi can come up with."

"Aye aye, sir," said Lynch. "I'll get the ship ready to commence Z-space translation."

"Very good. And ask Modi what we can do about the hole in the casemate; if it *does* come to a shooting match, I don't want a missile to come in through there and blast us all to dust."

"Will do."

Mattis left him to his duty and touched his earpiece. "Admiral Yim," he said, smiling widely. A pronounced feeling came from within, as though he had passed some kind of milestone, and for the very first time, talking with Yim didn't seem forced or unnatural, and he wasn't holding back a seething anger. "We're going for a jump. Care to join us?"

Chapter Forty-Nine

Hangar Bay
USS Midway
High Orbit Above New London
Omid Sector

Time passed. Hours. Corrick and Roadie sat, breathing recycled air with nothing else to do but watch their O2 gauges drop. She'd stuck a sealant square over the hole in Roadie's suit, and so far, it had held.

Running out of oxygen wasn't the problem, of course. It never was. The true issue was getting rid of the CO2 they were exhaling. Their suits had a device to break the carbon atom off and turn it back into oxygen, but it couldn't do so faster than they were producing the toxic gas. And there were always losses. Tiny wisps of gas that escaped the nominally sealed suits.

Suits which weren't designed for long-term habitation. But

with the shuttle stuck in the airlock—ahead inaccessible, behind only vacuum—there wasn't anything they could do until the *Midway* got around to rescuing them.

"You doing okay, there, Roadie?" she asked.

"Yeah. Just like I was the last time you asked. And the time before that, and the time before that—"

"Just making conversation," she said. "You got shot. It seems relevant."

Roadie groaned slightly. "Well, ask me something else. *Anything* else. Just not about the leg. It hurts like hell."

No doubt about it. Guano tried to lighten the mood. "Aww, come on. You got a bit of a boo-boo. You'll be fine. Betcha twenty bucks we get rescued before your tank hits a quarter empty."

"Twenty bucks, eh?" Roadie glanced at the meter on his suit—it showed just below half—and then managed a grin. "Hey, if you hate money so much, I'll take some of it off 'ya. Just ... talk about something else."

"Deal." She considered. "Okay, well ... tell me about your family, then. You haven't really talked about them much."

He snorted. "Sometimes I wish my mother had used a gun to kill herself instead of a bottle."

Guano blinked. "That's ... wow. Yeah, pretty personal. Thought we'd start with stuff like where they live, hobbies, that sorta thing."

"Well, drinking was her hobby. It's true," said Roadie. "I don't exactly keep it a secret. I just don't talk about it unless people ask. You asked. So I'm telling." He looked at her oddly. "You don't like to talk about your family either."

"True enough," said Guano. "Because, well, human beings

don't see things as they are; they see them as *we* are. The more I talk about them the more I'm, really, talking about myself." She paused to consider. "Wow. That was pretty damn deep of me, if I say so myself."

Roadie snorted. "Wonder what that says about me."

"Dunno."

Another period of silence. Then her radio crackled. "Hey, Guano?" It was Flatline. "You receiving me?"

Finally, someone else to talk to. Guano thumbed the comm on her hand. "You betcha," she said. "Good to hear your voice, you dipshit. Took your time already."

"Hey, screw you," said Flatline. "Damage control teams have *all kinds* of more important things to do than save a bunch of pilots." She could practically hear him smirking down the line. "You know what they say about pilots. They're just mouth-breathers who couldn't hack it as gunners. You guys are mostly expendable, priority level of: *eh, if we can get around to it*."

She muted the microphone, stifling a playful laugh, until her voice came back to normal. "Well, you damn idiot, we could kind of use your help right about now. Roadie got shot, and he seems okay, but if he dies in here I'm pretty sure the smell could travel through vacuum, so …"

Roadie punched her in the shoulder. In return, Guano playfully clapped on on the thigh, summoning a yelp of pain.

"He okay?" asked Flatline. Obviously one of them had left their mic open.

"Yeah, he's just complain' because he owes me twenty big ones."

"You can't take money from a sick man," protested Roadie, faking a little cough.

"What are you, Canadian?" Guano waggled her fingers. "Pay up, chief."

"I said not to call me that." Reluctantly, Roadie pushed a crumpled note toward her.

She caught it, pocketed it, and opened the frequency again. "Okay, Flatline. What do you need us to do?"

"Well," he said, "we can see you're wedged in there pretty tight. Damage control teams won't be able to cut you out of the wreckage, so we need you to reverse the ship out. I'll guide you on this side, and Frost will guide you on the other side. If something goes wrong, Frost will EVA and come get you. Make sure your helmets are on tight."

"Good morning!" said Frost, Roadie's gunner, her chipper voice beaming across the line. "I'll be your server today! Can I start you off with drinks?"

"Oh boy," said Roadie. "Saved by the gunners."

Guano fiddled with the switches in the cockpit, adjusting settings and diverting what little power the shuttle had left to the engines. "Get ready for full reverse," she said. "Hold tight, this might get a bit rough."

She pulled back on the throttle. The shrieking of scraping metal echoed all around her. The shuttle vibrated with the effort, engines straining. She diverted more power to the ship's propulsion systems. More power. *More* power...

Then, like a cork from a bottle, the shuttle tore loose. It flew across the hangar bay backwards, careening across the vacuum, smashing into the far wall. The hull of the shuttle cracked like an egg, and the ship broke apart into a several pieces, the cockpit detaching and rolling across the landing strip, finally coming to rest face-down on the deck.

Guano's head spun. Roadie had fallen on top of her. They struggled in their heavy space suits, finally disentangling from each other.

Frost's spacesuited face appeared at the torn-off lip of the cockpit. "Are you guys okay?" she asked, her earlier bright tone replaced but concern.

"I'm fine," said Roadie.

"I think I broke another ship," said Guano, staring blankly at the debris scattered over the landing strip.

Chapter Fifty

The streets of Glasgow
Earth

Reflex kicked in, and Bratta scurried out of the corner—

And into the path of his would-be assailant. Something got tangled in the leg department, and they both went flying. Bratta heard a nasty *crack* as his elbow hit the asphalt, pain flaring in his head, hip, and ulnar nerve—common name "funny bone" despite the fact that it was neither a bone nor particularly humorous. He heard another *crack* and winced.

Wait. That crack hadn't been from him. He looked up and saw leather jacket man braced against the corner. There was blood on the wall, at head height. He was in the middle of categorizing just how nasty a situation that could be when Jeannie appeared and shot the man in the back. He staggered backwards and fell on Bratta's prone form with the grace of a poorly-tossed caber.

Bratta yowled and wriggled out from the weight. His ankle hurt something *awful*, but that was nothing to what must have been happening in the big man's head.

Jeannie looked down and him, eyebrow hitting her hairline. "Well done, Steve."

"I am," he said, wringing a scraped hand, "the hero. That we both deserved, and needed. I need a theme song."

"You *did* hit your head hard," she snorted, rifling through the downed man's pockets.

"I did," he agreed from the road. He knew better than to try and sit up until the world had stopped visibly spinning. "What are you doing?"

"Research," she replied.

"When I do research, it usually doesn't look like that," he mused. "I don't use guns, for one."

"Stun-stick, Steve. It's a stun-stick."

"Oh, that's nice. Much less chance of death. I don't want to be an accessory to murder."

"For once, you're making sense. You should get knocked over the head more often. I could help with that, actually." She gave up on the jacket and turned to shirt pockets. "Ah, jackpot!"

"Um, OK?"

Jeannie held up a card. Bratta adjusted his glasses and peered.

"His name is … Callum McIntosh?"

She sighed. "Look. The company. Do you recognize it?"

He squinted as he tried to read in the dim light. "Uh …" It was called Pegasus Security. Didn't mean much to him.

She shook her head. "Damn. Well, I suppose we're waiting

until he wakes up, then."

A thought occurred. "Ah, hang on. Can I see it again?"

Jeannie handed him the card. "That's the security company they hire. I presume."

With the card in both hands, Bratta was able to actually get a good look at it. And then he saw it.

Even with his head pounding and his elbow probably scabbing onto his jacket, he knew that Jeannie had been having far too much fun being mysterious and all-knowing. It was his turn—he was, after all, the scientist here. And he knew something Jeanie didn't.

"The company," he said. "Pegasus Security? I read about them in—well, it doesn't matter. But they're all veterans. And there's only one place where these people are hired in force, apart from Zenith, and that's their home office, a little teeny place on the edge of nowhere. A place called Chrysalis.

"The asteroid?" she asked, her eyes bugging out a little. "You're shitting me."

"You're shitting *yourself*," said Bratta, angrily, then his eyes widened too. "That … came out wrong." He cleared his throat. "But, yes. Chrysalis. Apparently it's a bit infamous because of the mines. You see, the mines protecting the area use a unique gravimetric signature that—"

Jeannie held up her hand. "I know all about Chrysalis," she said, her tone a mixture of anger and … something else he couldn't quite pick up on. "We'll catch a shuttle in under some fake names. Ironically, even if we're caught, nobody will care; what happens on Chrysalis stays on Chrysalis or so they say. What a dump."

"Well," said Bratta, "if you're still keen on saving the

human race, we're going to that *dump*, so … best smile, Jeannie."

She glared at him and he wasn't sure, exactly, what he'd done wrong.

Chapter Fifty-One

Shuttle Zulu-4
High Orbit Above New London
Omid Sector

Mao had lost battles before. The last time she'd woken up in a field hospital on some desolate world, minus a perfectly good arm. This time she'd surrendered on a platform that seemed to be deliberately shut down.

The decision to do so was easy. No sense fighting a whole ship on her own with nothing but Jacobs for backup. When the Chinese marines had boarded, she hadn't resisted, even when they'd clipped on the binders a little too tight.

It only hurt one arm anyway.

The marines shoved her in a seat next to Bagram. The two of them exchanged a slightly defeated glance, but she saw something in his eyes that gave her a little hope. The edge of a smile.

She expected to be returned to the Chinese ship for a friendly chat with Admiral Yim in person, followed by a long stay in a Chinese prison, but instead, the shuttle took her to the *Midway*.

One part elation, one part confusion, one part suspicion. Why would the Chinese willingly give up their prisoner like that?

Mao kept quiet. The shuttle docked with the *Midway*. The shuttlebay was trashed; it had seen some kind of internal battle, almost certainly thanks to her people.

Nice work, ladies and gentlemen. Too bad you couldn't finish the job.

The shuttle loaded up her fellow Forgotten, space-suit clad warriors with their hands in binders. The sight took a little bit of the fire out of her belly. They weren't going to the *Midway* —they were just taking on more prisoners from her.

Soon, the shuttle was back in open space. Oddly enough, the guards who remained to watch them were a mix of Chinese and American soldiers, yet the ranks, the service patches of the marines didn't match up. Some were wearing service ribbons they couldn't possibly have earned, and some had way too many medals for someone of their rank; others, too few.

Mao had been serving with the Forgotten for years. She knew an impromptu, thrown-together unit full of misfits trying to be something they weren't when she saw one.

The shuttle orbited to the other side of New London. Mao saw glimpses of the west side of the planet through the dropship's tiny portholes. Were they going to stand trial on her homeworld? That would be bad. Ever since the Chinese fucked everything up, the courts had been notoriously corrupt. Their likelihood of receiving a fair trial was, ironically, higher with the Chinese. She hated the idea but was forced to concede, intellectually, that it was true. Red bastards … as long as someone could bribe them, or slip them some kind of payment … dammit. Not that it was going to be easy anywhere, but *this*?

Bias would be impossible to avoid. People tended to take a dim view of those trying to murder them all with nuclear fire from orbit.

The shuttle turned toward New London but, right as her heart sunk down into her gut, she realized it wasn't descending through the atmosphere. It was docking with another ship. A light frigate which had no recognizable markings, nor was it a ship in a style which she was familiar. It seemed almost to be a *combination* of Chinese tech, American tech, and some other influences she had no hope of recognizing.

With a faint hiss the shuttle and the strange ship docked.

Moments passed in silence, with the prisoners exchanging confused glances and hushed whispers.

Then, from the front of the ship, came a man she recognized instantly from the news.

United States Senator Peter Pitt. Thin and gaunt like a ghost, wearing clothes that draped off him like excess skin. He scanned the room.

Most of the prisoners had their eyes down, away from the newcomer, but Mao met his with a fierceness that surprised even herself.

Senator Pitt approached her, crouching in front of her seat. "Do you know who I am?" he asked.

She nodded, shifting in her seat, arms bound in front of

her. "Where are you taking us?"

"To a place where you'll be safe," said Senator Pitt. The perfect politicians answer. One, she imagined, that contained absolutely no truth to it at all. "I guarantee it."

"Your guarantee isn't worth much," said Mao, narrowing her eyes. "I wanna see my lawyer."

He laughed—a real, genuine laugh that, while warm on the surface, was cold as ice below. "I'm sure you do. My counterpoint is this: if I simply order it to be so, we could vent this shuttle and everyone in the passenger compartment would asphyxiate. Slowly. Painfully. Not a good way to go."

Threats didn't bother her. "Representation is my right as an American citizen. You can't deny me access to the legal system. And you certainly can't vent us into space without as much as a trial."

"Captain Mao, is it?" asked Senator Pitt. "Do you want a lesson in the American legal system?"

She glowered and said nothing.

"The truth is this: the *system* is and always has been designed to help the people up top and crush the people down low. I am one of the people at the top … and you, you middle aged, fat, broken-down soldiers with a grudge, are the people down below. You're going to get crushed by a system you do not even begin to understand. And besides, you're terrorists. Sending you out the airlock would be a mercy, and I'd be hailed as a hero for doing it."

Bagram spoke up. "Senator, I want your assurance that my men will be treated well; Admiral Mattis gave me his word that we would be."

Senator Pitt's expression remained cold and empty as it

turned toward Bagram. "Admiral Mattis cannot help you any more, little soldier." He stood up and turned toward the cockpit, moving toward the unseen pilots of their small craft. "Captain, set a course for Chrysalis. We have tremendous plans for our *guests.*"

Mao and Bagram exchanged a confused, frightened glance, and she could no longer see that little spark of hope in his eyes.

Chapter Fifty-Two

3:11am local time
Senator Pitt's Office
Washington, DC
Earth

Looking into this himself was proving a lot more difficult than Chuck Mattis had anticipated.

He'd considered multiple ways to break into Senator Pitt's office—pretending he had been un-fired and walking through the front door, trying to recover his old ID credentials, even creating a whole new set of identities and working his way in through an intern position—but the simple solution seemed to be the best. A brick through the window in the ground floor lobby.

No alarms, no sirens. Mattis gave it half an hour just to make sure the cops weren't going to show up. They didn't. So in he went.

Seeing his old workplace, several months removed and shrouded in darkness, was a strange experience. Everything seemed at once familiar and extremely distant; as though some strange, quiet miasma had seeped through every crack and pore in the building. If anyone was there, the *crash* of the brick through the window would have alerted them by now, but still, he crept around as though expecting to be caught at any moment.

Chuck made his way straight to the place where any information of value would be kept. Senator Pitt's office. The largest of all the rooms, but the one containing the least furniture. Just a desk, three filing cabinets stacked neatly up against the far wall, and a floor safe. Chuck knew about the safe. Senator Pitt trusted all his senior staff with the knowledge.

He felt pretty bad about that. Using Senator Pitt's trust against him. But at the same time, any help he had to get the job done was welcome. Speaking of help…

Chuck clipped on his earpiece and dialed Elroy. He picked up immediately.

"Here," said Elroy. "Are you in?"

Are you in? He sounded so excited, breathless even. It bought a smile to Chuck's face. "Yeah, I'm inside."

"Nice going, Secret Agent Chuck."

Cute, but he certainly didn't *feel* like a secret agent. Not even something as cool or interesting as a burglar or a spy. He felt like he was back working for the Senator—running errands, taking memos, and contributing on policy decisions. This was way, way out of his element. But it was necessary.

Chuck came to Senator Pitt's door and gently tested the

handle. Unlocked. He stepped into the office and saw the desk computer was still on. The whole desk was the screen, just how he liked it, and it was even logged in.

Was everything spy-related this easy?

"Okay," said Chuck, rubbing his hands together. "Looks like we're just about done. Just gotta take a look around, see what incriminating things I can find, and then I am *out of here*."

Almost two hours later, and he had found almost nothing.

He searched the desk, completely, and found absolutely nothing of interest. Just personal notes scribbled on pieces of paper and information about meetings long since attended. A scattering of pens and tablet styluses. A bent paperclip. Carefully, Chuck put everything back where he'd found it, giving it a firm wipe with his sleeve to hopefully smudge any fingerprints. He wasn't too worried about the DNA evidence —he'd worked here only a few months ago, so it would be easy to dismiss anything they found—but fresh fingerprints might be damning.

"Are you *sure* there's nothing here?" asked Elroy. "You still haven't searched the computer."

"I know," said Chuck, dejectedly. "Because if it sends out a signal to anyone, there's no way I'll know and frankly, it's the most likely thing to actually be alarmed here."

"Well, yeah," said Elroy. "Even *I* have an alarm on my system and I'm a nobody."

Chuck couldn't help but smile. "You aren't a nobody to me, El."

"How sweet. But still. Be careful, okay? At the first sign of an alarm, you gotta ninja-flip out there. I mean it. Full-cartwheel."

He snorted and, without anything else to do, plugged in his external storage and touched the desk. The screen built into it lit up, straight to the main operating system. Still logged in. Had been for eight days, according to the readout at the top left hand corner of the screen.

Eight days? Chuck frowned. He could understand leaving a machine logged in overnight by mistake, once, but for eight days … Senator Pitt must be off-world. During campaign season?

Something about this didn't feel right, but he had no time to think about it. "No sign of an alarm," he said, touching the screen and scrolling through various files. He selected everything and began copying it to the external drive; no sense reading it now, there would be time enough for that later.

One file snagged. It wouldn't copy; flagged as open. He told the computer to skip copying that one and made a duplicate of it, then started copying that one. The name stuck out.

SPECTRE

Ding. Both copies completed at roughly the same time. Spectre must have been big—lots of images, movies, and audio logs. Possibly even 3d scenes modeled with point data.

"Okay," he said, to Elroy, "I got it. Time to get out of here." Chuck unplugged his device and looked up.

A man stood in the doorway, a pistol comfortably cradled in both hands. He casually raised the gun and pointed it at Chuck.

"Well now, fancy seeing you here Mr. Pitt," said the man,

pulling back the hammer.

Chapter Fifty-Three

Captain's Ready Room
USS Midway
En Route to Kepler-1011 system

Mattis called Modi up out of Engineering and, with Lynch, the three of them retired to his ready room.

"Are you sure this is a good idea?" asked Lynch, his brow furrowed in worry. "We really don't know what we're sailing into over there."

"The gravity mines are a known problem," said Modi. "The technology behind them is very well understood. Granted, we won't have a simple way of bypassing their assault if it comes to that, but, at the very least, I'm expecting no surprises."

Mattis frowned slightly. "I was kind of hoping you'd tell me that there was a simple, risk-free way of disabling these mines, Modi." He held up his hand to cut off the guy's inevitable complaining. "And no. Obviously, that was sarcasm. Just—anything you can give me?"

Modi shrugged. "There is not much, to tell you the truth. Gravity mines work because they're dog-simple. A sensitive electromagnet detects the presence of metal hulls even at significant distances. Once detected, the mines activate a chemical rocket which propels them toward the target at high speed. When they get close—and close is more than enough—they activate, and everything in the blast radius is torn apart by the momentary gravity differential. The metal of the ship's hull might survive intact, but there is simply no way for a human crew to survive that kind of … stretching."

"Can we manipulate the ship's artificial gravity to help mitigate the damage?"

Modi snorted dismissively. "Our internal gravity system is rated for a maximum of 1.1g. That's like asking if wearing a pillow as armor will help protect you from a cannonball by reducing its velocity. Technically, yes, but by such a statistically small margin that it would make absolutely no practical difference to the outcome."

Lynch clicked his tongue. "Can Admiral Yim be trusted with this information?"

Nagging doubt tugged at him, lingering mistrust that whispered dark thoughts into his ear, but Mattis pushed it away. Yim had shown that despite their past, for now at least, he wasn't their enemy.

"He can," said Mattis, with as much strength as he could muster. "Pretty sure. He's just like me, in a way—obviously playing for a different side, but he cares about doing the right thing. He cares about his duty." Mattis thought of his brother,

Phillip—unstoppable images of his face flashing into his head —but for the first time since his death he felt vaguely at peace with everything that had happened, and he meant it when he followed with, "The past is the past."

"That'll do for now," said Lynch, nodding resolutely. "We can get through this, sir."

His communicator chirped. Mattis, almost on instinct, touched the answer key. It was the communications officer. "Sir, we're coming up on Chrysalis."

Mattis straightened his back. Time to be a commander and worry about everything else later. The three of them moved out to the bridge. Lynch took the XO's position and Modi hung around near the back.

"Commence Z-space translation," he said, moving up to the captain's chair and sliding into it. "Bring us back into the real world. And get ready to send out a signal to anyone who'll listen."

Chapter Fifty-Four

Senator Pitt's Office
Washington, DC
Earth

Chuck stared down the barrel of a gun.

He really had no experience with this kind of thing. He'd never been mugged, or attacked, and apart from schoolyard fights he'd never experienced any kind of violence in his life. So he just stood there, mouth agape, as the strange man pulled back the hammer and leveled the weapon at his head.

"W—wait," he stammered, thrusting his hands up above his head. "Stop. Don't shoot."

The man stepped forward, into the light. He was an older guy, about forty, grizzled, and clad in a finely pressed suit. He had a narrow brimmed hat on his head—like something out of a detective movie. The gun in his hand was polished chrome. Chuck didn't know much about guns, but this one looked deadly.

"I'm hoping," said the man, "that it doesn't come to that. But you're really putting me on the spot, Chuck Mattis."

The use of his name startled him and, for a second, Chuck almost completely forgot Elroy was on the phone to him. "Who are you talking to?" his husband asked.

"How do you know my name?" asked Chuck, ignoring Elroy for now. "Who are you?"

"Who I am is unimportant."

"What do you want?"

The man smiled uncomfortably. "It's not about what I want," he said. "It's about what *you* want. Assuming, of course, you value your continued health. You're asking the wrong people the wrong questions, and you need to just go home to your sick kid and your loving husband and give this whole thing up." The man's tone was at once kind and hard. "Live a good life, Chuck Mattis. There's no need for you to end up like your father."

He stared. "What's wrong with my Dad?"

"Nothing," said the man. "Yet."

The ominous threat hung in the air. The silence grew to be unbearable; Elroy was saying things into his ear that he didn't even hear, but that probably subconsciously made his growing panic even worse. Chuck, too, just started saying *things*; unconscious word vomit that in no way resembled sentences or meaningful information. Just words. Words about the aliens and mutants, words about the attack on Earth, words about Admiral Jack Mattis and his seeming predilection toward getting himself into every damn situation that cropped up.

None of it seemed to do any good.

"Enough," said the man, shaking his head. "Shut up."

It was time to be quiet. Chuck took a deep breath and composed himself, pointing a shaky finger to his external device. "I'm guessing you want that," he said.

"Only," said the man, seemingly full of patience for Chuck's display, "if you don't think you can send out the message yourself."

"What?" Chuck sniffled, wiping his face with the back of his hand. "What are you talking about?"

The man inclined his head toward the external device, sitting in the middle of Senator Pitt's desk. "Had a chance to look at any of that stuff yet?"

"No."

"You should. Check out files in the folder X-3711b."

With a shaking hand, Chuck touched the screen and scrolled through the folders. X-3711b … there. He opened it. It contained a series of video files with seemingly random names. Ten in all.

203301
446469
953427
293268
981326
038586
768594
564494
422634
471690

"What am I looking at?" asked Chuck.

"Videos. Videos that should interest you. Try it and see."

He tapped on one at random. *038586.*

It was a video shot in a starkly lit room, a heavy light casting sharp shadows across every surface. A creature lay splayed out on a metal table, its body pried open like a clam. Most of its organs lay in nearby jars or on metal trays. A woman dressed in a medical lab coat stood with something in her hand, inspecting a small thing the camera couldn't quite catch.

"-bject 0385868221, classification 211 bravo. We call this one Irene." The woman put down the device, her face a mask of frustration and disgust. It was a removed eyeball. "This one is contaminated just like the rest of the batch. The low gravity and solar radiation that bake every fucking living thing on this rock destroy their eyes. Apart from what we have in our labs, Chrysalis's general population seems to be unaffected. Must be some regression in the genome …" The woman sighed. "Like I fucking need more of *those*. Autopsy concludes at 11:39pm." She tossed the eyeball down in disgust. "Hopefully the next one will be—"

The video cut out.

"Interesting," said the man. "Don't you think?"

Chuck stared at him as, slowly, the truth dawned through his panic stricken mind. "You don't work for Senator Pitt, do you?"

The stranger's smile widened. "I do not."

"You're here for the same things I am."

"Naturally," said the man. "It's no coincidence we're here at the same time, I imagine. I'm guessing you saw the same thing I did; Senator Pitt travelled off-world three days ago, and surveillance of his house showed he packed enough clothes to be gone for at least a week. Last night was a bust, of course, due to the construction being performed across the road—too many security cameras, especially at night, always on the lookout for thieves—but tonight … tonight was perfect. No moon, and the block party down the street would muffle the sounds of intrusion. I came in through the car park, of course—a bug I planted a few weeks ago in the system's automatic doors. I'm guessing you came in through the ceiling however—bold move, but faster. I like your style."

Chuck stammered slightly. "Uhh, no. I, um, threw a brick through the front door and I came here because it was the first night I didn't have to look after my son."

The man stared. Then laughed. "I believe you, Chuck Mattis." He held out his hand. "Call me John Smith."

John Smith? Chuck hesitated, then took the hand, giving it a firm shake. "That sounds like a fake name," he said, before he could fully think through what he was saying.

"Of course it is." Smith nodded to the portable hard drive. "I have a contact in the media who'd be dying to get hold of these files. If you don't mind—" he held out hand, touching a switch on the underside of a ring on his right finger. The device flashed as it copied—hopefully copied, not moved—the data from Chuck's device. "If the next piece of the puzzle is on Chrysalis, we should probably consider going there right away."

"Yeah," said Chuck, nodding. "I … guess so. I can send Martha a message, let her know what we've found. She can meet us there."

"Martha? Martha Ramirez, the reporter?"

Chuck nodded.

"My, you are more resourceful than I anticipated. Do it." Smith pulled out his phone. "I have a chess piece near Chrysalis, I'll reach out to them. See if I can get them to do a bit of the digging for me before we get there."

Chess piece? "Okay," said Chuck. He tapped out a message on his device, sent it, then considered. "Before we head out, though, you should know: there were more files there. On Pitt's computer."

"Mmm," said Smith. "Mostly trash. Nothing relevant to our interest. Election promises made in public which he didn't intend to keep, and election promises made in private which he did. The usual political fare. Nothing at all special in any way."

"Except Spectre," said Chuck, warily. "That directory was encrypted."

Smith's eyebrows shot up as he casually slid his gun into his holster. "Spectre?"

"Yes," said Chuck. "It was spelt the British way. With an "re" at the end."

Smith's expression fell. "If that's who I think it is, Chuck Mattis, you are in *way* over your head."

Chapter Fifty-Five

Six hours journey from Chrysalis
Kepler-1011 system

The *Midway* dropped out of Z-space, reappearing into reality in a sea of multicolored light. Right away, Mattis touched the button to open communications with Chrysalis.

"Attention Chrysalis station, this is Admiral Jack Mattis, commanding officer of the USS *Midway* of the United States Navy. I'm here with Admiral Yim of the People's Republic of China Army Navy, and although our presence must be alarming to you, I want to assure you that we're not here in force. If we were, we would have bought more ships." He paused to gather his thoughts. "We're aware of the minefield you have protecting your section of the belt. It's not our intention to harm you or your inhabitants in any way. I understand you'll be reluctant to let a United States naval vessel and a Chinese naval vessel dock at the same time, but now hear this: we're here to speak to John Armitage for the express purpose of hearing his grievances so that they can be peacefully relayed to the governments of both our nations. It is not our intention to do anything else while at Chrysalis station." Another pause. "Please transmit your reply when you are ready."

He sat back in his chair as the communications technicians primed the long range antenna and dispatched his message. They didn't have to wait long for a response.

"USS *Midway*, this is Chrysalis station. You are cleared to proceed through the minefield."

Lynch grimaced. "Guess we find out if they want to kill us now, right?"

"Pretty much," said Mattis.

The next six hours were spent in relative silence, the *Midway* steaming toward the largest rock in the system's asteroid belt, the eyes of all her crew on the long range radars. The mines drifted in a lazy orbit around Chrysalis, gentle and predictable in their paths, but their presence was unnerving. Mattis kept the Z-space drive fully charged with the hope that, if a mine did start towards them, the ship could jump away before the destructive device pulverized them.

Thankfully their precautions seemed unnecessary, for as they drifted further and further into the minefield the lethal devices gave no sign they were hostile.

After a full shift, the *Midway* docked at Chrysalis station.

"Get Modi," said Mattis. "You're with me again. We'll meet Yim down there."

"Sir," said Lynch, his tone a little more formal than normal, "we shouldn't go alone this time. There's no need for the three of us to get onboard Chrysalis together." Lynch took a steadying breath. "As your XO, I should warn you, taking half your senior staff off the ship and putting them onboard this 'roid where we don't know the lay of the land—that put your ship at a high degree of risk."

He knew it was true. And he'd even promised himself that next time he wouldn't just go down there but, well, the only one he was accountable to for that was himself.

"Unfortunately," said Mattis, "as much as I agree with you—and I do—I feel like if we show up with armed marines that undermines our stated goal of diplomacy, don't you think?" He smiled slightly. "We should do what we would do if this was a leisurely dock at some US-friendly port. Just waltz on in like we're about to spend a whole bunch of money on overpriced booze. If nothing else, it'll be disarming. Might put them off balance."

"Guess so," said Lynch. "Just doing my job."

Mattis clapped him on the shoulder. "I know. C'mon. It'll be fun."

"That's what you said about New London," said Lynch, his face souring instantly.

"Everything turned out okay in the end," said Mattis.

Lynch looked like he inhaled a lemon. "That's a matter of opinion, sir," he growled.

"Trust me," said Mattis, "this time will be different."

Chapter Fifty-Six

Chrysalis Station
Kepler-1011 system

Chrysalis Station was at once so alike New London, and yet so different. An asteroid with hollowed out sections, it had gaudy shopfronts and markets packed with people. It more resembled a center of commerce rather than a corporate headquarters, although Mattis had to begrudgingly accept that a planet's population, even a tiny one, had to shop somewhere.

Despite the heavy commercial presence, the people of Chrysalis seemed much more interested in partying than anything else. Glass lined the streets, trash piled up in places where it had obviously spent some time decaying, and if there was any kind of law enforcement or security on the entire rock, there was absolutely no sign of them.

Still, as he, Modi, Yim, and Lynch wove their way through the raucous, bustling crowds he couldn't help but feel his earlier words—that they should pretend they were all here to spend money—were eerily prophetic.

"How far away is our rendezvous point?" asked Lynch, struggling to keep up. His eyes flicked from side to side as they passed people. "I hate this place."

"You hate every place we visit," said Modi, matter-of-factually.

"I *especially* hate this place," said Lynch, bitterly. "Lots of remote outposts have problems with pirates, thieves, criminals—all that crap. But not Chrysalis. Why? The mines keep them honest. Nobody attacks this little rock. Nobody steals from it—at least nobody hoping to escape with their lives. They wouldn't get far before, you know, *boom*. So nobody tries." His voice was painted with sarcasm. "Death by minefield for stealing. Just lovely."

"It doesn't seem so bad," said Mattis, stepping around a person in the middle of the road. He *hoped* they were merely sleeping. "And I don't plan on stealing anything."

Lynch's whole face contorted. "Just doesn't seem right to me."

"It might seem odd," said Yim, "to have business spring up in the area, but businesses want steady streams of customers and security to make sure they don't get robbed. What does Chrysalis have? A huge supply of veterans, and, thanks to the Chinese Navy's mine-laying devision, a unique security element. It's safe, it's prosperous, and we have the People's Republic to thank for it."

"Great," snapped Lynch. "Feel free to pass along my congratulations. Where are we meeting this Forgotten guy again?"

"The communication was simple," said Modi. "At the *Blessed Humanity* coffee shop. Apparently Mister Armitage has a fondness for the product."

Mattis didn't like it at all. "Yim," he said. "I thought you said that the only non-Chinese worlds that *Blessed Humanity* has license to operate is on Zenith and New London."

"That's what I thought," said Yim, shrugging helplessly. "Who knows. Maybe it's an illegal rip-off."

Maybe, but even so, it seemed odd. Suspicious. Out of place.

Soon the sign loomed, familiar to him now. The neon flashing, steaming cup. "Looks legit to me," said Mattis, and with no further ado, pushed open the narrow door that lead into the shop.

Surprisingly it was empty. The stools were clean and barely marked, the floor waxed but covered in a thin film of dust. Behind the bar, casually polishing a glass, was a man Mattis's age—grey around the temples, with a neatly clipped beard.

"Admiral Mattis," he said, smiling politely. "Heard you're looking for me."

"John Armitage." Mattis sat at one of the stools. Yim sat to his left, Lynch on his right, and Modi stood around awkwardly. "We've come a long way to have a chat with you."

"You look tired," said Armitage, appraising them all in turn.

Mattis smiled half-heartedly. "It's been a long trip, and a six hour journey through a minefield to get here. But I'm used to it. Nobody knows tired like parents or soldiers."

"What about soldier parents?"

A thought of Chuck flashed into his head. "We long for

the sweet, sweet release of death. Or, you know, so much caffeine our hearts explode."

Armitage nodded politely. "Here," he said, reaching below the bar and withdrawing three steaming mugs of brown coffee topped with foam. "This will help." There were eight more mugs, similarly steaming.

"You expecting more guests?" asked Mattis, cautiously.

"Only you. I expected more of your team, to be honest. And none of these people have the look of marines about them."

Yim seemed to almost snatch the drink, sniffing it eagerly, a broad smile crossing his face. He muttered something eager in Chinese and sipped it, nodding approvingly.

Encouraged by this, Mattis sipped his, too. It was rich and quite sweet, but delightful. "Never understood why," he said, putting his mug down on the bench, "that sane, God-fearing men would even consider polluting perfectly good coffee with milk and sugar."

"But Admiral," said Yim, a milk-moustache on his face, "that's the best part."

"Coffee's just like my old girlfriend," said Lynch, sipping it cautiously. "Bitter, overrated, and it's not even worth considering unless you can change some essential part."

"Mister Lynch, I'm not sure there's room on my boat for filthy coffee heathens."

Lynch raised the mug and drank again.

"All very amusing," said Armitage, "but I'm guessing the four of you didn't come here to compliment my hot drinks."

"No," said Mattis. "We're here to talk. Specifically, to listen to you and what you have to say. To see if we can't defuse the situation we find ourselves in. These attacks on military assets is unacceptable, and to be blunt, if you don't stop, you're all going to die."

"Good." Armitage casually folded his arms. "I just want to let you know, Admiral, that this shop might seem empty and safe, but I want you to know that if any of your hands touch the metal on your belts, the only thing left of you will be the 'Admiral Jack Mattis And Friends Memorial Crater' where this fine establishment once stood. I'm sure I don't need to go into the details of exactly how this will be accomplished."

The threat, so boldly stated, stole a little of the humor from their faces. Yim's in particular, who seemed to take the destruction of the coffee house as a personal affront.

"So," said Mattis, "we're here to listen. That won't work unless you talk."

Armitage pulled up a chair. "Of course." He took a breath. "Admiral Mattis, I'm not sure you remember, but we actually met before. Once, right after the war. It was at the memorial for the *Saragossa*." The ship his brother had died on. Destroyed by Admiral Yim's ship.

Yim looked away, unable to look at Mattis.

"I don't really remember much about that day," said Mattis, honestly.

"I'm not surprised." Armitage sipped his drink, smiling wistfully. "Ahh, Admiral. If only you'd seen her. The *Saragossa* was the finest ship I'd ever served upon. Transferring to the *Yorktown* was bittersweet. I didn't go down with the ship, but, at the same time, my post just wasn't the same. I got out when my tour was done. No war, no need for me to be there."

"I understand," said Mattis. "I stayed in, but … the last

war isn't something easily left behind. I think, in some ways, we're still fighting it."

Armitage smiled like a jackal. "I knew you'd understand." He leaned forward, over the counter. "Sir, you need to listen to me. Friendship Station was the beginning. The Chinese—"

Mattis held up his hand. "I brought Admiral Yim to talk to you because I *knew* this was going to be an issue. Admiral Yim, the man sitting right there, was the CO of that station and I *hated* him. I, too, thought it was a Chinese fleet coming for us in the beginning." He took a deep breath. "But I promise you this, Armitage, I promise you; I've seen the face of our enemy. It's not the People's Republic."

Slowly, slowly, Armitage's face fell. "You can't honestly believe—"

"I was *there*," stressed Mattis. "I fought them myself. I saw the—" he almost said *bodies*. "*Ships* they had. The technology. It wasn't just an evolution of Chinese tech, it was something else entirely."

Armitage sipped his drink. "I thought," he said, at length, "that you were one of the good guys. A good man. That when I explained things to you, you would help us."

"I like to think I am a good man," said Mattis. "Maybe I'm not. But if you're just going to peddle the same conspiracy theory crap that the other Forgotten are trying to shovel, I'm not buying." He knew he was mangling his metaphors but he didn't care.

"If so, you're on the wrong side of this war. I hope you can see it in time."

Mattis had always been in the military. It had been his life, his career. Unlike Armitage he never got out; he knew the system better than basically anyone.

The military kept secrets. It had to. A nation's armed forces couldn't exist as an open book. But secrets bred conspiracies; from Area 51 to the F-117a "Stealth Fighter" Nighthawk, to the first combat starship, there were always conspiracy theories.

But, just like the F-117a, sometimes a conspiracy theory turned out to be true. Maybe there was something more to it—not the Chinese, of course. But *something*. Something that had been missed by all and sundry.

Like that the alien attackers were not, in fact, aliens, but humans from the future. Kind of a pretty big detail, and one he didn't want to let slip.

So Mattis lied again. He was getting mighty sick of doing that.

"Here's what I can do," he said. "I can talk to the President. I can get her to look further into this. Open another—yes, *another*—inquiry into what happened. I can't guarantee it, but I can lean on her as hard as I can. But you should be prepared for the possibility the results will be the same."

"Which is why," said Armitage, "I cannot accept it."

It was tempting to tell the truth in that moment, but his rational side prevented him. Mattis held his hands out. "I don't know what else I can do for you."

Armitage groaned softly as he slid out of his seat, onto his feet. "Then I guess we're done here," he said. "Talk to your President. Get her to look into this again, and don't take no for an answer." He considered, almost as an afterthought, "and Mattis, tell her: *There's a beautiful symmetry to all this. A lie got you into this problem, a lie might get you out.*"

He squinted. "What's that supposed to mean?"

"She'll know," said Armitage, and then he slowly turned toward the door toward the kitchen. "I'm sorry, Admiral Mattis. I wished this had gone better for us both."

Mattis sipped his coffee gently. "So do I."

Chapter Fifty-Seven

Bridge
CNS Luyang III
Orbit above Chrysalis
Kepler-1011 system

They'd hit a dead end. Yim played through everything in his head, his neurons lit up by the infusion of the galaxy's best coffee. There was a way past this. He could feel it.

A video had been leaked to the galaxy's media, showing that the alien creatures who attacked Earth were out there. Being kept under wraps. That had taken place on either New London or Zenith. They'd investigated, found links to a steroid company that employed veterans.

The Forgotten were, almost exclusively, American veterans of the Sino-American war. So they were here, at Chrysalis, to speak to the leader of the Forgotten and hear their complaints. Which they had done. They didn't want to walk.

But now where? Where was the next step, the next piece in the puzzle?

It didn't make sense. It felt like a dead end but it shouldn't have been. Yim put his chin in his hands, staring at the various monitors and displays around him. What were they missing here?

No answers came. Only the soft beeping of his monitors and the occasional report from his bridge crew.

Was Mattis holding something back? That seemed unlikely. There was still bad blood there, it was true—he could expect no less, given the death of Mattis's brother at his hands—but they had come a long way. Mattis had trusted him and in return Yim knew he should show some trust back. The American wasn't betraying them.

So what was it?

Yim watched Chrysalis spin slowly, a rock in the middle of nowhere. He reached out his hand, closing his fingers around it as though squeezing it. No answers came out. Blood from a stone…

His implant vibrated, signaling an incoming transmission.

John Smith. The *other* American he didn't quite trust.

Well, now. Yim opened the connection, once more dropping his voice to a whisper. "This is Yim."

"Admiral," said Smith, a voice he had hoped not to hear from again. "I need a favor from you."

"Favors," whispered Yim evenly, "do not come cheap. What kind of favor?"

"Rook to E4." They had all kinds of code words for these kinds of things. This one meant *infiltration*. "You'll want to head down to Chrysalis, assuming you haven't already been there, and check out the east end of the market. There's a factory there, a small one, but you'll want to go light. Bring a friend if you have to."

"Why?" asked Yim, squinting slightly. "There's nothing—"

"Go to the factory," said Smith. "And you'll find your answers."

The communication ended. Yim took a deep breath. "Okay," he said to the room. "It's time for us to make our move. Prepare a shuttle."

Chapter Fifty-Eight

MaxGainz Facility
Floor 1
Hidden Genetics Lab
Chrysalis
Kepler-1011 system

Senator Pitt stepped out of the elevator. Floor One was accessible only by a special key; it was an industrial level formed in a naturally occurring fissure in the asteroid. Craggy and broken, with antennas and computers jutting out of the rock walls. Row after row of large oval tanks, each big enough to hold a person, stood vertically. Hundreds of them. They shone with a green, inner glow. A gantry extended above each tank, complete with a thick guard rail.

The last time he came here, he had been alone. Not this time. General Lok Tsai—tall bastard he was, like a willow tree—stood beside someone he didn't recognize. A short,

European man in a bowling hat, with an enormous gut and a round, childlike, clean-shaven face. He carried a briefcase in his left hand and couldn't have been more than twenty.

"Who's this?" he asked the General, eyeing the rotund man.

"This is Spectre," said General Tsai. "One of our most powerful assets."

Strange, General Tsai was not usually the kind of man who would fall for such simple deceptions. Senator Pitt immediately shook his head. "That's not Spectre. Spectre is a woman."

"Appearances," said the man, in a chipper, educated, male English accent. He put a small device to his throat and his voice immediately changed to female. "Can be deceiving. And, have a care, General. You are as much my *asset*, as I am yours."

It seemed absurd. Senator Pitt squinted. "You don't look like the kind of spy who has access to the secrets of various world governments."

Spectre—or at least the person pretending to her—smiled happily. "And what exactly should such a person look like? A black leather clad femme-fatal with a pistol in each hand? A sexy, tall, suited man able to seduce anything with two legs, and sometimes not even that discriminatory? If I looked like a spy, Senator Pitt, I would not be doing my job very well at all, would I?"

That was a good point he was unable to refute. "I just didn't imagine you to be," he paused, giving the man a critical eye. "So … out of shape."

"You wound me with your assumptions of my incompetence." If Spectre was in any way offended he didn't show it, turning to General Tsai with a smile on his face. "Now that the very good Senator has bought us what we need, shall we proceed?"

"Of course," said General Tsai, motioning over his shoulder. From behind and above him, the prisoners Pitt had brought were being led onto the gantries. Each one of them had hoods over their faces, and they shuffled forward, chains on their arms and legs. The guards led them before the tanks, one each, and they were made to stand over them.

"You did well bringing these to us," said Spectre, finally turning back to him. "They're *perfect*."

"As I said," said Senator Pitt. "Untraceable people, in exchange for my son."

"Of course," said Spectre, tilting his head back slightly. "Commence stage one."

As one, the marines pushed the prisoners into the tanks. They fell in with a splash, sinking into the green fluid, and then the top sealed over them. A mesh, keeping them in.

"What are you doing to them?" demanded Senator Pitt.

Spectre turned to him, a confused look on his face. "What do you think?"

Each of the prisoners kicked and struggled inside the tanks, trying to force their way up through the grates that sealed them in; to bend them, break them. The bars were thick metal, holding them under. The liquid churned as they kicked, frothing up bubbles that overflowed and ran down the sides of the tanks.

Soon their struggles ended, and, one by one, they began floating limply in the water.

"There," said Spectre, "much better."

"You killed them," said Senator Pitt, a bitter edge to his voice he was unable to disguise.

"Come now," sand General Tsai, simply. "What did you *expect* to happen?"

He'd expected a lot of things. Most notably, a clean death for them, but not this.

Spectre touched something inside his jacket. The tanks churned again as some force agitated them, making them vibrate as though they were experiencing some kind of seismic distress.

The bodies inside began to hiss and smoke, dissolving as though suddenly exposed to some kind of intensely powerful acid; their flesh was stripped away, followed soon by their muscles and tendons. The corpses broke apart, drifting down to the bottom of the tank, leaving only their skeletons and the occasional implant. One of them had a prosthetic arm that sank to the bottom with a faint *clink*.

"Can't make something from nothing," replied Spectre, as though he were discussing composting techniques. "Don't worry. The biomass will be put to very good use."

Senator Pitt said nothing, staring wide-eyed at the metal arm floating in the tank as it settled down toward the bottom.

"Cheer up, Senator," said Spectre, watching the prosthetic arm as it, too, started to smolder, "soon you'll have your request fulfilled."

Chapter Fifty-Nine

Blessed Humanity *Coffee House*
Chrysalis
Kepler-1011 System

Bratta poked his signal booster with a screwdriver. The dratted thing had been working a minute ago, why had it decided to disconnect from the external hard drive now? The device tended to be finicky, but this was outside its usual range of deviant behavior. Which was a pity, because it meant he'd lost signal, and he wasn't about to connect to the café's free wifi. He pocketed his miniature toolkit, and closed down the news websites he'd had open on his third phone this month. So much for background research.

Jeannie had been gone a long time.

Bratta looked around, scanning for anyone who looked like a threat—not that there would have been much he could do if he did find anyone, he was still sore from the Glasgow *incident.* His injuries weren't medically significant—he'd escaped a concussion by what felt like a hair—but they'd stiffened up in a most inconvenient way. This kind of outcome, he thought indignantly, was why he made a habit of avoiding any physical exertion past the healthy minimum in the first place.

Surely Jeannie should have been back by now.

He spun the phone around on the table's dubiously-clean surface. It had been a mistake to let Jeannie go talk to the home office alone. Certainly, they knew his face better than they knew hers, and she *was* a trained investigator, but they'd already threatened her with violence once, and she deserved—

He put that train of thought on hold. Actually, as far as he could tell Jeannie didn't really *deserve* anything from him. She was rude, cold, obsessively dedicated to the pursuit of justice, and had always been. That, he knew better than anyone. She'd put his life back in danger without so much as asking, and dragged him into a life of crime with no consideration for what he might have wanted. *And* she'd mocked him when he'd brought out his favorite toy to go through his files en route from Earth, which was deeply unfair when one considered that he could say with 98.1% certainty that the combination battery and hard drive was no longer a fire hazard. To be perfectly frank, she could go to damnation for all he cared—not that he saw any particular benefit in adhering to a religious creed. It was the metaphor that counted, he assured his disgruntled inner atheist.

"Penny for your thoughts?"

"I don't like you," he replied before processing that Jeannie's voice meant that Jeannie was back, and Jeannie's expression meant that Jeannie was now feeling insulted.

"Thank you, Steve, you make my day."

He glowered and said nothing.

She pulled out a chair on the other side of the table. "Well, the corporate scumbags didn't give me anything. *"Of course, Ms. Tafola, we will investigate your concerns as appropriate in the shortest possible time frame."* "*No, Ms Tafola, we are not manufacturing aliens in an attempt to destroy the human race, that would be against company policy.*" "*If you will please leave now, Ms Tafola, then there'll be no trouble.*" Just really fascinating stuff, you know? How did it go on your end?"

Bratta held up the signal booster. "My net connection broke."

Jeannie seemed to take that remarkably in-stride, which was worrying. "And did you find anything out? Anything at all?"

He set his lips as he pocketed the booster. Realistically, resistance was futile. She'd probably find a way to drag him into conversation, anyway. "It depends how you define 'anything,' really. I couldn't find any coverage about the aliens, but there's been a lot of resistance activity about the US and Chinese peace. Old US marines—um, leader was this old bloke called Ryan or something?—they took over a Chinese embassy and then they got into a space battle over New London. Apparently, they hijacked the planet's Goalkeeper. Other than that, only your zombie-less zombie apocalypse. Lots of supply shortages, no security or military action taken by governments, but people are forming their own groups."

"Huh. Even quieter than I would have thought."

"Germany is asking questions. But other than that, yes—I haven't even seen *one* expert opinion on the video."

"The Chrysalis network might be censored."

He nodded. "That seems likely."

The conversation dissolved into silence. Jeannie was glaring at something on the back wall, over his head. Bratta got the signal booster out again and started tinkering with the connector. It didn't really help his mood, especially when a tiny nut rolled off the table and he realized he didn't have spares. He stopped to retrieve it, looking at the coffee line on his way up. Then froze.

"Jeannie?"

"What?"

He pointed to a woman wearing a thick coat, hair done up in a bun. "Is that … Martha Ramirez? Your reporter? Getting coffee?"

Jeannie snapped around. "I—you're right. Yes, it is. Oh my god."

"Um. Do we do something?"

She shook her head like she was trying to clear it.

"Yes, we do," she said, and left the table.

Bratta found himself left to fiddle with the connector for five or so minutes—not that they were particularly productive minutes, he couldn't help but to glance up every few seconds.

Eventually, Jeannie started making her way back, reporter in tow. Bratta swallowed. Science Communication had been his worst subject at college, and he'd found it extremely uncomfortable to deal with reporters and journalists since. The art of employing psychological *tricks*, rather than data and logic, had always been a distant, unknowable, and vaguely disreputable discipline.

"…And this is Steve Bratta, the man who took the video I

gave you." Jeannie's voice gave him little time to react.

The other woman, Martha Ramirez, nodded and treated him to a polished smile. "It's a pleasure to meet you, Mr. Bratta."

Bratta scrambled to his feet to shake her proffered hand. "It's a pleasure to meet you too, Ms. Ramirez."

Jeannie offered Ms. Ramirez a seat. "We were just pooling resources, Steve."

Despite himself, a spark of hope started to incubate in his chest. "Do you know anything more about the situation, Ms. Ramirez?"

"Please, Martha," she said. "And, well, perhaps. I understand you have some ideas about what might be going on here?"

"Well, er, I wouldn't say 'some ideas,'" he replied, wondering just what insane pile of leapt-to conclusions Jeannie had fed her. "I have a hypothesis but it's quite unfounded, really. We haven't actually been able to find out much. MaxGainz, ah, don't seem to be interested in our own gains, so to speak."

Martha smiled tolerantly. Not that he could complain, it was a better reaction than he got from most. "Ms Tafola thinks they might be participating in illegal human experimentation."

He adjusted his glasses. "That certainly *could* be the case. In fact, I rather suspect it is the case, or rather, at least part of it. The creatures' anatomical structure is remarkably familiar. But, just because they're human-like, doesn't necessarily mean that MaxGainz are involved in … *manufacturing* them. It could be they split off from humanity some time ago and this company is really a government front to keep that a secret. Or … the company could have been targeted for their resources. That's what they told us at any rate. I could be simply *wrong* … without an open mind, one cannot expect to learn."

Jeannie rolled her eyes. "Thanks, Steve. Look, we know they're hiding something—they all but sent someone to *assault* us, the guy tailing us had a stun-stick—and Steve was mugged on his way from Zenith, and we know they got uncomfortable when Steve started telling them their labs could make monsters like that. I tried to drill the home office here—wouldn't have been safe to send Steve, they know him—and they gave me hours of red tape and some hot air. Martha, we want to help. Is there anything else we can do?"

Martha nodded. "My other sources have led me to Chrysalis, too. Something's up with this place, and I can't for the life of me get a *why*. Although if even one of Mr. Bratta's hypotheses are right," she laughed a little, "I'm not surprised by the security.

"Still," she continued, glancing at her phone for a second "if you want to help, I have a … friend, who appears to still be in the system that might help us get the answers we all need. If nothing else, he's good for barging into places and getting peoples' attention.

"Who's that?" said Jeannie.

Ramirez smiled uncomfortably. "I hope neither of you have any issues with the US Navy?"

Chapter Sixty

Bridge
USS Midway
Orbit above Chrysalis
Kepler-1011 system

The shuttle back to the *Midway* had been a short trip that felt much longer than it really was. No ideas presented themselves as he, Modi, and Lynch made their way to the bridge. No solution to their problems.

"Well," said Mattis, a dejected edge to his voice as he sank into the Captain's chair, "that sucked."

"I concur," said Modi, standing beside him. "I certainly anticipated things going differently."

"Useless," said Lynch from his console, his face an angry, frustrated scrunched up ball of Texan anger. "A waste of our dang time. We're back to square one."

It was almost impossible to believe that they had come so

far to get *nothing.* "Great," said Mattis, more darkly than he intended. "I'm sure that will be a big comfort to the poor dumb bastards who get torn in half the next time these creatures get out. And who knows what the hell else is locked away in those vaults…."

Whoever was behind this, whoever had managed to capture and control these creatures, it wouldn't stay contained on some far-away asteroid. Mattis didn't know *why* these creatures were being kept here, but like the secrecy around developing a weapon, nobody operated that way unless there was a plan, even theoretically, to *use* said weapons.

Where would next be hit? Earth? What would be the result then?

They couldn't fail. It was too dangerous. And if they just walked away now, whoever was on that asteroid would burn everything to the ground and they would never know the truth.

And where had these creatures been captured from? One invading vessel had escaped six months ago, and disappeared into Z-space. Had they been found by some ultra-secret deep state government cabal?

"At least the ole' girl's space legs got a stretch," said Lynch. "Beats hauling her around the same patrol route every damn day."

"And nobody was nearly killed in a car accident," said Modi. "Or shot."

"And," said Lynch, obviously trying to lighten the mood. "At least the coffee was good."

That got a smile from him, although Modi didn't react at all. Which he anticipated. "It was pretty damn nice," said Mattis. "Tell you what. When we get back to Earth, we should franchise that company. Start up our own little coffee shop on the edge of nowhere and make our fortunes that way."

"Sir," said Lynch, "you sure your hamster hasn't fallen of its wheel?"

"Just kidding," he said, grinning a tad. "The shop would be aboard the ship of course. Traveling around the galaxy, dispensing delicious drinkables in all flavors and sizes. We'd sail around space, dispensing coffee and freedom, and—"

Mattis's communicator chirped, stealing away the joke. His personal one. Curiously, he pulled it open, his chest tightening. A text message.

MARTHA RAMIREZ: Hi, Jack. It's Martha. I'm on Chrysalis. I have some people you need to talk to immediately.

She's here. She's actually here.

The very notion that Martha could be within metaphorical stone-throwing distance blew the air out of his lungs.

"You okay?" asked Lynch. He and Modi were staring.

"I'm fine," said Mattis, managing a little smile. "Looks like for once, it'll be me pulling information out of Martha."

Chapter Sixty-One

Bridge
USS Midway
Orbit above Chrysalis
Kepler-1011 system

Mattis watched the shuttle Zulu-1 drift toward Chrysalis, then return almost an hour later. A glance at the readouts on a nearby monitor confirmed it was full of passengers. Martha … Martha Ramirez was aboard that shuttle.

He hadn't seen her since the battle above Earth. Because he was a piece of shit, too cowardly to confront her about their feelings. Just like he'd always been. Running away from her; not because she was going to hurt him, but because of what she might represent.

Mattis didn't fear Ramirez saying no to him. He feared her saying yes.

The closer the shuttle got, the more his fear intensified.

Putting off talking to her hadn't helped at all, something he was more than old enough to know. He felt like a child again. *Running away from the woman like a teenager with a crush.*

Zulu-1 docked. For a time there was nothing as, presumably, the people aboard made their way through the ship to the bridge. The more time passed the more nervous he got. What was taking them so long? The ship was still battle damaged, maybe they had found some kind of hazard, maybe the emergency bulkheads had failed and they'd been sucked out into space, or maybe—

The ruined remains of the door to the bridge, patched haphazardly with welded-on panels, creaked open.

"Martha," said Mattis, smiling as widely as he could. "It's a pleasure to—"

A short, mousy looking man wearing civilian clothes poked his head in the door. "Um, no. It's, uh, Bratta. Steve Bratta. Can I come in?"

Awkward. Mattis gestured for him to do so. "Permission granted, Mister Bratta."

Gingerly, Bratta stepped over the cooled lumps of metal—the destroyed remnants of their casemate—and moved onto the bridge. Behind him, he saw the vague outline of a woman. Definitely a woman this time. He took another deep breath. "Miss Ramirez, it's a pleasure to—"

"Nope," said the woman, stepping fully into view, a hard looking civilian with a powerful looking stun-stick strapped to her hip. She wore a dusty blue coat and had her hair tied up in a neat bun. "I'm Officer Jeannie Tafola."

Bloody *hell*, he was making a hash of this. Mattis rubbed the bridge of his nose in frustration and waited. And waited.

"Oh?" came Ramirez's voice from the other side of the door. "Not going to embarrass yourself a third time?"

Did she mean anything more from that? The *first* time would be them in the past, the *second* time just before the battle of Earth—so this would be the third time? He was overthinking it and he knew it, but his mind suddenly felt frazzled. Like he'd stayed up for two nights in a row then had ten cups of coffee. As it stood, it was about twenty hours and two cups of coffee, but—

More overthinking.

"I'll try to keep the embarrassment under control if I can," said Mattis, a little later than he really should have. "I hope."

Ramirez stepped into the room smiling lopsidedly and, for just a little fraction of a second, *she* actually seemed to be the nervous one. It was actually quite endearing. "A'right, well, these are the two I told you about."

"The two people I just had to meet?" Mattis flicked his gaze over to each of them in turn. The cop seemed to have potential, but the little scientist guy seemed to be too busy nervously fiddling with a strand of his hair to be any use to anyone. "Unless there's someone else?"

"Hey," said Bratta, somewhat nasally and defensive, "I'll have you know, *Mister Mattis*, that Jeannie and I broke this whole thing wide open. We tracked down the plant at Chrysalis, and we are more than capable of taking care of whatever—"

"Steve," said Jeannie, a distinct note of frustration in her voice, "stop trying to look tough for the admiral, please."

"Okay," said Bratta, his shoulders slumping.

"Excuse me," asked Modi, the first words he'd said in a

while. His eyes were drawn to Bratta's hip. "Is that an X-39?"

Bratta's whole face lit up. "Why yes, it is indeed! Although it's been heavily modified. My own personal blend of alterations. I managed to induce a signal resonance in the casing, giving—"

"A substantial boost to signal performance. The Takashima effect." Modi practically slid across the floor to him, holding out his hand. "May I?"

"You absolutely *may*," said Bratta, with something akin to a mix of fatherly pride and childish delight. "Just one moment, I'll show you how it all works. You see…"

The two of them began talking over each other in increasingly excited tones, huddled over the seemingly normal-looking phone, chattering away in techno-babble that Mattis had no hope of understanding.

His eyes met Jeannie's briefly, and he saw within them a deep seated, but long subdued, frustration. Nerds and their toys. His eyes strayed next to Martha's, who met his gaze with her own. They held it, and after a moment he felt the need to distract them all before he felt … something … he didn't want to feel at this point.

"So," asked Mattis, a little louder than necessary so he could move past that momentary weirdness. "Enough about phones and stuff. You haven't really answered my question."

Jeannie grinned slightly. "I don't think you believe us, Mattis," she said, with a slight impish edge to her tone that reminded him of Ramirez.

Ramirez looked to Jeannie, then back to Mattis. "It's true that Steve and Jeannie investigated this," she said. "These two really did find out most of what you and your crew also discovered. I know that doesn't *sound* like much, but there are just two of them. And I have an idea how they can help us a fair bit further."

"How's that?" asked Lynch.

"Well," said Jeannie, "we found out that everything is connected. The Genetics corporation on Zenith. MaxGainz. Even the damn fucking coffee shop. They're all companies owned by shell companies, parent companies and umbrella corporations, but there's one piece of the puzzle we haven't looked at. I know it."

"I know," said Mattis. "That's exactly what I think."

"Sir," said Lynch, cutting into the conversation, "the *Luyang III* are sending a transmission our way."

Maybe Yim had an idea. "Send it through," he said.

"It's not audio. It's text only. It reads…" Lynch cleared his throat. "MaxGainz facility on Chrysalis. East end of market. Get inside." He tilted his screen so that Mattis could see the message himself. It was just as he'd described.

Odd that Yim would send through a text. What was happening over there?

Jeannie snapped her fingers. " I know just the person to get inside," she said, looking right at Bratta.

Modi looked at Bratta.

Ramirez looked at Bratta.

Lynch looked at Bratta.

Bratta looked at Bratta, self-conscious that everyone else was suddenly looking at him. He noticed his fly was unzipped, and, eyes widening in embarrassment, struggled to close it.

"You've got to be kidding me." said Mattis, eyes widening slowly. "Am I losing my mind here?"

"You've got to admit," said Jeannie, watching Bratta fight with the stuck zipper, "nobody'll be expecting him."

Mattis grimaced. "All right. I'll inform fleet command what's going on. Maybe they can give me more insight on what this company is really doing." He pointed his thumb towards Bratta. "That'll give the good doctor here more time to—" he regarded the small man struggling with his fly, "get ready, so to speak."

Chapter Sixty-Two

Bridge
CNS Luyang III
Orbit above Chrysalis
Kepler-1011 system

"Prepare a shuttle," said Yim. "I have to go back there."

"Of course, sir," said Xiao, straightening his back. "I'll have it ready again." A playful smile crossed his lips. "Going back for more coffee, sir? I'll have to get you to get me some, too."

Yim managed a smile of his own. "I'll do that. Send me your order, and I'll make sure you get it." He eased out of his chair with a groan.

Xiao turned back to his console, and then his tone became professional again. "Sir, we're receiving a Z-space transmission. Wide band. Priority one."

Priority one? Well, they were popular today. "What's the

origin?" asked Yim. It felt good to stand after sitting down for so long.

"Unclear," said Xiao. "It's from General Tsai. And …" he squinted. "It's addressed to the … *bridge crew* of the *Luyang III*."

A strange and improper way of addressing a communication. Either a ship or the CO was normally specifically called out. "Very well," said Yim. "Put it through."

"Mister Yim," said General Tsai, his tone almost accusatory. "Where is your ship at the present moment?"

Yim blinked and touched his neck, dropping his voice to a lower tone. "Sir, I'm—"

"Speak out loud," said General Tsai, "if you please, Admiral Yim."

He scowled. "Sir, the Luyang III is currently investigating a matter of utmost importance to the People's Republic. We are in orbit of a large asteroid, Chrysalis, and I believe it holds the key to many of the mysteries surrounding the alien invasion upon Earth."

"I understand," said General Tsai. "Now hear this, Admiral: we have detected long-range transmissions from the *Midway* and we believe that they are planning to move on Chrysalis. For reasons of national security, this cannot be allowed. The *Luyang III* is hereby ordered to revert, immediately and without delay, to its previously assigned mission. This order is to be followed without delay or hesitation of any kind, Admiral. Do I make myself clear?"

What the hell was the General saying? "Sir, if you just listen to me, I've been speaking to Admiral Mattis about this place. It's not what you think. There is a *lot* going on here, and if you give me a minute, I'll fill you in on the details of—"

"Is Lieutenant Commander Xiao present?" interrupted General Tsai. "Is he listening to this conversation?"

Yim and Xiao's eyes met. "He is," said Yim, uncertainly.

"I'm here," said Xiao, equally uncertainly.

"Admiral Yim," said General Tsai, his voice iron. "The grace of the people has expired. Remove your sidearm and give it to Lieutenant Commander Xiao, and then have him relieve you as the Commanding Officer of the CNS *Luyang III*. Lieutenant Commander Xiao, marines on the bridge, if Admiral Yim refuses this direct order from the Joint Chiefs of Staff, you are ordered to force him to comply in any way you see fit, including putting a bullet in him."

This was—Yim spluttered for a moment, trying to find the right way of arguing against this madness. Standing down the CO of a ship like this was *absolutely* improper. Ordering his XO to *shoot* him on the bridge of his own ship was beyond improper. It was insanity.

Slowly, with obvious reluctance, Xiao drew his pistol, cradling it in both hands. "I'm sorry, sir," he said. "We can sort this out later. I promise."

Barely able to disguise his disgust, Yim drew his pistol with two fingers, reversed it, and handed it grip-first to Xiao. "Commander Xiao, I stand relieved."

"General, sir," said Xiao, taking the pistol and laying it on his console. "I have the admiral's weapon."

"Excellent," said General Tsai, his tone painted with obvious relief. "Lieutenant Commander Xiao, you are hereby ordered to use the capabilities of your ship to engage the USS *Midway*. We have classified the demilitarized orbital space of Chrysalis as financial importance to the People's Republic and its integrity cannot be compromised; that minefield remains Chinese property, after all. Your objective is the following: disable that ship's engines or weapons, and once that has been accomplished you are then to jump away from the system and head toward Earth to be properly debriefed. Do I make myself clear?"

Xiao hesitated, and then nodded firmly. "Yes, sir. Launching fighters and spinning up heavy guns."

He only had a few minutes to act. Mattis had to be warned. Yim sunk into his seat and, using his keyboard, typed out a brief message to the *Midway*. Text only.

"Alert fighters away," said one of his bridge officers—although they weren't *his* bridge officers anymore, were they?

"Thank you," said Xiao.

Yim scowled as the watched his ship's fighters fly out of the hangar bay, turning and banking toward the *Midway*. "I'm not getting you coffee anymore," he growled.

Chapter Sixty-Three

Senator Pitt's Office
Washington, D.C.
Earth

Chuck had no idea what Spectre meant, but just mentioning the name had rattled John Smith something fierce. He had stepped away from Chuck to make some kind of long range phone call. It felt odd to just stand there while an armed guy made a call to another star system, speaking quietly and deliberately about something he simply couldn't overhear.

"Hey," said Elroy, his voice strained. "You still there, Chuck? I'm about to call the cops."

"Don't," said Chuck, reflexively. "I'm okay."

Smith glared at him, as though considering taking some serious action, then went back to his call.

"You sure?" asked Elroy, "you were crying for a long while there, Chuck. I'm really worried."

Chuck moved over to the other corner. "Look," he whispered, "something's come up. I'm fine. I'll call you later." He hung up. It hurt him to be so callous, but things had gotten suddenly way out of hand and Elroy was a distraction he simply couldn't afford right now.

A few moments later, Smith finished his call too. "Okay," said Smith, "change of plans. We're getting the fuck out of here and we're taking your data disk and throwing it into a furnace and then scattering the ashes in the ocean. Then we're splitting up and we're never speaking again."

That sounded crazy. "That's a little paranoid, isn't it?" asked Chuck, skeptically. "We can just erase it if you're feeling like the files we recovered were dangerous."

"That won't be enough," said Smith, shaking his head firmly. "You can always recover things from a file system, even if they've been securely erased. These spooks are good at what they do. We simply can't take the risk." He gave a low chuckle. "Like I said, you're in *way* over your head here."

Chuck frowned. "Pretty sure I was in over my head when I broke into Pitt's office. What we're doing *is* a crime you know."

"This isn't some youthful misdemeanor," said Smith, exasperatedly. "Or even a felony. This it outside the law—outside the shared lie we call society. This is *dangerous*. And I mean bullet-in-the-back-of-the-head, dump-your-body-in-the-swamp-for-the-gators dangerous. The people you're missing with—they don't play by the rules."

As if breaking into the good Senator's office would be safe. Or legal. "Hey, you're here too," said Chuck.

Smith smiled. "Hardly the first time for the CIA. We're experts at this kind of thing by now."

Well. That explained that. Chuck grimaced internally. What *had* he got into? "What the hell is Spectre, anyway, that's got you so upset, CIA tough guy?"

"Not a *what*," said Smith, "but a *who*. An extremely dangerous assassin and spy, made all the more dangerous by how innocuous they look. They picked their name because of some old James Bond movie, and it's apt. If they're hunting you, you'll quietly have an accident and nobody will raise an eyebrow, because the circumstances will be entirely believable to the forensic analysts who examine it."

It sounded crazy, but Smith definitely seemed to believe it. "Okay," said Chuck, slowly. "Why are you telling me this?"

"Because I know who your old man is. I like him. I want to help him find what he's looking for, but I can't do that if I'm laying at the bottom of some bog."

"What *is* my dad looking for?" asked Chuck. "He never really talks to me."

Smith snorted. "Lots of things," he said. "This goes deep. I'm talking a deep state—a shadow government running things from behind the scenes, performing genetic experiments, operating within and outside nations, doing things nobody in their right mind should ever even consider. They're waist deep in every distasteful thing you could ever imagine."

"Why don't you go public?" asked Chuck. "If you have the proof…"

"That's the problem," said Smith. "I don't. Yet."

Spoken like a very sane man with extremely normal beliefs. Chuck couldn't help but let his eyes drift back to the man's pistol. Suddenly, Chuck trusted him a whole lot less. And yet…

No. It was crazy. "Okay," said Chuck, lying through his

teeth. "I believe it. What do you suggest we do?"

Smith shrugged helplessly. "I know what I'm doing. Leaving. I suggest you do yourself a favor, kid, and drop this. It's way too deep for you. Hell, it's probably too deep for *me*." He affixed Chuck a firm glare. "You never saw me, kid."

Chuck nodded and then Smith turned and left the office.

So much for going to Chrysalis, thought Chuck, and then he backtracked too, looking for the hole he'd smashed in the window and hoping there wasn't a parade of police cars outside waiting to arrest him.

The moment he arrived at the broken glass, the howl of a police siren started up, and a floodlight lit up the whole area, white glare blinding him. He could barely see flashing blue lights.

"Freeze!" shouted the a police officer. "Don't move, you're under arrest! Hands above your head!"

Well, thought Chuck as he slowly raised his hands above his head, *shit. I jinxed it.*

Chapter Sixty-Four

Commander Modi's Workroom
USS Midway
Orbit above Chrysalis
Kepler-1011 system

Bratta stared at the prototypes on Modi's glistening bench.

Modi appeared to take note of his interest. "Of course, these are purely recreational projects, hardly military standard. I would never field test them under regular circumstances, but of course, I estimate that the odds of your dying due to lack of support are significantly higher than the odds of significant injury due to equipment malfunction."

Bratta nodded, throat suddenly dry. "That … does sound reasonable. Ah, thank you, Commander Modi."

Modi nodded seriously. "You are welcome."

"So," he ventured, "what do all of these do?"

"This," said Modi, "is a camera that can be easily fitted to any regular pair of glasses. Hardly an innovation in and of itself. Comes with a miniature ear piece and microphone. It's reverse-engineered Chinese technology; just speak in a whisper and it should work."

Bratta took the mic and carefully touched it to his neck. "What next? How will the heads-up lens, attach to my glasses?"

Modi reached for a pair of gloves, then picked up the tiny transparent screen. "It is articulated to clip onto the frame itself, so the lenses are not damaged. Some minor modification may be necessary before it adheres to your frames, unfortunately. May I have your glasses?"

Bratta complied, blinking as his vision suddenly blurred. Modi seemed to be fiddling—it was hard to tell—and when they came back, the right-hand lens was slightly blurry.

It shouldn't be a big problem. "So," said Bratta, "these are communication devices. Um, no offense, but how helpful will they really be? It's not like there can be anyone else as backup if things go horribly wrong, is there?"

"You underestimate the tactical value of a command center, Doctor Bratta," Modi said. "Not only will all visual and verbal feed be instantly transmitted to the *Midway,* but the ear piece and heads-up 'lens,' as you put it, can be used to show maps, enemy positions, and any other relevant information that is best presented in a visual format." He tapped on a few more keys. "Furthermore, the communicator will cycle through frequencies once you reach the office until I have detected their security personnel frequency, although your microphone will be muted on that channel. I think this will be a helpful feature."

There wasn't much he could say to that, really. "You're

right, Commander Modi."

Modi blinked. "Thank you."

"Um," he frowned, "for what?"

The commander's expression settled back into blankness. "Usually people are insulting me at this point."

Bratta snorted. "Believe me, I'm familiar with the experience."

Silence reigned for a moment.

Modi turned to the far end of the bench. Bratta, feeling about as awkward as he usually did this far into any social encounter, picked up the ear piece and fiddled with it. It looked like it would be comfortable, at least. The design was incredibly size-efficient.

The engineer reappeared, a dull metal cylinder about the size of Bratta's two fists in hand. "This is an extremely powerful electromagnet. Place it near any hard drive you wish to wipe in order to destroy its contents." he said, handing Bratta something that looked like nothing so much as a wristwatch and indicating a switch on the side. "It is remotely activated, which is a safety feature as much as it is tactical. I would not activate this device while wearing metal within a six-meter radius. I would prefer this device returned in working order, if possible."

Bratta hefted the cylinder gingerly. "I've worked with powerful magnetic equipment—and its safety regulations—before. I'll keep that in mind when it's in my pocket. Um. I don't think I'd be able to forget it if I tried, to be honest."

"Good," said Modi.

"Do you think I'll have to use it?" he asked.

"The destruction of electronic records is certainly not

within your mission parameters. However, survival is, and while I am currently unable to contribute to an ideal degree, it is a goal often greatly helped by having many options available. This includes instigating crises and running in the other direction before security can converge upon the crisis position."

"That … um, that is a very good point. I like that plan."

"I have one further item that will likely be of use to you." Modi picked up a strange arm-length contraption of lengthy wires, straps, plates, and a rectangular case. "Lockbreaker Mark 1."

Bratta's throat dried up all over. "Mark 1, version…?"

"Version zero. This is the first step beyond theory."

A montage of Bratta's own version zero prototypes flashed before his eyes. Several things were on fire, and many prominently featured an *extremely* put-out Jeannie—once literally, with an extinguisher. His heart sped up a little more than a little. "Er, what does it do?"

"Theoretically," said Modi, "it sends out electrical pulses to fool electronic locks to open or seal, depending on the setting, although extremely preliminary testing suggests a seven percent outright failure rate, full effects unclear. It should otherwise function like a normal glove with a secondary power and processing unit."

Just like he had made! A *very* wise design decision. Bratta beamed. "How does it work?"

"Knowing how standard military and industrial electronic locks function is part of my job description, Doctor Bratta. The interface is designed to trick a wide variety of standard designs."

It had been years since Bratta had read up on *this* kind of technology. He resigned himself to having to blindly trust the engineer on this one.

Jeannie stood on the other side. "You ready, Steve? Everyone is getting antsy."

Modi nodded. "You now have a statistically significant higher chance of success, I believe. I will brief Captain Mattis as to the nature of the technology I have given you."

Jeannie looked concerned, but didn't comment. "Steve?"

"Coming," he replied. "Thank you, Commander Modi."

"You are welcome, Doctor Bratta." Modi inclined his head, then turned towards his computer.

The door hissed shut behind Bratta with a disturbing sense of finality.

"Was that useful?" Jeannie asked.

"Yes," he said. "I hope. Uh, well, at least Commander Modi thinks they will help. You'll have a direct line to a mic and ear piece, at least. And I have a magnet and a lockpick."

Her expression drew tighter. "I should be doing this. You are *not* an expert."

Bratta paused. "I … they know us both, Jeannie. But you don't know where the labs are. I don't want to, we both know I *really* don't, but I can find them. And I get to play with Commander Modi's prototypes," he said, abruptly feeling a lot more cheerful. "Do you have any *idea* how inventive—"

Jeannie chuckled quietly. "Alright, Steve. Here, have this," she said, handing him a plastic card. It was the ID card of the man who'd tailed them in Glasgow. "Or should I say, alright, Mr. McIntosh?"

Bratta pocketed the ID. "I can do this."

Her face set into hard lines. "You can. And you're not about to get hurt on my watch. Even with your twit head."

"Excuse me?" his pitch skyrocketed. "I have been *bruised* and *scraped* and *battered* and my ankle still hurts!"

"Walk it off, sissy," Jeannie punched him in the shoulder. "I'll be just outside the facility, so if everything turns pear-shaped, well … not sure what I can do with a facility full of moderately-paid security guards. Just … try not to die. Now come on. Our shuttle is this way."

Chapter Sixty-Five

Bridge
USS Midway
Orbit above Chrysalis
Kepler-1011 system

Mattis watched the shuttle fly toward Chrysalis with something approaching glum despair. Bratta was smart, there was no doubt about that. And the others—once he'd calmed down a bit—had made good points. Bratta was a civilian, and therefore significantly less likely to attract the kind of attention a military presence would. Jeannie didn't know the tech, and Ramirez was far too noticeable a celebrity to even consider making the attempt.

It still felt kind of crazy to send in a lone civilian, no matter what equipment Modi could give him. The guy was a geneticist, a scientist. Not a spy. Not an infiltrator. Yet he was, paradoxically, the only one aboard a ship of military personnel who could even potentially pull this mission off.

This day kept getting better and better.

"Sir," said Lynch, tapping keys on his console. "We're detecting an incoming transmission. Wide beam."

A wide beam transmission meant that anyone could pick it up, but such things were inevitably encrypted. "Any idea who it's addressed to? Or where it came from?"

"Not sure," said Lynch, "on both counts. Wide beams are good for that…." He consulted his instruments, his voice suddenly painted with surprise and adrenaline. "Sir, I think we have our answer. The *Luyang III* is launching strike craft."

No. No, it couldn't be possible. Yim wouldn't—after all they had been through recently; they weren't friends before, certainly, and there was some lingering anger there too, but—Yim, seemingly, had proven that he was simply a soldier doing his job. The war was over. Maybe the fighters were just performing a combat sweep. Or maybe there was some kind of danger the *Midway* wasn't aware of.

Yet, as Mattis watched the *Luyang III*'s fighters roar across space directly toward the *Midway*, he knew the true reason.

Betrayal.

The words he needed to say next were *launch strike craft* but he just simply couldn't bring himself to do it. "Mister Lynch," said Mattis, slowly, "what's the status on the hangar bay? It was damaged, wasn't it?"

"Aye sir," said Lynch, perhaps sensing where Mattis was trying to go with his line of questioning. "It was. But the pilots fixed it. There's some minor debris remaining but it should be okay to launch ships."

No excuses.

Lynch grimaced. "It's not your fault, sir. You couldn't have anticipated this…."

He knew that. Yet still it hit him hard, right in the chest.

"Open a channel" said Mattis, his heart heavy in his chest. "Broadcast it on all frequencies, and to all craft. Put it out on radio, Z-space, hell even via signal light in Morse. Message reads: ten kilometer exclusion zone established around the *Midway*. Any ship crossing this line will be destroyed."

Lynch tapped on keys, writing down his message. "Transmitting."

Mattis took a deep breath. "Launch strike fighters. Order them to engage and destroy any aircraft that cross the ten kilometer line."

"Aye aye, sir," said Lynch, eyes fixed on his monitors. "Scrambling strike craft—" he turned and looked at Mattis, the corners of his mouth turned down. "The Chinese strike craft are accelerating to attack."

His mouth became a thin line as he watched his monitors, and the two clouds of fighters drawing closer and closer.

Chapter Sixty-Six

MaxGainz Home Office Staff Entrance
Chrysalis
Kepler-1011 System

Bratta stared at the MaxGainz staff entrance and wiped his palms against his jacket—only for the mostly-translucent panels of Modi's Lockbreaker to catch on the fabric. He winced and tucked his hands behind his back. Yes, Jeannie wasn't that far away. Just around the corner, really. But still … he felt awfully alone. He couldn't believe he was doing this.

He could *not* believe he was doing this.

He couldn't believe he was *doing* this.

And yet, here he was. He stared at Callum McIntosh's ID. It stared back. In a twist of fate that might have been amusing under different circumstances, it looked about as much like him as his own ID did, although the security guard had been a *lot* bigger than him. He scrunched his face up experimentally, trying to mimic the expression in the picture.

He was stalling.

Bratta squared his shoulders, and strode across the street.

The staff entrance was unobtrusive, a plain door set in the side of the building overlooked by at least one security camera. He held the stolen ID up to a reader on the wall. It buzzed, and the door clicked open.

That had been easy, hadn't even needed to use the Lockbreaker. Maybe this wouldn't be so bad, after all. Almost like a regular day at work.

"Steve, there's a guard." Jeannie's voice hissed through his earpiece.

He jumped and looked around. Sure enough, a security guard was stationed at the end of the entry corridor.

"Don't worry about it," Martha Ramirez' voice came through, calm and steady. *"Walk up to him and say you left some work in an office yesterday, and you're coming in to pick it up. Walk up to him now."*

He did as she said, ambling cautiously over.

Jeannie spoke up again. *"If he says you were acting suspiciously, laugh and agree with him. Mention hearing something, probably the wind. Keep talking. Your story isn't that interesting and it's probably near the end of his shift. Flash your ID and he should let you past."*

Up ahead, the guard crossed his arms.

"Alright, sir, what's your business here?"

Bratta's palms went from *damp* to *drenched.* "O-oh, I'm just here to pick up some work I left in the office yesterday."

The guard raised an eyebrow. "At this hour?"

Bratta did his best to set his face into an assertive expression. "Yes, I haven't been able to come in earlier than this. Is that going to be a problem?"

That had felt so *brave!*

"It shouldn't be, sir. You seem awfully nervous."

"Steve, you've got to calm down." Martha whispered.

Bratta's eyes widened in shock. For a brief moment, he didn't say anything.

"Steve," said Martha, *"repeat exactly what I tell you: Oh, right, I guess I do look nervous, ha ha ha."*

"Ah, of course, I must look a little nervous, don't I? Ha ha," he repeated almost as she spoke.

She continued whispering through the speaker. *"It's the wind—I'm just imagining things, I'm easily distracted, keep going."*

"Sorry, it's just the wind, I thought I heard something—very distracting, you know how it is."

"I can't say I do," the guard replied.

"Oh, I'm making such a *hash* of this," Bratta tried. "I'm sorry," he forced a smile, "it's been a long day, my wife just *isn't* listening to reason and the cleaning robot's broken and—"

The guard sighed. "Alright, sir, may I see your ID?"

Bratta scrabbled through his pockets. The card actually turned up on the first try. The guard glanced at it.

"Doesn't look much like you."

"It's the flash," Bratta grimaced, familiar at least with *this* conversation.

The guard squinted, shrugged, and held the ID under a scanner. It beeped, and he handed the card back to Bratta.

"On your way then, sir. And see the main office about getting that ID re-shot soon."

Bratta stammered out a stream of promises and fled.

"You probably didn't need to coach him that far, Martha," Jeannie said. *"That was a fairly normal conversation for Steve."*

"Hey!" he muttered. Laughter crackled in his ear. He shook his head and looked around.

"Detecting security frequency now," Modi's voice came through. *"I will monitor chatter for now. If it becomes relevant to you, Mr. Bratta, I will patch you in."*

Bratta nodded. "OK."

There was a plaque that looked like it might have been a sign on the far wall. He wandered over, and yes, reception was that way, offices were there ... Well, if the layout of this place was anything like the Zenith facility, the laboratories would be behind the offices, near the back, where they could be properly ventilated and fitted with emergency exits. The more expensive equipment, however, would be at the center of the complex, where it could be more thoroughly secured. Which wasn't exactly ideal for him, but that was probably the idea.

"I'm going to start looking for the labs now," he whispered, and set off deeper into the building.

Chapter Sixty-Seven

MaxGainz Home Office
Chrysalis
Kepler-1011 System

Bratta tried to look normal and purposeful, but it was hard when he was moderately lost and there were three voices in his head. At least the building had been quiet, so far. Like the grave. He hadn't seen a single other living soul.

"Steve, what are you doing?" Jeannie demanded, helpful as ever.

"Trying to find the labs?" he whispered.

Chatter streamed back at him. He did his best to filter it out, eventually settling on humming softly as he tried to study the latest sign without *looking* like he was studying it. He'd already been told in no uncertain terms by both Martha and Jeannie not to do that—according to them, there was nothing worse than appearing lost. Bratta was fairly certain he could name any number of diseases, injuries, and genetic defects that would produce a more discomfiting effect than their proposed worst-case-scenario, but he'd decided hadn't been worth the time or effort to list them all.

"Are you alright, Doctor Bratta?" Modi's voice broke into his reverie.

"Yes, yes, just trying to *think!*" he responded, a little more forcefully than intended.

"Judging from your current position within the building and the information provided in the previous signage—"

"I turn left!" Bratta interrupted, before feeling abruptly guilty. Modi hadn't been the one causing problems.

"Well done."

Not really knowing how to respond to that and about as interested in being seen muttering constantly to himself, he started down the new corridor in reply. It was essentially identical to the previous ones, although the increased spacing between doors at least suggested that he might be getting to larger and more important offices. Although ... there were at least three floors above ground, and who knew how many might be below? Bratta felt a clammy sweat break out at the mere thought of how long it might take to explore the whole building.

New junction. He'd been walking for ten minutes or so, and heading generally back and inward, so ... straight on. Hopefully.

About halfway down the new turn, Modi's voice stopped him. *"Doctor Bratta, could you please obtain some more precise images of the locks? I believe they may have changed."*

"What if someone comes down the corridor? I can't really

explain stopping to peer at the locks, can I?"

This time, Jeannie came through. *"No, that would be a terrible idea, you're right. Stop near one of the doors and polish your glasses on your shirt, though, and that should do you fine. Your head doesn't need to be near them after all, just the camera."*

Modi agreed. *"Officer Tafola's idea is sound. Please ensure that you hold your glasses relatively steady, and if you are able to obtain coverage from all angles that would be ideal."*

Bratta did as they said. His hands were shaking a little, and Lockbreaker's plates were slick with perspiration—whatever adhesive seal Modi had used to stick it to his hand, it was performing admirably—but he managed to get a reasonable view of the electronic locks. Well. He hoped.

Modi *hmmed* and said nothing.

"I'd suggest you get going," Martha told him.

"I'm on the guard channel and it sounds like there might be a patrol headed your way," Jeannie added.

He set off.

Another turn—right this time, he decided.

"Doctor Bratta, you need to reconfigure your Lockbreaker, now," Modi said.

"What? Why?"

The head of engineering's tone turned urgent. *"Those are state-of-the-art devices, and they are* extremely *sensitive. The ID card you possess is not compatible with their design. There are however, certain weaknesses in the design that may be exploited, provided the Lockbreaker is adjusted precisely as I tell you. If you fail to do so, or you attempt to use the ID, the system will detect inconsistency and set off an alarm. I expect this would be disastrous."*

Bratta swallowed. "What do I have to do?"

"First, find a bathroom. Unfortunately, you will need to perform some small amount of rewiring to the power source."

"Er, sure," he whispered, backtracking. He entered a bathroom he had passed earlier. "What now?"

"Do you have access to the battery?"

"Er … how long do I have?"

"Only as long as you can manage without drawing suspicion."

"Whatever you're doing, make it quick, Steve," Jeannie added. *"Please."*

As long as he could manage without drawing suspicion? Well, that was … negative a few hours on a normal day. He wouldn't have time to doff and don his shirt and Lockbreaker, which had taken five minutes to arrange in the first place.

He winced at the inevitable solution. He was wearing his best shirt again. Not for long.

Bratta scrabbled around in his bag for his tiny pocket-knife. Trying to keep his hand steady, he pulled the shirt away from oh-so-tender armpit flesh and proceeded to slice the fabric until Lockbreaker's power and processing unit was easy to access. Then he switched his phone to its front-facing camera and propped it up on the back of the toilet, so he could see the unit on screen—which, as long as his glasses were pointed at it, Modi would be able to see. Ready.

"Alright, Doctor Bratta. Firstly, you will be working on a live device, because the off button is temperamental and tends to shock the user."

"Come again?"

"Do not be concerned. The rest of the device, barring the functional surface of the plates, is well-insulated. The odds of electric mishap are significantly less if you simply leave the off-switch alone."

"Uh … good?"

"Now, if you simply follow my instructions…"

Teeth clenched, Bratta carried out Modi's commands as they came, only shocked himself a little once.

"Congratulations, Doctor Bratta. Lockbreaker should have been successfully reconfigured."

"How am I for guards?" he asked.

"No suspicion yet," Jeannie replied. *"But the sooner you get going, the better."*

He rested his hand on the stall's latch. Now that it came to it, he didn't want to leave. It felt safe, hidden here. No one was looking for him. *How sad is that?* The thought came to him unbidden.

No, he couldn't spend the rest of his life shivering in a toilet stall. Bratta squared his shoulders and headed back out into the corridors.

Not much further down the hall, the doors changed. Square windows looked into dark labs, and glowing panels beside them monitored for temperature, gas leaks, and other hazardous contents within. Even better, the laboratories were clearly labeled, although none of them seemed particularly interesting. The same black locks protected each door.

He passed by "Sequencing," "Computer Lab 3," "*Mus Musculus* Trials" and "*Macaca Mulatta* Trials"—the muted sounds of macaques cooing and grunting to each other coming out from the latter—and stopped by "Incubators."

He held up Lockbreaker, and did everything he could—which wasn't much, honestly—to prepare himself for the moment of truth.

Silently, the door swung open.

Hoping against hope that no one would happen past,

Bratta turned on the lights and headed to the incubators. They were definitely the kind that could be used for, say, human fetuses, rather than developing bacterial cultures. There were viewing screens next to the machines. He recognized the technology, not from his years of research, but from his time in medical practices, so it didn't take him too long to switch one on.

Jeannie cursed in his ear, Martha not far behind her.

"Are those … humans?" Jeannie asked. *"They don't look … right, do they?"*

"That's because they're monkeys," Bratta sighed. "We use them for near-human testing. Nothing wrong here. Well, I mean besides the ethical implications of using monkeys as—"

"Alright," Martha said. *"Keep going, then, I'm sure you'll—"*

"Steve, they're talking about you," Jeannie broke in. *"On the radio."*

"Indeed they are," Modi confirmed. *"Although they currently appear to be merely gossiping."*

"We need to patch him in, now," said Jeannie.

"I am currently occupied with video analysis, Officer Tafola, but if you simply click there … make sure he's muted first. Don't want to hear him breathing over the line."

A whole new channel assaulted Bratta's ear. The guards, he discovered, *were* indeed talking about him. Or, more precisely, laughing. Mocking him for how he'd acted. Knowing he was muted, he indulged himself in an indignant sniff. It wasn't *his* fault awkwardness had been the plan.

"Get going, Steve." That had been Jeannie again.

So he switched everything off, and left.

Next corridor over, he came to a door marked "Restricted

Access Only."

"Lockbreaker should be sufficient, Doctor Bratta," said Modi.

He followed the engineer's advice, and found himself in a much darker, plainer space. About ten meters away was a steel door with no windows, labeled "Productions." There weren't any other openings, and there were no signs anywhere to be seen.

"Good work!" Martha chimed in, *"This looks like the jackpot."*

Bratta walked up to the door. Its mechanisms looked entirely different to everything he'd seen before. He pretended to polish his glasses again.

"Commander Modi?"

"Yes, Doctor Bratta?"

"Is there … anything I should be doing about the lock?"

"I am formulating the optimal course of action as we speak."

"Oh. Alright."

He listened to the security guards for a minute.

"It … appears to be unlocked. I suggest being prepared to run."

Bratta gulped.

"Steve, you—" Jeannie began.

He opened the door.

About thirty faces looked up at him.

Oh. So that's where everyone was.

Oh *dear.*

Chapter Sixty-Eight

MaxGainz Home Office
Chrysalis
Kepler-1011 System

Bratta quickly took in the scene before him. A lowered laboratory floor was filled with rows of metal slabs. On each slab, a body. Most were covered by white sheets, like corpses at a crime scene, but a few bodies—a mix of Asian and others, all physically robust, mostly male—lay exposed. Judging by the color in their skin and the ease with which a host of spidery-limbed robotic surgeons moved their limbs, they were heavily sedated, but alive—or at the very least, only recently dead.

Scattered throughout the room were white-coated figures —he assumed doctors, scientists, and technicians—as well as a number of well-dressed Chinese people who were guarded by twenty or so strong-armed marines, just like the ones who had smashed his phone on Zenith.

In the stunned silence, his gaze landed at the back of the room, where a Caucasian man in a suit stood by a table separate from the rest. On it lay the untended body of what appeared to be a young man—distance made it difficult to tell —less physically impressive than the rest, and so pale he was nearly blue.

"Jack needs to see this," Martha whispered unsteadily. *"The* world *needs to see this."*

The room exploded into action. Guns swung up and the unarmed personnel ran for the back of the chamber, the well-dressed ones shouting into phones and mouthpieces. Bratta shook, but his muscles had completely frozen.

"Unmute him, unmute him!" Jeannie's voice screeched through the line. *"Quick, while they're all still receiving him!"*

"Why?" Modi retorted.

"Here, I'll do it!"

Bratta found his voice.

And screamed.

Around the room, armed guards clutched at their heads and ripped out their earpieces. That was … that was good, right?

"RUN, Steve!" Jeannie yelled.

He ran.

"And that *is why, Commander Modi,"* she added, sounding smug. "Steve's scream is … bracing."

Bratta wondered if this was really the best time for gloating. But then, Jeannie was the expert.

He skidded out of the restricted access door.

"Doctor Bratta, I am sending through a map of what you have seen of the facility so far to your heads-up-display. It will direct you to the most

likely route of escape."

A green map marked with a red trail flashed in front of his right eye, and he nearly stumbled into a wall. He held out a hand to brace himself, wincing as Lockbreaker cut into the flesh of his palm, and pelted onward, following the trail.

"He can't make it alone," Jeannie said, voice hard. *"I'm going in there to get him. Get an extraction team ready. I'll meet them outside the facility."*

"Officer Tafola! Don't go in there, it's too dangerous—"

"It's done," said Jeannie. *"Hang on, Steve, I'm coming."*

Modi groaned into his ear. *"It would appear I am the only remaining member of your handler team with sense, Doctor Bratta. Please take the next left."*

Bratta wheezed for breath in reply.

And caught the sight of a troupe of guards running towards him from the other end of the junction.

"Nope nope *nope*," he managed.

"Doctor Bratta, take the next right and loop back around, perhaps they might—"

He rounded the corner, only to see another group of marine-types charging at him from the other direction. He shrieked a little.

"I can't outrun them!"

"No you cannot." Modi's voice was frustrated. Frustrated, but subdued. "A shuttle is being prepped for launch, it will be there in—eight minutes."

"I'm coming," said Jeannie, puffing through the microphone. "Eight minutes is seven minutes too long."

No. He wasn't going to die here, he was *not*, he had a million and one things on which to lecture Modi on user interfaces and the very least, and he had to rub it into Jeannie's face that he'd *done it* where she'd failed, and …

The guards were closing. Even in the labyrinthine corridors, they'd have a clear shot in moments.

Bratta drew the electromagnet from his bag and pegged it behind him towards the oncoming guards.

"Grenade!" one of guards yelled, and they scattered.

He had a good lead on them by the time they realized it wasn't exploding.

"Decoy!" the same guard yelled, and they swarmed around the corner.

Past the waiting electromagnet.

Bratta grinned at them and pressed the switch on his "watch." Their expressions went from confident to confused screams as their weapons were ripped from their hands, their belt buckles were pulled towards it, and at least one high-speed wallet hit someone in the face.

He ran.

And he never switched the electromagnet off.

"Well done. I am recalibrating your path—I identified a side entrance you passed on your way here, it should be extremely close."

The red line flickered and reappeared. Bratta gasped for air, heavy bag bumping against his leg painfully, but he kept running.

Before him, a door.

"Your card! Lockbreaker is misconfigured for this one!"

He rifled through his pockets madly—ah, there it was!—and hit the sensor.

The little light turned green, and he stumbled into a narrow alley.

Safe. Or close to, anyway. The streets of Chrysalis shouldn't be too hard to lose pursuers on, surely. He slumped against the wall to catch his breath.

"Doctor Bratta!"

"Wha—"

A giant hand closed around Bratta's throat. He smelled… cheese? Old cheese, and black and blue flesh and a grip too strong and oh *no no no*….

"Well, *hello* there," the … the *creature* said in a voice of gravel and strain and … American accent? A strange dialect—Louisianan, or something?

Beyond the fact that definitely, yes, quite definitely indeed, this appeared to be the third of these … entities that had tried to kill him so far—which was just *hilarious*, almost certainly made him a galactic expert—it looked … *familiar.* Where *had* he seen it before? It was a rather strange moment for déjà vu, but then again, it might have been the oxygen deprivation.

Then the thing lifted him up, and he got a good look at its face.

"Rya—Mitch Ryan?" he choked.

Oh God. He … *it*, was. The old veteran marine captain that had taken over that embassy.

It answered with a broad grin, black-scabbed lips stretching and cracking over darkened gums and approximately seven rotting teeth.

Bratta was no dentist, but—well he wasn't really *breathing* right now either, although Modi was saying … something?

The creature rolled its shoulders and tossed him across the alley like he weighed nothing. As he slammed into the opposite wall, Bratta heard a *crack*.

Through swimming vision, he saw it walking towards him. He heard it speak, its voice dark and guttural, even through the accent. "Game over, intruder."

Chapter Sixty-Nine

Lieutenant Patricia "Guano" Corrick's Warbird
Hangar Bay
USS Midway
Orbit above Chrysalis
Kepler-1011 system

"Lieutenant Corrick, Alpha flight is green light for launch."

Exactly what she wanted to hear. "Roger that." Guano punched the throttle, opening it fully. Her Warbird leapt towards open space, flying out of the hangar bay like a dart, leaving an expanding silver trail behind it. To her left and right two other craft—Biter and Spud's ships—flew out alongside her, similarly painting space with glittering water vapor.

With Roadie in the infirmary with a gunshot wound, leading the attack wing was left to her. Her first time commanding a whole strike group—her feet tingled against the rudder pedals.

"So hey," said Flatline, behind her, "how're you doing over there? How's things going? You feeling stressed yet?"

"Actually feeling pretty good," said Guano, turning toward the swarm of Chinese fighters. "Guess we get to see how good these J-84's really are."

Flatline didn't seem impressed. "You know how good they are," he said. "Better than us. And we're the first wave going up against them—"

"Cut to the point," said Guano, fiddling with the dials on her console. Her HUD was full of green contacts. Chinese fighters. They hadn't been cleared to engage yet—only when they crossed the line. "What are you trying to ask?"

"I'm asking," said Flatline, "if your weird combat meditation bullshit is working, because now would be a very excellent time for it to be working, if you know what I mean."

She took a deep breath of the oxygen mixture in her suit and let it out slowly. She knew the feeling the strange *thing* gave her. She felt nervousness, flying into battle against overwhelming odds. She felt excitement, doing what she loved. She felt fear, knowing she might be killed.

She should have felt nothing at all.

"It's—it's not working," she said, but there was no time to dwell on it. "Doesn't matter. We'll make do." She had to lead her wing. Guano flicked onto the shared channel with Biter and Spud. "You boys ready to take down some reds?"

"Roger that," said Biter, his voice charged. "I'm primed and weapons-hot."

"Maintain weapons safe," said Guano, shaking her head even though the guy on the other end of the radio couldn't see it. "I say again, do not engage unless they cross the line."

Her ship sped towards the Chinese fighters. Eight targets—no, ten. She locked up the first one, painting it with her targeting radar. The space-fighter equivalent of pointing a gun at them. A giant *fuck you* to their former allies.

"What if they shoot over the line?" asked Biter. "Does that count?"

She thought for a split second. "If its owned by the PRC, and it crosses the magic ten click mark, light it the fuck up. And whatever fired it."

"Copy," said Biter.

Eight kilometers. Seven. Six. The Chinese ships were a similar distance away and doing the same speed. The white box around the green dots flashed an angry red, missile lock tone blaring in her ears.

Five. Four. Three.

"They ain't stopping," said Spuds. "They're just picking up more speed."

Two.

"Wait until they cross the line," said Guano. "That's our orders."

One. Guano switched from radar guided to heat-seeking missiles.

The first Chinese ship flew across the invisible ten-kilometer sphere her computer projected around the *Midway* and instantly turned red.

Her finger hovered over the fire button and then, as quickly as the dot had changed from green to red, she *felt it.*

Absolute, total calm and control.

"Fox two," she said, losing the missile and breaking hard,

passing through the Chinese ship's silver jet wash. It splashed across her screen, condensing on the glass.

No time to see if the missile found a home or not. She thrust the stick forward, diving her ship, the g-forces thrusting her up into her seat. She spun the ship around, flying backwards, her own silver engine exhaust washing over her cockpit. Through the mist, she locked up another Chinese fighter and squeezed the trigger.

Her ship vibrated slightly as the missile tore free of its railing. Again, no time to look. She accelerated, the force crushing her back into her seat, then locked up a third.

"Good hit," said Flatline behind her. "On both missiles. Splash two Chinese fighters."

"Did they bail?"

"Yeah," said Flatline. She could hear him pounding away at his keyboard behind her. "I got two distress beacons. The pilots are drifting out of the combat zone, life signs healthy."

Guano touched her radio, transmitting in the open. "Flag those pilots as neutral," she said. "And make sure all ships understand that ejected pilots are to be avoided. Do not engage them, and avoid collisions."

Flatline's voice spiked up. "You're feeling it, aren't you?" he asked. His gun chattered behind her, sending a stream of tracers flying off into space. "You're feeling it!"

"Oh yeah," said Guano, much more deadpan than she intended, switching targets to a third fighter. "I'm feeling it."

"They're on me," said Spuds, the panic in his voice clear. "I got a tail. Two bandits, right on my six. They're painting me."

His distress seemed so out of place to her. She swung her

ship to the right, following her HUD's directions to her wingman. "Drop flares, chaff, and engage ECM. Break right and maintain defensive posture."

Two Chinese fighters up ahead, their twin silver streams like snakes trying to bite Spuds. Guano lined up her gunsight on the lead fighter, gently squeezing the trigger. A tiny burst—twenty rounds or less—leapt out from her ship, well beyond the maximum effective range of that weapon.

She watched the rounds fly out, toward the dodging, weaving Chinese spaceship. Flying, flying, flying …

For a moment she thought she'd missed, then the rounds burst against the rear of the ship, little flashes of light in the black.

"Splash three," she said.

The remaining Chinese fighter strafed Spud's ship, blasting the wing off it with a well placed stream of gunfire. His smoking ship careered away, spinning violently.

"Spuds, eject, eject, eject," she said. The ship spun faster, faster—and then it broke up, bursting silently in space.

"Damn!" shouted Flatline. "I'm looking for a distress beacon. Scanning …"

No way he survived that. Guano lined up the Chinese fighter who killed him, and let loose her two remaining heat seeking missiles. At that range they barely had a few seconds of flight time before they speared into the Chinese fighter, blowing it to atoms.

Blood for blood.

"Guano, look," said Flatline, pinging her HUD.

She followed the flashing light, eyes seeing what he meant immediately.

Three Chinese bombers on an attack run to the *Midway*.

Chapter Seventy

Bridge
USS Midway
Orbit above Chrysalis
Kepler-1011 system

Anger. Confusion. Sadness.

Mattis ran the emotional gauntlet as he watched his forces meet those of the Chinese. Little dots on their screens, flying around and around, blasting each other with missiles and guns. From the distant vantage point of the bridge it all looked safe, quiet, even serene. A couple of little red dots winked out. Then a blue one. Pilots fighting and dying. Over what?

"Open another channel," said Mattis, grinding his teeth together. "Get Yim on the horn. I don't care what it takes. I want to speak to that bastard. Right now."

"Aye aye, sir." Lynch was trying. He knew that. "We've got every dang antenna on the ship pointed straight toward them, broadcasting at maximum power. Six hails a second. We can see outgoing communications to their strike craft, providing them with coordination and telemetry. Their comms are working. They should be able to see our hails, bright as day. Practically screaming across the void at them, sir."

He knew that. He *knew*, deep down in his gut, that there was no way known that Yim couldn't see what they were doing. It was stupid, pointless to continue down this path but, he had to. "Keep trying," said Mattis. "Just keep trying."

The bridge crew avoided looking at him, eyes down on their consoles even though there wasn't all that much for them to do. He hadn't ordered weapons free yet—and he wouldn't. Not yet. Not before he'd spoken to Yim.

What was going *on* over there?

"Sir," said Lynch, twisting around in his seat. "We have three heavy strike craft making a direct run for the *Midway*. We're detecting radiological signatures from their weapons bays. They're carrying torpedoes, sir. Looks like they're targeting our engines."

A good torpedo strike could cripple the ship or worse if the reactor core failed. The threat shook him out of his melancholy.

He had to act or they could all die.

"Spin up point defense," said Mattis, his commander's voice returning. "Flak barrages, go. Target those bombers and anything they launch, then target the scrap we make out of 'em. Order Alpha wing to break engagement and intercept. Protect the *Midway*, Mister Lynch."

"Aye aye," said Lynch. "Rerouting strike craft." He tapped a few keys, and then looked directly at Mattis, a pointed expression on his face. "Our torpedoes are standing by."

That wasn't enough. He knew what he needed to do. What his crew needed him to do, his country ...

He had to fire.

"Arm torpedo warheads and load them into the tubes," said Mattis, forcing the words past his lips. "Target the *Luyang III*; center of mass, no messing around. Full spread, maximum yield, straight burn until impact."

"Just confirming," said Lynch, "you want to fire on the *Luyang III*?"

He did *not* want to do that but the situation was rapidly spinning out of his control. "We have logs of everything, right?" asked Mattis. It felt horrible to be covering his ass in a time like this, but there was more at stake than simply his ship. If tensions escalated to another Sino-American war it would give *whoever* his real enemies were the opportunity they needed to crush them both.

Mattis had to make sure his actions were justified. And documented.

"Logged in triplicate," said Lynch. "We have everything. The Chinese strike craft, our hailing attempts, the targeting data for every damn ship out there, theirs and ours."

"Good." Mattis took a deep breath. "Fire torpedoes."

Chapter Seventy-One

Outside MaxGainz Home Office
Chrysalis
Kepler-1011 System

Bratta blinked what was either sweat or blood out of his eye and stared up at the towering monstrosity that may or may not have recently been a militant extremist. It—he?—was closer than before. He thought. His vision was … funny, although his glasses did appear to be missing, which probably wasn't helping.

"So, rat," the creature began in that drowning-eating-sandpaper voice.

"Actually, according to the Chinese zodiac, I'm a horse," he interrupted, tittering. He got a boot to the ribs for his trouble, and found himself whooping in air on the asphalt, curled over in pain.

"You think you're here to joke?"

"At least—" Bratta gasped, seized by some utterly insane impulse, "you think …" he had to stop to choke down more air, "… I'm funny."

The creature hunkered down beside him. Its eyes were too bright, almost—almost as if they were displaying some form of bioluminescence. "You," it growled, "are the funniest little creature I have *ever* met. Which is why you're going to tell me who you're working for. Won't that be a *great* joke?"

"Not really," Bratta decided. "You have very pretty eyes. Though you might want to work on the complexion. And the smell."

The giant bared its teeth. "*You'll* smell of blood and piss when I'm done with you."

"That is likely accurate," he agreed. "Bladder voiding is a typical reaction to danger and stress."

The creature grabbed him by the throat again. At this rate, he was going to be as black and blue as *it* was.

"So *answer me*, before you die."

Bratta pointed pointedly at his extremely constricted windpipe. The creature released it a little.

He blinked back a spate of tears. "Nope!"

Its pretty eyes narrowed. "You have no idea who you're dealing with, here. No one can stop what's been set in motion."

Bratta propped himself up on an elbow, which hurt. "Would you … would you like to—" he hacked a cough, "—tell me the rest of your evil plan while you're at it?"

The Ryan-like thing drew back a fist, snarling. "Don't mind if I *don't!*"

And then someone shot it in the head.

Someone with sensible brown hair and a sensible blue-gray

coat.

Someone who was now running towards him. They seemed worried.

"Hi, Jeannie," he managed.

"Steve! You're OK!" she knelt down beside him. "Or—or not. That's—a lot of blood."

Bratta nodded. "Unfortunately it's all mine."

"That's … that's alright, Steve, there's a shuttle nearby, we'll get you back to the *Midway* just fine, provided there still *is* a *Midway* to get back to—"

"I expect you will," he said. "I don't think my injuries are life-threatening."

Jeannie let out a choked laugh. "You are the doctor."

"I am. Can you get my glasses? I seem to have lost them."

"Oh, sure," she said. "I see them, over there. Give me a second."

She walked over to the other side of the alley and bent over to pick up some indistinct blur.

And the rotting giant's prone body leapt up off the asphalt and slammed into her. Jeannie ducked and twisted, and they both ended up on their feet, circling each other in the narrow street.

Even without his glasses, Bratta noticed a deep line along the side of the thing's head, seeping surprisingly regular-looking red blood.

"Tried to shoot me, eh?" hissed the *thing*.

Jeannie's smile was sharp as a razor, and about as warm. "More than *tried*."

"Should have aimed better, bitch," the creature snarled, and snapped an arm practically thick as a tree trunk—and again, far too long for its body—out at her.

She twisted away on the ball of her foot. "Not my fault you're a zombie-looking-freak who doesn't know when to die."

"Zombie?" he practically roared. Privately, Bratta thought it was a little excessively villainous. "That would require me to be *dead!* No, we are *homo insequens*, the future of the human race!"

Jeannie feinted and shot forward, trying for a trip. The thing weathered the attempt like it was made of stone. She stumbled as she recovered, and was rewarded with a glancing blow to the face.

"You do kind of look like you've been six feet under a while," she retorted, sounding more Glaswegian with every passing second. "No offense or anything."

"An acceptable sacrifice for this kind of *power!*" the creature slammed its fist at her head.

She barely ducked in time, and danced behind it. Once it drew its fist away, Bratta could make out a crater in the wall where its fist had connected.

It occurred to him that Jeannie was not going to win this fight. The thought was like a bucket of cold water to the face.

Jeannie was in too close with it to draw the gun, and against that much force—which should have shattered the thing's fist, he noted—her luck and reflexes would only hold out so long. And, she didn't have the hitting capacity herself to damage it in the slightest.

But, he realized, he might.

He grabbed his bag and began searching desperately for his phone's charging cable.

"If you never want a date, I guess," Jeannie taunted from

the other side of the alley.

The creature only chuckled and swept a leg under Jeannie's feet. She turned the resulting fall into a shoulder roll and came back up out of the range of its swiping fist. Barely.

Bratta jammed the charger under his armpit. *Come one, come on, come on.* He'd seen a charging port on Lockbreaker's processing unit, all he had to do was find it and trust that Modi was the sort of man who used standardized ports....

"There's no point, you know," Jeannie panted. "The information's already out there. Killing us? Does nothing."

It replied by flashing its handful of rusty teeth. "Killing you is a good way of not having to care if you're lying."

The device was ready. Bratta clawed his way upright, using the brick wall behind him. Jeannie saw him and her eyes flew wide. The creature saw *that* and paused. Apparently it shared the human instinct of the *look behind you* trick.

And in that moment Bratta charged. And for the first time, hoped against hope that his device would break. And as he flew at the behemoth of a pseudo-man, he pressed Lockbreaker's off-switch.

Bratta yelped as a painful current shot through his finger. The creature that had once been Mitch Ryan *screamed* as a rewired Lockbreaker short-circuited the full charge of Bratta's combination external hard drive and battery into its body, and it fell.

He felt a burning sensation all along his right arm, and collapsed on top of its body. Oh. Lockbreaker's wires must have overheated. And his ankle hurt, that was bad.

"Steve?" he heard Jeannie say. "Steve? Oh my god, he's *dead*, are you OK?"

He tried to respond, but his vision was going really funny, and he hurt a lot, actually.

"I'm getting you out of here, now."

The last thing Bratta saw before everything went dark was Jeannie's back, as she slung him over her shoulder.

"M'hard drive just saved your life. Can't be mean to it now," he whispered into her coat.

"Of course, Steve," she said, a little too … affectionately. And then there was nothing.

Chapter Seventy-Two

Bridge
USS Midway
Orbit above Chrysalis
Kepler-1011 system

The instruments around him flashed as the *Midway*'s torpedoes leapt away from their tubes, engines flaring as they streaked toward their target, each leaving a thin silver stream behind them to mark their trail.

Right as they fired, the *Luyang III* fired as well, an identical volley of missiles.

"Torpedoes away," said Lynch, followed immediately by, "incoming torpedoes. Gun batteries are maintaining rate of fire and scoring good hits on the target."

Thanks for telling me what I already know!

Mattis took a breath and pushed the anger out of his mind. Feeling angry at Lynch, or at Yim's apparent betrayal, solved nothing. There was no sense in being annoyed at things he could not change. All he could do now was work towards solving it. "Adjust flak batteries to fire on those torpedoes. Bring them down. I don't want to ruin the *Midway*'s paint job."

That was standard procedure. But, of course, torpedoes were armored against such things. As he watched, the *Luyang III* fired up its own gun batteries, blasting the *Midway*'s torpedoes with salvo after salvo of fire.

Twin lines of torpedoes sailed out, crossing paths in the void of space where, for a brief second, both sets of ordnance were exposed to gunfire from both ships.

"Ready a second volley," said Mattis. "And fire when ready."

"Still loading," said Lynch, tapping furiously at his console.

Suddenly, all around them, shouts of alarm sprung up. "Captain," called the comms officer. "The *Luyang* has fired another barrage of torpedoes, headed our way."

Again? So soon? Mattis scowled. Intel on Chinese torpedo capacity had been underplaying their capabilities significantly. "Have their *advantage* recorded in the ship's computer," he said, bitterness painting his words. "Intelligence are going to have a lot to answer for." The *Midway* shook as a wave of Chinese fire splashed across her bow, mostly deflected by her armor. The Chinese guns weren't the problem....

Lynch finished typing, standing up and straightening his back. "Well sir, you know military intelligence. The oxymoron division." He grimaced at a monitor, showing the torpedoes streaking across space towards them, fire from the *Midway*'s guns streaking past, or bouncing off the armored hull. "We should get ready for those things to join the party."

"Aye," said Mattis, nodding firmly. "Turn our bow into them, Mister Lynch. The armor at the front of the ship will absorb the impact."

"So much for not ruining the ship's paint job," said Lynch. "Executing the turn. Bearing 084 mark 279."

The view began to change, rotating around as the ship turned, presenting its most heavily armored section to the incoming nukes. The hull on the *Midway*, as with all warships, was specifically designed to absorb nuclear detonations, but each impact stripped off layers of their protective armor. It was temporary, but such was the nature of space combat. Fighters were like dancers, swirling with impossible speed and precision, engaging each other with finesse, grace, and dexterity. Battleships, however, were armored boxers, bashing each other's heads in with brute force.

"All hands, brace for impact." Lynch studied the incoming torpedoes. "Impact in five, four, three, two, one …"

A roar filled the room, like a gong, as the whole ship vibrated from the impact of the half-dozen torpedoes, their nuclear warheads bursting in space, the impacts tossing the ship around like a rag doll. The metal of her struts groaned in protest, the noise reverberating around the ship until it faded into a barrage of alarms.

"Damage report," said Mattis, hands holding onto the arm rest with such force his knuckles turned white. "How bad?"

"Breach in forward storage compartment A15," said one of the bridge officers. "Sealing."

Casualty reports came in from all over the ship. Falls, trips, crew members struck by debris—nothing critical, but certainly not good.

"We can't take too many more of those," said Lynch, picking himself up off the floor.

"Effect of our own torpedoes?" asked Mattis, trying to determine it for himself. The monitors were all washed out from the radiation.

Their radar operator pulled up her screen. "Detonations on the front quarter of the *Luyang*," she said. "We hit 'em pretty good."

And they'd been hit back in return. "How long until we can fire again?"

"Two minutes," said Lynch. "And probably, by that time, the *Luyang* will have another salvo coming toward us."

Damn. Twice as fast—that was a huge gulf in capabilities.

"We have to even the odds," said Mattis. Maybe they could use their strike craft to attack the *Luyang* directly. Or perhaps they could call for reinforcements—which would never arrive on time, but it was an idea.

Or they could retreat.

Before he could make a decision, Ramirez, a tablet held in both hands over her chest, pushed past the marine guards at the ruined entrance to the casemate. "Jack!" she shouted. "Jack!"

"Get her out of here," hissed Mattis. A civilian busting onto the bridge during a firefight was a *massive* breach of protocol. If they survived this, he was going to have words with her. That kind of thing simply couldn't happen.

"Wait," shouted Ramirez, as the marines grabbed hold of her shoulders. She threw them off. "Jack, the feed from Chrysalis—from Bratta—you have to see this, right now!"

Chapter Seventy-Three

Lieutenant Patricia "Guano" Corrick's Warbird
11km from the USS Midway
Orbit above Chrysalis
Kepler-1011 system

"You know," said Guano as she lined up a radar-guided missile shot on a Chinese bomber, "I promised to go get myself checked out when I got back to the *Midway*." She squeezed the trigger, sending the projectile leaping off the rail toward her enemy. "We never got around to doing that."

"This isn't really the best time for this!" shouted Flatline, his guns chattering behind her. "We got a contact coming in, bearing 270 mark 015!"

She tilted the ship so that Flatline had a better angle of fire, touching the rudder with her foot to adjust the ship, dragging her gunsights over the path of the second bomber. The computer plotted its course, making it so easy to aim. "I also promised Roadie that I wouldn't break his shuttle."

Brrrrrrrt. Spent shells flew out from the underside of her ship as she sent a stream of death toward the ship trying to destroy her mothership.

"Yesyesyes," spat Flatline, "you're a terrible person and I will have Roadie spank you later, but for now, *please* focus on the dogfight we are right-fucking-in-the-middle-of!"

She laughed, watching with something approaching almost boredom as the first of her missiles smashed into the Chinese bomber and blasted it into a billion glowing pieces, while her gunfire blew holes in its friend, causing it to slowly spin, aimless, obviously damaged. The crew punched out. "How are those ships behind us?"

"Oh, they're *real* friendly, trying to—no wait, they're firing again!"

Guano had anticipated that and was already turning the ship. The stream of fire flew past her ship, drifting off endlessly into the void.

"Shit," said Flatline breathlessly, "they almost hit us."

"But they didn't." Guano flipped the ship, spraying a burst of gunfire she knew wouldn't hit, but accomplished her primary aim—the two Chinese fighters broke away. "Take care of the bomber, will you?"

Flatline's gun spat flame and death behind them—way too much ammunition for her liking—and she locked up the fighters that had pursued them.

"Fox one," she said, dumping all of her missiles. "We are winchester on missiles."

"Almost out of gun ammo too," said Flatline. "I got that bomber good. Look at him burn."

A glance in her rear view mirror confirmed it. The Chinese bomber, belching quickly dissipating smoke, began spinning aimlessly toward the *Midway*, engulfed by the flak barrage. For a moment all she saw were bursting shells in space, and then the Chinese fighter's torpedoes exploded, vaporizing the ship. The nuclear tips wouldn't detonate like *that*, of course, it was the conventional explosives inside the warheads that blew, but still. A radiological mess scattered all over space, yes—but not a nuclear blast.

Otherwise they would all be dead.

"A'right," said Guano, flipping the ship again and aligning her nose to the *Midway*. "Time to rearm. Let's burn for home. Alpha-1 to *Midway*, we are RTB, intent to rearm and re-engage. Prepare the hangar bay for combat landings."

"Confirmed," said a welcome voice, Roadie, in her ear. "Come right in, we got plenty of missiles. Call the ball."

She grinned, steering for the open mouth of the landing bay. "That's what I like to hear, my CAG. ILS engaged, Alpha-1 has the ball. Skids down in forty seconds."

"Hey, you didn't wreck your ship this time," said Roadie, stifling a wet cough in her ear. "And I'm not your … well, I *am* your CAG, but don't say it like that." He sighed. "You aren't Tango-Uniform, that's what I like to see. Good job. Maybe you can get through this one without costing the US taxpayer a fortune."

"Mmmhmm," said Guano. *Tango Uniform. Totally useless.* "I'm learning. I lost a full centimeter of height when I ejected —if I keep that up I'll be a midget in a few short years. Which, honestly, would be pretty damn awesome if you ask me."

"You'd make a cool midget," said Flatline, somewhat

unhelpfully. "I like little people. They're awesome."

Roadie, on the other hand, just snorted. "Oh, so, she *does* learn. Just saying, if you get bored of the creature comforts of your cockpit, don't just pull the ejection handle, okay? It's not an *I'm sick of being in a cramped spaceship and wanna take a walk outside* button."

She snorted dismissively. "Roger that. Hands off the boredom button."

There was a faint crackle on the radio as the *Midway* loomed larger in her cockpit canopy. "Hey, Corrick," came Roadie's voice again. "This is a private line. You, uhh … you feeling okay?"

"If you're asking if I'm *really calm*," she said, hoping he would get the hint. "I am."

"No, I meant, are you in the … *you know*. The trance thing."

Normally him missing the point so widely would piss her off, but instead, she just calmly thumbed the radio. "Yes."

"Great," said Roadie. "Okay, you're coming up on the hangar bay now. Don't mess up the landing."

Never. The ship touched onto the landing strip, all three skids touching the deck at once. The perfect landing, a so-called first kiss. Space-suited technical crew ran out to her, frantically clipping missiles to her ship's hard points and feeding in belts of ammunition.

"Okay," she said, waving off the ground crew. "Let's get back out there."

"Good thing," said Roadie. "Bag a couple more for me, will you?"

Chapter Seventy-Four

Bridge
Luyang III
Orbit above Chrysalis
Kepler-1011 system

Yim could do nothing but watch, helplessly, as his ship fired salvo after salvo of gun fire, flak, and torpedoes at the *Midway* and their strike craft.

It wasn't supposed to be this way. His own ship stolen from under him. He sat in the captain's chair—the irony of that fact not entirely lost on him—as Xiao gave the orders, directing the flow of battle and coordinating weapons strikes.

"Reload torpedo tubes," said Xiao. "I want a third barrage ready to go in moments."

"You're stressing the autoloaders too far," cautioned Yim as the ship groaned underneath their feet, still reeling from the American nuke strikes. "They aren't designed to be used for sustained fire."

"Then what good are they?" spat Xiao, the stress of the situation obviously mounting on him. He wasn't anywhere near as experienced as Yim—this was his first actual battle.

Yim folded his arms in front of his chest. "Commander Xiao, this is crazy."

Obviously rattled, the man shook his head. "I have to follow orders. The Joint Chief of Staff—"

"Is obviously in the wrong here," said Yim as another volley of fire washed over the *Luyang* and the ship shook with the force of the return barrage. "Think about this. There's a *reason* he wouldn't let me talk to him, because he *knew* I was on to something. There's something on that asteroid that will blow this whole thing wide open and we *need* to find it. And to do so, we need to stop shooting at the only friendly ship in this system!"

The cogs turned over in Xiao's head, and the man began pacing back and forth, obviously trying to balance his conscience with his intellect. For all his faults Xiao wasn't a bad person. Just … loyal to the state. A little too loyal.

"Xiao, we can't—" said Yim.

"Shut up!" Xiao grabbed the XO's console and focused on it. "I can't deal with this right now. I have a battle to win."

"You have a battle to *lose*," said Yim, matter-of-factually. "Our rate of fire advantage with our torpedoes is designed to be balanced with striking and moving. It's not designed to be fired like this. You'll burn out the articulators and jam it."

Xiao's eyes flicked from console to console, as though searching for the one that would tell him what he wanted to hear. "They'll hold," he said. "These machines were forged in

Tsingtao. That's my home. The people who made it are family. They're strong. Master craftsmen. The articulators will hold."

Right on cue, the whole ship shook from stem to stern, and a massive explosion tore through the port side of the ship, nearly throwing Yim off his feet.

"Articulator failure," reported one of the crew, muttering a dark curse under their breath. "The torpedo launchers are down."

Without their primary weapon the fight was lost. Yim moved up beside his XO, resting his hand on Xiao's shoulder. "Come now," he said. "I know we haven't served together long, but must trust me. This is pointless. We need to cease fire and answer the hundreds of hails the Americans have left for us. It's time."

Angrily, Xiao shrugged off Yim's hand. "No, we can still win this—"

Yim drove his foot into the back of Xiao's knee, knocking the man down, his free hand snatching the pistol out of Xiao's holster. Xiao fell face down on the deck, rolling onto his back. He groaned in pain, propping himself up with an elbow, suddenly finding himself looking down the barrel of Yim's pistol.

"Admiral, wait—"

Yim shot him in the face. Twice.

A tense silence fell over everything, broken only by the rumble of gunfire and the chirping of the communications computer.

His ears rang. Gunshots in enclosed spaces were known to cause hearing loss, but so did death. It was better than the alternative.

"Cease fire," said Yim, slowly holstering his still smoking pistol. "And answer those damn hails. Get the *Midway* on the line."

Chapter Seventy-Five

Bridge
USS Midway
Orbit above Chrysalis
Kepler-1011 system

The incoming torpedoes shut off their engines, drifting for a split second before detonating silently in the vacuum of space.

"Sir," said their communications officer, her tone almost disbelieving. "The *Luyang*. They've answered our hails."

Oldest salesman technique in the book. Keep ringing till someone picks up. "Put them through," said Mattis. "And call off our birds—all ships, return to base, weapons safe. While I'm talking to Yim and trying to sort this mess out, get damage control teams to inspect the bow of the ship. And anywhere else that needs it."

"Aye sir," said Lynch. "Opening the channel."

The connection that came through was full of static. "Admiral Mattis," said Yim, somewhat breathlessly. "I apologize for the outburst. We had a minor case of … *mutiny* over here, but we've resolved the situation to my satisfaction. Our strike fighters are returning. There'll be no more unpleasantness heading your way."

Normally Mattis would be ready with a playful quip, a sarcastic response, or something else to deflate the tension, but all he felt was relief. "Resolved?" he asked. "Do you need us to take care of some prisoners for you?"

"No need," said Yim. "Our morgue has space enough for them. When my XO took my gun he might as well have shot himself with it. Turns out I had to do the heavy lifting, which is obviously a nuisance, but there you go. Apologies, once again, for the uncivil behavior."

Well. That explained that. "Thanks for taking out the trash."

"Any time," said Yim. "Hold please." The communication fluctuated for a moment, then went totally quiet, as though muted. When Yim came back he seemed to be talking to someone else nearby. "—that the damage is shored up. And someone get that body out of here." A faint click. "Mattis, we're having some minor issues over here with the aftermath of the battle. I'll have to call you back."

"Wait," said Mattis. "Let your men put out the fires. I have something to show you."

With a tap of his keyboard, Mattis sent the feed from Bratta's camera straight to Yim. Everything. He knew that when all this was over, and the paperwork was being filed and the reports written, he would have to explain why he transmitted the information he had straight to the Chinese, but that was a problem for the future. In fact, given the secrets and misdirections surrounding Chrysalis and the Forgotten and *everything* that had happened since the Battle of Earth, it felt good to send through absolute, unmitigated truth. Just the facts. No filter.

"*Ó, wǒ de shàngdì*," exclaimed Yim, aghast. No doubt he was seeing the same thing Mattis was. "Oh my God…"

"This thing—this conspiracy. It runs deep," said Mattis, his hands clenched by his sides. "Deeper than we probably know. The people you're looking at will do *anything* to accomplish their aims. We need to expose them. I'm going to take this video, give it to our local friendly reporter, and broadcast this thing to the galaxy. No more secrets. No more lies. Let everyone see what we're up against."

"I understand what you're saying," said Yim, a slight hesitation coming into his tone. "But Admiral, do you really think we can go public with this?"

"We don't have a choice." If they waited, someone else would do it before them. And they might not tell the full story. Half-truths mixed with falsehoods could be far more damaging than any lie. "I need you to be onboard with this, Yim."

"How can I refuse?"

Mattis smiled grimly. "Okay." He took a breath. "I need to make a call to Chrysalis. I have a man down there, and I want him back. We'll send in the marines as soon as you're ready."

"There might be civilians," said Yim, somewhat unconvincingly. "I'm concerned about casualties."

"There might be," conceded Mattis. "If you're concerned

about that, we can start a controlled evacuation."

"Not sure there'll be time enough for that. One of our governments is bound to interfere."

Typical. "Well, let me talk to them, maybe they'll have some kind of solution for us."

Yim's voice became painted with curiosity. "How do you propose to do that? Through your man?"

Bratta was in no position to relay anything to anyone. That guy—it had been a wonder he was still alive. "Nah. I figure if I send them a message, they'll pick up."

Yim seemed to consider, pausing for a moment. "Okay. Do it. I'll listen in."

With a gesture to Lynch, Mattis patched in the Chrysalis communications systems. He broadcast the message to as many people as he could reach.

"Attention Chrysalis Station. As you're no doubt aware, there's been a minor bout of uncivilized behavior in your orbit. I wish to advise that the hostilities have ceased and to apologize to your good people for our … unsettling outburst." He paused for effect. "That said, we have become aware there exists a secret genetics lab hidden within your planetoid. Gaining access to that facility is our only goal. I assume I can count on your full cooperation in this matter." Another pause. "And Senator Pitt? If you're hearing this, I want you to know that you'll be treated fairly if you cooperate." He ended the transmission.

"Yeah," said Lynch, grinning sardonically. "We have all the guns. They're going to cooperate a'right."

Mattis wasn't so sure. "Pitt won't."

"That ain't our problem."

Good point. "Get Modi up here," he said. "I want a report on the damage we've taken. I don't like having to fight without an intact casemate protecting us. If we're going to need anti-rad shots, I want to get them in us as soon as possible."

"Sure thing, Admiral. I'll go round up the space janitor."

Mattis grimaced. "Don't let him hear you call him that, he won't be happy."

"Is he ever?" asked Lynch, and then turned back to his job.

Mattis stared at the slowly spinning rock of Chrysalis and wondered just what Senator Pitt was thinking at that very moment.

Chapter Seventy-Six

MaxGainz Facility
Floor 1
Hidden Genetics Lab
Chrysalis
Kepler-1011 system

"And Senator Pitt? If you're hearing this, I want you to know that you'll be treated fairly if you cooperate." Mattis's voice echoed throughout the station like the screams of the prisoners who, only moments ago, Senator Pitt had watched dissolve into nothingness.

His hands clenched so hard his fingernails dug into his skin.

That bastard. That bastard Mattis was screwing everything up. *Why* did he have to come here—why now, when they were so close to giving him what he wanted? Couldn't he have just gone away for a few days? A week? Thoughts of politics, of power, flew out of his mind. There was only one thing he wanted.

And he was so close to getting it.

Anger. Anger so raw and hot it burned like a white hot road flare. Senator Pitt snatched his communicator up from his belt and thumbed the dial. General Tsai looked like he was going to say something, protest or complain or bitch pointlessly, but Senator Pitt silenced him with a raised finger.

"Get me the President," he hissed into the small device. The voice recognition chirped and began dialing. It rang and rang. The secretary answered, and then more waiting….

"Mister Pitt," came President Schuyler's voice, drenched in sleepiness. "I hope you have a fucking good reason to wake me up at three am."

If Schuyler was swearing then he must have really pissed her off, but he had no time to worry himself about her sleep schedule. "Actually there is. I need you to bring the fleet in to destroy Admiral Mattis's ship, the USS *Midway*."

The absolute, stunned silence on the other end of the line was deafening. It took President Schuyler several seconds to give her answer, which came as a halting, confused laugh. "I swear, I thought you said you wanted me to—"

"Destroy the USS *Midway*, which is currently in the Kepler-1011 system in the orbit of the Chrysalis planetoid, yes. That is correct."

More silence. "Is this some kind of sick joke?"

"No, Madam President. I know as well as you do that there is a fleet of frigates and destroyers no more than two hours away from Chrysalis through Z-space, and I want you to order them by whatever means necessary to come to Chrysalis and destroy that miserable fuck's ship. No survivors."

President Schuyler's voice hardened, sounding stronger than iron. "Senator Pitt, I will *not* be authorizing the US Navy to destroy one of its own vessels because you say so. The very fact that you are asking this of me shows you are out of your mind. Come morning, I will be investigating this fully, and I will be having your metaphorical head for this." Her tone became ice. "Metaphorical, *dear senator*, because that is how our society operates. Within a system of laws and checks and balances. We don't shoot our own people in the back. Good night, and never, ever call me again."

"Before you hang up," said Senator Pitt, his tone even and controlled. "Since you're throwing me to the wolves, and I'm forced to burn my credit—I know about Matthew. Matthew Schuyler."

Silence so sharp it could have cut glass. "And what," said President Schuyler, her voice suddenly quiet, "do you know about him?"

"I'm not going to insult you by claiming to know *everything*," said Senator Pitt, his voice slipping subconsciously into a malevolent purr. "But I know enough. Enough to bury you. I know how he died and why that information terrifies you, both personally and politically. The media are sharks, as well you know, Madam President. And this story has plenty of blood in it."

He heard the sound of rustling sheets, as though President Schuyler was sitting up in bed. "Are you blackmailing me, Senator Pitt?"

No sense in sugar coating it at all. "Yes. And, frankly, it's going to work because the only way you get out of it is to hit me back with something, and I know you have *nothing*."

"You know I don't collect dirt on my political rivals." Her tone developed a desperate edge. A faint crack in her verbal armor. So rare in a woman of her caliber. "I prefer to play fair."

"This isn't a game; it's war, and a fair fight is a sign of poor tactics." Senator Pitt smiled to himself. "Now, Admiral Mattis isn't the only one with reporters in their contacts list, Madam President. If you like, I can call them up now, patch you into the call so you're on the line with them when I'm giving them the scoop of the *century* on you and your dirty little secret...." he clicked his tongue. "Unless you think it won't be necessary."

She didn't answer which told him more than enough. Now he had her. "I'm a busy man, Madam President. Lemme just pull up their contact information..." he selected a number from his contact list. Miss Ramirez's boss. Chief Editor at GBC news. That should be fine—he hit dial. "Here we go," he said, as the phone dialed. "You can see the number on your caller ID."

"Wait," said President Schuyler. "Stop. Okay."

The call connected. A sleepy sounding man picked up. "Who is this? Do you know what time it is?"

"Sorry," said Senator Pitt, "I accidentally pressed your number by mistake. Real sorry. Go back to sleep, Christian. Say hi to Jennifer for me in the morning."

The guy didn't need to be told twice. He grunted and hung up immediately.

"So I think you'll agree," said Senator Pitt, "that it is *imperative* that the nearby fleet get word that Admiral Jack Mattis's ship has been taken over by the Forgotten—or, in fact, that he's decided to join them. Such a story will be easy to sell; the good Admiral is a veteran of the same war as all of them, isn't he? And he's a known malcontent, at least when it comes to the Chinese. Everyone will readily believe he's joined up with those bastards. I'm sure you see as well as I do how easily the pieces fall into place. It practically writes itself. Beautiful."

He could practically *sense* President Schuyler glaring down the line at him. "You'll pay for this," she warned him. "You think you can get away with blackmailing the president like this? Destroying a US Navy asset? The dead soldiers?"

Senator Pitt thought for a moment. "Yes. That's why I'm doing this."

She sighed angrily. "I'm sending the fleet. But mark my words—you'll pay."

Warmth flowed through him, a mixture of emotions being released like a cork from a bottle; anger, the succor of revenge, and some other pleasurable emotion he couldn't quite quantify. Relief? "I don't care," he said. "Just remember—no survivors."

Chapter Seventy-Seven

Bridge
USS Midway
Orbit above Chrysalis
Kepler-1011 system

Nothing to do but wait. Mattis let the minutes tick away, monitoring Chrysalis with every single system he had on hand. No sign of a civilian evacuation, but neither did the mines activate and blow them all to smithereens. Probably because the *Luyang* and the *Midway* were far too close to the planetoid for the gravity mines to hurt them without catastrophically damaging their own systems.

Maybe that's what they delay was. The leadership on Chrysalis was slowly working this out for themselves. Overall, a good thing. It was about time cooler heads prevailed.

When he was reasonably certain there was no more he could do at his post, Mattis visited his ready room and splashed some water on his face. When he came back, everyone seemed to be waiting for him with anxious eyes.

"Report," he said, slipping into his CO's seat.

"Sir?" asked Lynch, frowning at his console in mild confusion. "Did you request reinforcements from the fleet while you were taking a leak?"

Mattis blinked. "There's a ship incoming?" he asked.

"Significantly more than *one*," said Lynch, pointing to the long range sensor array, at the dizzying list of ships closing on their position. All American.

Something about that many ships coming so quickly ate at him. "Open a hailing frequency," he said. "I want to talk to those ships."

The hail went out. Followed by another. And another.

Nothing.

"Maybe we should check if our hailing system is working," Mattis joked half-heartedly.

"I don't like this, Admiral." Lynch shook his head firmly, not seeming to find the humor in the situation. "They look like they're spoiling for a fight. I'm reading a *lot* of inter-fleet communication from them, but no answer to our hails."

"What do you think?" asked Mattis, staring intently at the screen. "Do you think they're on our side? Maybe they're just trying to find out what's going on."

"Doubtful. If they were here to talk about Chrysalis, they would have, you know, talked to us."

That was a good point. Mattis cursed under his breath. He'd had his eyes glued on Chrysalis, but it turned out he should have been looking for threats elsewhere. Now he had a big problem. The might of the US Navy coming to—well, he didn't know exactly *what* they were coming for, but it wasn't good.

There wasn't any way he could fight that many ships, nor would *want* to. The idea of firing on his fellow Americans made him feel ill—but he couldn't simply pull up stakes and move on. This was *his* mess. He had dragged everyone into it. So many secrets and lies … if he pulled back now, he'd never be free of them. His enemies would spin a tale out of what had happened at Chrysalis and, while it might not all stick, at least some of it would. Fighting it would be a distraction they couldn't afford.

So it was time for the truth.

He pulled out his personal communicator and thumbed through the contacts, selecting M. RAMIREZ. It rang twice before she answered.

"Jack?" She sounded surprised, struggling to keep a stammer down. "Aren't you a little busy to be talking to me?"

"Actually," said Mattis, "I'm kind of hoping you'll be the key to solving my most recent little problem. Did you bring your broadcast gear?"

"Only the portable stuff," said Ramirez. "It's not as good as the full kit."

"Can it reach the news network?"

"Of course," said Ramirez, confused. "It wouldn't be much good if it couldn't."

That was good enough. "Bring it up to the bridge," he said. "To my ready room. I want to make another broadcast. Like the one we made before."

An acidic edge crept into her tone. "Like the one where you gave me nothing and made me look like an absolute idiot in front of the whole galaxy?"

Mattis chewed on the inside of his cheek. "It won't be like that, this time. This time—I got something *big* for you. I promise."

Her hesitation was plain, but finally she relented. "Okay. I'll be up in a bit." She blew out a low, long sigh. "You better be right about this, Jack," she said.

Minutes later, she arrived, skeptical but with an edge of hope on her face. Together they went into Mattis's ready room.

Ramirez set up her camera. It was a dinky little thing, about the size of a fist, balanced precariously on a too-thin tripod.

Into it, Mattis told the galaxy the truth.

He told them that the aliens who attacked Earth were not extraterrestrial beings, but humans. Humans, that they had thought were from the future, but now believed were created by a secret government project.

He told them that the world governments had created a system called the Ark Project.

He told them that Senator Pitt was deep into the conspiracy.

He told them that President Schuyler knew all of this and had done nothing.

He mentioned the Deep State. That it was behind these human experiments, through a front company, MaxGainz.

He told them … everything.

The whole thing was cathartic. Searing, hurting, but like ripping off a scab, strangely pleasurable. It felt good to come out from behind the wall of half-truths and barely-kept secrets.

And when it was done, Ramirez stood up, slowly, as

though in shock, and turned the camera off.

"That'll be beaming out to the whole galaxy in a minute or so," she said, a slight tremor in her voice. "Once it's finished compressing. You have about … twenty seconds to change your mind."

Mattis smiled confidently. "No changing my mind. We've told all of humanity everything there is. Named names, shown them where the bodies are buried. Should have done it a long time ago."

"Well, I hope you know what you're doing," said Ramirez. "There's going to be consequences for this, you know."

He knew that. One simply couldn't do what he'd done and expect that things would just be okay.

But, right at that moment, it felt good.

Mattis's communicator chirped and, with a cautious hand, he pulled it open. "Yes?"

"Sir," said Lynch. "The fleet's turned away." He laughed and, in the background, Mattis could hear the bridge crew celebrating. "They're leaving."

Ramirez smiled and Mattis smiled back.

"Nice work," she said, casually folding up the camera. "You did the right thing, Jack."

"You're right," said Mattis, standing up out of his chair. "Now I gotta go make sure my ship is okay."

"This isn't over," cautioned Ramirez as she slid her camera into her bag. "It's just beginning."

A problem for another day. Mattis managed a little half-smile—it *really was* good to see her again. "So," he asked, "what have you been up to?"

Chapter Seventy-Eight

Private Office
Genetics Lab
Chrysalis
Kepler-1011 system

"What do you mean," hissed Senator Pitt, his hands clenched by his sides, "that the fleet has turned back?"

President Schuyler's voice was, on the surface, apologetic, but he could tell—could sense below the level of her politician's lies—that she was secretly glad. "I had no choice," she said. "The US Chairman of the Joint Chiefs telephoned me personally and asked me to explain why I was giving direct orders to a navy battle group. I couldn't do anything but tell him that I was acting on a personal tip I'd received. One of an urgent nature. One I couldn't share with him or it would compromise national security. He didn't buy it."

"You realize," said Senator Pitt, "that I do not *care* if he bought it or not, right? I expected results, and I—"

"Will not be getting them," said President Schuyler, flatly. "Mattis's broadcast implicated you in all of this—hell, he did more than implicate you. He flat out said you were partially responsible. When you finally make your way back to Earth, Senator, you will find yourself embroiled in a shitstorm the likes of which you cannot possibly imagine." She chuckled. "I daresay your political career is over, Peter."

He knew it was likely true, but he almost didn't care. "Fine. You know as well as I do—you have to protect me. If I burn, you burn, Madam President."

"If you burn," said President Schuyler, "I might get singed on my finger. I'll weather this storm, Senator. You, on the other hand, will not."

"Do something," growled Pitt angrily. "Do something!"

"Now is not the time for haste," said President Schuyler, her politician's voice in full force. "Mattis is seen as a hero. I have my own reputation to protect—even if you run crying to the media with what you know, they'll be too distracted by this, a far more newsworthy issue. And frankly, I will be too. To cover my ass with this I'm going to have to appoint a blue-ribbon commission, have the attorney general call up a special prosecutor, sign executive actions, and all manner of unsightly business. I'm going to be *very* busy." She paused. "You might think I need you, Senator Pitt, but the reality is, you need *me* instead."

She hung up.

Slowly, Pitt returned his communicator to his pocket, simmering with fury.

Mattis and Schuyler would pay for what they'd done. For

taking it all away.

Everything that he had done, his entire political career, gone in an instant. Every scrap of political credit, every favor, every—everything. Lost.

All he had left was …

He smiled. It would all be worth it.

Everything.

Chapter Seventy-Nine

Hangar Bay
USS Midway
Orbit above Chrysalis
Kepler-1011 system

Guano guided her Warbird back to the *Midway* and, just as the ship touched down, the strange feeling drained out of her.

She powered down the ship and, as the energy left her Warbird, she too felt exhausted, like she couldn't keep her eyes open. She stifled a rippling yawn.

"What," said Flatline, playfully patting her on the back of the helmet. "Was that boring to you, Guano?"

She snorted and shook his hand off. "Naw, I just … I dunno. I just feel really sleepy. It's nap time for the bat."

The playfulness drained out of Flatline's voice. "Is it the *thing*?"

"No," she said firmly, although in truth she couldn't know.

"Maybe."

"Well, I'm convinced." Flatline coughed. "Hey, we're back. Time to go see the medical staff."

She knew it was true. "Okay," she said. "Fine. Fine." She pushed the cockpit canopy open button, the hinge unsealing itself with a hiss, then she hooked a leg over the edge of the starfighter.

Dizziness. The sensation of falling. Then, suddenly, she was on her back, sprawled out on the landing strip, facing the roof.

"Patricia!" called Flatline, struggling to get out of his seat. "Oh my god! Hey! Wake up!"

She groggily tried to sit up, but her head swam. That was a bad idea.

"No, no!" said Flatline, his helmeted face appearing at the edge of the fighter's cockpit. "Stay there. Stay down. I'm calling the corpsman."

"I'm fine," she insisted, her voice groggy. "I just … fell."

"You freaking passed out." Flatline scrambled down the side of the fighter, jumping the last meter or so onto the deck, his metal boots hitting with a *thump*. "You didn't just *fall*."

Guano searched for a good lie, but none of them came. "I…"

"You," said Flatline, hooking his arms around Guano's shoulders and pulling her up, "are going to get yourself checked out. Right *now*."

Try as she might, Guano was simply too tired, too dizzy, to resist. She went limp in the arms of the medical technicians who arrived to carry her away.

Chapter Eighty

Captain's Ready Room
USS Midway
Orbit above Chrysalis
Kepler-1011 system

Mattis felt free.

He'd been keeping other peoples' secrets for too long and to have them all out in the open was liberating. The consequences for his actions would be serious, even dire—but at least his conscience was unburdened. He sat on the couch in his ready room, tablet in one hand, mug of black coffee in the other.

The ratings started to come in. His interview was the third most popular broadcast that day, after reruns of the initial video of the aliens, and some *really* cute video showing a cat eating spaghetti.

"How's my star doing?" asked Ramirez, smiling as she

returned with a warm cup of coffee, tired but seeming, as he was, to be quite glad that they had let everything out of the bag.

"Much better now that I have some coffee and a little breathing room." He smiled back. "Feeling good."

Ramirez slid into the couch beside him. "Good." She sipped her drink. "Thank you again."

"Naw," said Mattis. For a moment, he almost put his arm around her shoulders—a sudden impulse he suppressed just in time. "You did all the work. All I did was talk."

"Talking is work," said Ramirez, and then she put her arm around his shoulder. "At least, it is in my world. And it was brave, too."

A funny comment given that he'd considered, and chickened out, of doing exactly what she'd just done. Mattis found words hard to come to his throat. "I … suppose so."

"Don't worry," she said, grinning playfully at him. "I think we have a lot more chances for you to tell the galaxy about important stuff. You'll be in front of my cameras again."

"Great," said Mattis, groaning teasingly. "Just what I always wanted."

There was a bit of silence as the two of them sat, their sides touching, pretending like it wasn't a huge deal when it was.

"I really do think you were brave," said Ramirez, finally.

Brave? He didn't feel brave. "Like I said, all I did is talk.""

"Important talk," said Ramirez, a firmness in her tone that surprised him. "And not just because you told the galaxy a whole bunch of stuff that frankly it didn't want to hear but *needed* to, but because of what it meant to you." She squirmed around on the couch, facing him squarely. "You went for transparency, and that's what's so good about it—you went out of your comfort zone. I could see you squirming as you spoke, trying to find some other way of delivering the news that would make it hurt less, even though such a thing wasn't possible. So you just did it anyway. Bravery means overcoming a challenge. That's what makes you a hero."

"I suppose so," said Mattis, unable to refute what she was saying, but also unable to accept such flattery from her. "Maybe if I'd done a better job, it'd be the number two trending video instead of number three. That damn cat is tough to beat, though."

Ramirez stifled a giggle. "As much as this was important, even I'm forced to concede that the cat was really cute. The way that noodle dangled out of its mouth…"

"Very cute," said Mattis, and he leaned in and kissed her.

She sat there. For a moment, he thought—feared!—that she was going to do nothing, but then she leaned back, settling in on the couch with him once more.

"Jack," she said, "sometimes I feel like you're the last hero in the whole damn galaxy. Even if you are number two to a cat."

He gently squeezed her. "For now," he said, smile widening. "Humans live longer than cats. If nothing else, I'll outlive the bastard."

She laughed and squirmed around. "You're insufferable."

Maybe, maybe not. Going public like he had could not be good for his career, but … it had been necessary.

"So," asked Mattis, "why the hell were you even on Chrysalis in the first place?"

"Anonymous tip."

He frowned, rolling his eyes. "Cut the crap."

Ramirez hesitated before she answered. "It was your son, Jack. Chuck sent me this message out of the blue—I think he's conducting his own investigation or something. Anyway, something about it spoke to me, and then, what do you know. I found what I was looking for."

"Resourceful kid," said Mattis. "Hope it doesn't get him killed. Or worse, arrested."

"I hope *you* don't get yourself killed." Ramirez looked up at him.

"I won't," he said. "Promise."

Another moment of silence passed, then Ramirez—sounding almost sleeping—spoke up again. "Do you think … these experimented-on humans, these future-people … do you think they'll come back?"

Mattis sipped his coffee. "They're not from the future. I think that's clear now. I never thought that time-travel explanation was very believable. Whatever this … Deep State is up to, they not only created these things, but they supplied them, in complete secrecy, with a fleet. A fleet that took out Friendship station and nearly took us out with it."

"Mmm."

Mattis wanted to talk more with her, but he had work to do. With palpable reluctance, Mattis pulled out his communicator. "Mattis to the infirmary."

The on-call nurse, the same one who had struggled to inject Modi with a simple inoculation, picked up. "Good evening, Admiral. What can I do for you?"

Mattis gave Ramirez another gentle squeeze. "Just

checking in on Doctor Bratta."

"He's resting," said the nurse. "He's pretty beat up, but he has company and plenty of painkillers. He'll be fine. We gave him a video of some cat eating spaghetti, and that seemed to make him happy. We're mostly focused Guano. She was recently admitted."

He made a mental note to check up on that. "Good. Keep me apprised. On both counts."

"Aye, sir."

He cut the connection. The moment he terminated the call, another came through.

"Sir?" asked Modi, a tinge of concern in his voice. "You and Martha have been in there for a while, I'm worried that—"

There was the faint sounds of a scuffle. "Give me that!" he heard Lynch hiss in the background. Then, louder, "Sorry, sir, Commander Modi's come down with a case of the stupids. Sorry to disturb you both. Sorry!"

And then he hung up, too.

The two of them shared a laugh which took a long time to fade. It was partially Lynch and Modi's stumblings, but also relief. Relief they were alive. Relief the truth was out. Relief that they were sharing that exact moment together, happy … or at least, something like it.

"They'll be back," said Mattis, unable to keep the levity in his voice despite it all. "Sooner, rather than later."

"I know," said Ramirez, her eyes drooping closed, snuggled up to Mattis, her slowly cooling cup of coffee almost forgotten. "This isn't over. Not by a long shot."

He wanted to reassure her, to convince her that everything was going to be okay, but the words didn't find their way to his lips, and so he just sat there, waiting, until she was asleep, their drinks were cold, and the ship's lighting changed to signify a shift change.

Mattis was alone in the silence with his own thoughts and his own words echoing in his ears, twisting and reforming until they shaped a new, realized thought:

The war was just getting started.

Epilogue

Private Office
Genetics Lab
Chrysalis
Kepler-1011 system

With the *Midway* and the *Luyang* in orbit of Chrysalis, and nothing else left to do but wait until they came down to arrest him, Senator Pitt was reduced to watching the news coverage of the events.

"*Breaking news on the Chrysalis station incident: we are now receiving reports that the President herself is scheduled to make a speech on the developing situation within the hour.*"

He flicked to another station, seeing a familiar face. Chuck Mattis.

"*I don't know anything about this,*" said Chuck, his lying face obviously withholding something. "*Uhh, as far as I'm aware, there is no quote-unquote deep state within the United States or the People's Republic of China at this time.*"

Lying son of a liar. Pitt angrily changed the channel again.

"*—orts indicate that neither the* Midway *or the* Luyang *have* *launched marines or ordnance into Chrysalis at this time, but we remain vigilant and remind our viewers that this remains a developing situation —"*

Liars. Probably. If the American or Chinese ship were going to attack they wouldn't broadcast it onto the news. Another channel, this time, Mattis's face himself.

"The MaxGainz genetics corp is a front for illegal research, and we will see to it that—"

Not in time. Whatever that idiot was planning on doing it wouldn't be done anywhere near fast enough. Senator Pitt would get what he needed and get out.

Right on cue, his private communicator chimed. A message from General Tsai.

TSAI: We're ready. Come to Productions.

Barely able to keep his nerves in check, Senator Pitt leapt up from the table and darted out of the small office. All around him alarms blared and sirens wailed, although he wasn't sure—or didn't care—if they were in relation to the technical-wizardry being performed, the presence of the two warships in orbit, or something else entirely.

Rounding a corner, Senator Pitt came upon a simple steel door labelled "Productions." He swiped his card at the reader. Strange, it had never been locked before. He practically fell down the stairs leading to the laboratory floor.

Within the wide open lab space lay row after row of surgical slabs. Each contained a body draped in a white sheet; multi-armed surgical robots tending to them beneath the covering, stitching and sewing, and injecting pulses of the glowing green fluid, some of which dripped into the floor, pooling beneath each of the bodies.

As he watched, one of the bodies jerked as it received an electrical current. Then, slowly, as though waking from a deep sleep, the body sat up and pulled the sheet away from his head.

Senator Pitt's face split into a wide smile. "Hello son," he said.

Commander Peter Pitt looked at him, and blinked in surprise. "Hello, dad," he replied.

And it was all worth it.

Thank you for reading *The Last Hero.*

Sign up to find out when *The Last Dawn*, book 3 of *The Last War Series*, is released: smarturl.it/peterbostrom

Contact information:
www.authorpeterbostrom.com
facebook.com/authorpeterbostrom
peterdbostrom@gmail.com

Made in the USA
Las Vegas, NV
23 April 2022

47909550R00236